*continued . . .*

# the
# TENTMAKER

##  michelle Blake

**BERKLEY PRIME CRIME, NEW YORK**

This is a work of fiction. Names, characters, places, and incidents are either the product of the author's imagination or are used fictitiously, and any resemblance to actual persons, living or dead, business establishments, events, or locales is entirely coincidental.

THE TENTMAKER

A Berkley Prime Crime Book / published by arrangement with the author

PRINTING HISTORY
G. P. Putnam's Sons hardcover edition / 1999
Berkley Prime Crime edition / September 2000

The Penguin Putnam Inc. World Wide Web site address is
http://www.penguinputnam.com

ISBN: 0-425-17668-1

Berkley Prime Crime Books are published
by The Berkley Publishing Group,
a division of Penguin Putnam Inc.,
375 Hudson Street, New York, New York 10014.
The name BERKLEY PRIME CRIME and the BERKLEY PRIME CRIME
design are trademarks belonging to Penguin Putnam Inc.

PRINTED IN THE UNITED STATES OF AMERICA

10  9  8  7  6  5  4  3  2  1

**TENTMAKER:** an ordained priest who works at a trade outside the church, sometimes serving as interim priest for parishes in search of full-time rectors

*And, because he was of the same trade, he stayed with them, and they worked together— by trade they were tentmakers.*

ACTS 18:3

# THE TENTMAKER

# chapter ✳ 1

Lily leaned back in the old-fashioned desk chair, closed her eyes, and prayed. She prayed for compassion, she prayed for insight, and she prayed, if it was anywhere in the scope of God's will, for release from this job, which was driving her crazy. She had worked as an interim priest several times before, taking over while a parish searched for a new rector, but this time it was different. For reasons she hadn't yet discovered, the people at St. Mary of the Garden seemed determined to keep her out of their lives and out of the life of the parish. Over the past two weeks she had felt like a ghost in the church building—invisible, pointless—while the parishioners posted their notices, collected their messages, and conducted their Bible study without her help.

So now, the sudden loud creaking of the door from the chancel not only startled her but also gave her a shot of hope. Maybe somebody was paying a visit. Maybe somebody here needed her.

The woman who appeared in the office doorway did not look like a person in need. She was round and solid, in a lightweight cloth coat, and clearly unbothered by the cold. Her short, gray hair seemed to have been recently permed; her shoes were sturdy, lace-up oxfords. She stood for a moment, studying Lily, then spoke in a businesslike voice with a hint of her Irish Boston ancestry.

"I suppose you're the replacement," she said.

"I'm the interim priest-in-charge, Lily Connor."

"And what do they call you?" asked the woman.

"Who?" replied Lily.

"Your parishioners. They can't call you 'Father.' "

"No, we don't call our priests 'Father' in the Episcopal Church—not anymore, at least. I mean, *I* don't," said Lily. She had just realized that this woman must have a key to the street door of the church, since she hadn't entered through the garden. Very few people had that key. Who was she?

"Is that so?" the woman asked. "I called him Father Barnes until the day he died, and he never objected."

Lily stood and walked toward the woman to shake hands. "Are you a parishioner? I'm afraid we haven't met."

The stranger stepped back, away from Lily, and folded her arms across her chest. "I am not," she said. "I'm a member of St. Luke's Roman Catholic Church."

Lily awkwardly withdrew her hand and leaned against the desk, mostly for support.

"I took some time off after I—after he died," continued the woman. "You won't owe me for that. I looked for you the past couple of weeks, but you're not in the office much, and I didn't like to intrude over at the rectory." She inclined her head in the direction of the two-story shingled house across the courtyard. "I'll finish up here today, but I can't come back." She paused, then added, "It wouldn't be right."

"I'm afraid I'm confused," said Lily. "Do you mean it wouldn't be right because—well, what do you mean?"

"I've cleaned the church and the rectory for Father Barnes all these years because of the kind of man he was and the kind of church this is. Honest, safe, respectable. But I can't go on doing it now. I've talked it over with my priest, and he feels the same. You need to get some-one else."

After a moment, Lily felt indignation replace confusion. Apparently, this woman believed it besmirched her good name to clean a church in which a woman served as priest.

"Of course that's up to you," said Lily. "But I'll have to ask you for more notice, since I've just started and don't really know the procedure for finding someone new. Could you stay on for at least two more weeks?"

"I can," she answered. "Will you be wanting me to clean the rectory as well?"

The question caught Lily off guard; she had not ex-pected such quick compliance. "Sure," she said. "Yes, that would be fine."

"I'll just get started here," said the woman, turning from the door, clearly softened by the encounter.

It's probably how she's used to being treated by church superiors, thought Lily. I've given her orders and made her feel right at home. And those two thoughts made Lily her-self feel worse than she had all morning. She followed her visitor out into the hallway.

"I'm afraid I didn't get your name," said Lily.

"I'm Mrs. Hanlon," she said over her shoulder as she headed for the stairs to the church hall in the basement. Then she turned and added, "I'm sorry for being rude. I've never had to talk to a woman in a collar before—not a priest's collar." With that she turned again and disappeared down the stairs.

Back in her office, Lily sat once more and stared through the leaded windows into the church courtyard. Though green lingered on the clipped lawn and among the hedges, the color had been absorbed by a gray October sky. Water dripped from the dark overhang of the building where mist condensed and pooled in the clogged gutters. She watched a car roll past on Lee Street, splashing through a shallow puddle near the corner.

After a moment she swiveled the chair to her right, toward one of the walls of books that lined the small office—theology, philosophy, church history, all predictable and all alphabetically arranged. So far, she had not found one out of place: Abelard, Anselm, Aquinas, Athanasius, Augustine, Barth, Bonhoeffer, Buber, Bultmann and the rest, many of whom Lily had read in seminary, few of whom she still read. She had formed an opinion of her predecessor, the late Reverend Mr. Barnes, as a straight-backed, tight-lipped conservative—that is, as the enemy. His obsessively alphabetized library only confirmed her suspicions.

As did his perfectly empty desk, she thought, though that was irrational, since Barnes couldn't have cleaned it out after he died. But someone had. When she'd first opened the drawers, not a dry pen or a loose tack rattled anywhere. The files were full of the regular mailing lists, minutes from vestry meetings, parish correspondence. But there were no personal papers, not a sign of the aging priest who had used this room for more than ten years.

Lily turned to the desk and glanced down at the list of messages she had collected that morning. Bishop Spencer had called, but, since he was the person responsible for her being at St. Mary's to begin with, she didn't feel like talking with him anytime soon. He was a longtime friend and ally in the church, but right now she could have killed him. Besides, he had waited two weeks to call and check in with her; he could wait a few more days.

John Neville, senior warden of the vestry, had left a message (desultory, unenthusiastic) agreeing to have a special coffee hour—some sort of informal discussion group in which she could get to know parishioners, and vice versa—but he wouldn't have time to do anything about announcements. Could Lily get something typed up and talk to another vestry member, maybe Cynthia Babcock or Stanley Leonard? Stanley Leonard hadn't returned Lily's call, but Cynthia had called to say she was awfully sorry they had been so lax. Could she ever forgive them? Unfortunately, she wouldn't be around this week, maybe Lily could call Stanley's wife, Jo . . . ?

More of the shell game she'd been getting from the start. At that moment, Lily couldn't come up with a decent explanation for the behavior. This dogged avoidance had begun to appear purposeful, even secretive.

# chapter 2

The second in line for blame regarding her current employment was Charlie Cooper, her best friend since their seminary years together in Cambridge; he, too, had urged her to take this job. Charlie was now a brother in the Anglican order of St. Peter on Brattle Street, just two blocks from the seminary where they had studied years ago. Lily had agreed to meet him for an early dinner in Harvard Square, but she regretted it. After a day of hunting elusive vestry members, Lily was in no mood to navigate the rush-hour crush on the Red Line train to Cambridge.

On the elevated platform at the Charles Street station she watched a group of teenagers, a matched set of girls and boys in fatigue pants, army boots, and black watch caps, shoving one another dangerously near the edge. For at least five minutes she stared disapprovingly but stayed silent. Then, when two boys took hold of a girl—slender, pale, with dark circles under her eyes—and pulled her toward the track, Lily stepped forward.

"Don't fool around like that—if you slip, you could kill someone," she said, keeping her voice level.

The boys stopped for an instant, their grimacing smiles still intact, then the one closest to her turned and said, "Fuck you," loud and clear on the crowded platform.

The couple to Lily's right backed up two steps.

"Be that as it may," said Lily. "Let go of her."

At that moment, the train pulled into sight so she was spared the follow-up requisite defiance. The girl, who seemed to be partly in charge now, said something with the word "bitch" in it, then led the way to a car farther up the track. But Lily had attracted the attention of everyone around.

By the time she had boarded the packed train and found a handle on the overhead right-hand railing, halfway down the car, she felt as if the entire crowd were staring in her direction. As uncomfortable as it made her, she drew on a longtime history of ignoring curious glances. In the most peaceful of settings, she still gave off an incongruous set of messages in her jeans, hand-tooled cowboy boots, army surplus slicker, and clerical collar. She wore her thick, dark hair pulled back in a braid, but in wet weather she could not control the strands that curled around her forehead and the nape of her neck.

In high school she had been the skinny, overgrown geek, the outcast, the reader of poems and nineteenth-century novels. She still pictured herself that way. During one of their chronic conversations about the lack of romance in her life, Lily had told Charlie, "You're not on the dating circuit, but I've got news for you—people don't date geeks."

Charlie had let out a surprised laugh. "I've got news for *you*," he had said. "You're not a geek—a difficult person, maybe, but a good-looking difficult person. You're tall and skinny, the cultural icon. Don't you know that?"

Lily had left it there. But in truth, even at age thirty-six, she still thought of herself as a geek. She had even come to suspect it was what she preferred. She refused to take her looks or her clothes seriously, though she indulged a weakness for expensive shirts.

And there was the added problem of the clerical collar. After ordination she had come to mistrust people's responses to her when she was "frocked," as she called it. But the bishop had suggested she take to wearing it again, temporarily, for her work at St. Mary's. So she had. She was conscious of it at that moment as a mild abrasion on her neck.

She was also conscious of the way the tall, older man beside her leaned crazily away, as if scared of brushing her arm. He's afraid I'm going after him next, she thought. At Kendall Square he got off, and the small cleared area around her closed up with unsuspecting newcomers.

The sense of being universally shunned made her think of Mrs. Hanlon. Could the woman really be afraid of a female priest? Had that been Mrs. Hanlon's problem? If so, what did "honest" mean? And hadn't she also said "safe"?

Lily stared at the dark window across from her, at the image of her pale face, her large eyes. When the inbound train hurtled past, she startled. For the next few minutes, she tried to reason away the growing certainty that something was wrong at the heart of St. Mary of the Garden. But she couldn't entirely. By the time she reached the top of the escalator in Harvard Square and felt the cool evening air on her face, she had quit trying.

At a crowded Indian restaurant overlooking JFK Street, Lily reported her encounter with Mrs. Hanlon to Charlie, word for word.

Charlie's response was predictably fair-minded, compassionate, and irritating. "Poor thing," he said.

Lily studied him for a moment. "I hope you mean me."

"I don't," he replied with a half-smile, "I mean poor Mrs. Hanlon. Think what a shock you must be to her system."

Lily finished chewing. Then she said, "I think you miss the point."

"Yeah?" he asked quizzically. "So, what's the point?"

"Gee, I don't know, Charlie," she said, in mock bafflement. "Maybe the point is that I find myself in this throwback, country-club parish with its own cleaning lady, and at a very, very hard time for me. I've just spent six months in Texas doing—you know what I was doing. I get dragged back to Boston by you and Spencer to baby-sit rich people, I've got no place of my own to live, and I can't figure out what the hell is going on over there."

Lily's voice had gotten loud on the last few lines and carried out into the high-ceilinged room. The couple at the next table quickly averted their eyes from the two clerics when Charlie glanced at them.

"Thanks," he said. "This is terrific PR. I think I'll leave my collar at home the next time we go out."

Lily stared through the window at the sidewalk population of the Square on a drizzly evening. Even in dripping parkas, the students looked, to her at least, smug and self-satisfied. On the corner, a skinny, young Latino man in an oversized raincoat was selling copies of *Spare Change,* an advocacy newspaper for the homeless. No one was buying. She could think of nothing to say to make either Charlie or herself feel better, so she kept quiet.

They had been friends since their first-year New Testament seminar, bound by temperament, theology, and the odd coincidence of conversion: they had both been raised Catholic and had not been confirmed in the Episcopal Church until they were in college. And when Lily had decided to stay on in Boston after seminary, they were both ordained in the Diocese of Eastern Massachusetts, in the same ceremony at the Cathedral of St. Michael and All Angels.

Charlie now lived in the Cambridge monastery of the Society of Saint Peter, an Anglican order he had entered just after graduation. He had changed very little over the years: his dark hair was cut short, his body was still lanky, his face narrow and aquiline. In general, he had developed that ageless quality Lily noticed in monastics, as if the reward for abstinence were a better complexion.

"I take it this is my fault," said Charlie.

"That's ridiculous," said Lily, bristling at being found out. "It was time for me to come back here, back to my life. It's just . . ."

"What?" asked Charlie.

"I don't know. I just wish I'd thought more clearly about taking this interim thing. Maybe I grabbed it because it solved my housing problem."

"People have done much worse in Boston to solve their housing problems, believe me," said Charlie. "But I don't think you're giving yourself enough credit. I seem to remember your spending a lot of time and prayer on this one."

"I did," said Lily. "But lately I can't tell if it's God answering me or just my ego speaking in a deep voice."

Charlie laughed. Then he asked, "Why did Mrs. Hanlon say 'safe,' do you think—about the parish?"

"I don't know," said Lily. "I wondered about that myself. What do you think?"

"I haven't the slightest idea. Does St. Mary's strike you as unsafe?"

Lily glanced across the large, bright room at an older man with his college-age daughter. The two were looking out the window at the roofs of Harvard buildings, just visible in the evening light. Finally, Lily turned back to Charlie and said, "Yes, it does. But I couldn't tell you why."

"Maybe that's why you're there, then," said Charlie. "To sort it out for them."

"You see this as part of the larger plan, do you?" she asked, smiling tolerantly. "You think there's some reason for all this to be happening now?"

But Charlie didn't smile back. "What did God say to Job?"

"Yeah, yeah, I know. 'Where were you when I laid the foundation of the earth?' I get it. I get what it's supposed to mean, but I don't always like it."

"Nobody likes it," he said. "Who do you know who *likes* God?"

When she didn't respond, Charlie said, "You're there for a reason, Lily. It's not clear to you yet what it is, and it may not be clear for a long time, maybe not until way after you leave, but eventually you'll see it. There is an order at work here. Trust me."

"You, I trust," said Lily. "But that's about all."

# chapter ❊ 3

what Lily had been doing in Texas was watching her father die of advanced Hodgkin's disease. She thought of it as "watching," because there wasn't any way she could help, or not any way she could *feel* helpful. Even though she had uprooted her life in Boston, given up her beloved apartment, taken a leave from her work at the Women's Center, and moved to Texas to live with him, it had not seemed enough. Nothing had seemed enough.

When Bishop Spencer had called her in Texas to talk about the job at St. Mary's, her father had been dead only a week. She had been numb and, she thought now, vulnerable. Spencer was a persuasive man, and he had made the parish sound needy, almost pathetic. Their beloved rector of more than ten years had just dropped dead of a heart attack, brought on by insulin shock; the parishioners were sheltered, conservative; they required a compassionate, experienced priest to guide them through this time of change. Even through her numbness, pride had worked its special magic. She was clearly the one for the job—maybe the only one.

On her way home from dinner with Charlie, Lily could conjure the words "vulnerable" and "pride." But, of course, she had not been conscious then, in Texas, of all the forces at work. She had seen a rope dropped down to her and grabbed it, without asking too many questions. She was paying for that now, she thought, as she descended the stairs from the Charles Street stop. She walked quickly, head down, aware of the sharp rap of her boot heels on the wet sidewalk.

Halfway down the block, Lily glanced up and saw a familiar figure approaching, but she had no idea, at first, who it was—a woman, carrying two shopping bags, trudging down Charles. The person looked just like Lily felt, oddly out of place. As she got closer she recognized Mrs. Hanlon.

"Hello," Lily called out.

Mrs. Hanlon saw Lily, and a look of bewilderment crossed her features.

"I'm Lily Connor, from St. Mary's. We met today . . ."

"Yes," said Mrs. Hanlon. "I know who you are. I was just surprised to see you. Father Barnes was a great one for evening walks. He walked three miles a day. Somehow, when I saw you, I got confused." She shook her head. "Age is a fine and interesting thing."

"Are you headed for the train?" Lily asked.

"Yes," said Mrs. Hanlon.

"On your way home?"

Mrs. Hanlon nodded.

"I wish I had a car," said Lily. "I'd give you a ride."

Mrs. Hanlon glanced sideways at her. "That's what Father Barnes always said to me," she told Lily. "He said the only reason he'd like to have a car is to give me rides back and forth. He would have, too, good man that he was."

"I guess he and I had more in common than I would have imagined," said Lily, doubting, even as she spoke, that it was true. "Can I help with the bags?"

Mrs. Hanlon shook her head. "No, thanks. I'm used to

it," she said. "So, good-bye then." She started off toward the station.

Lily turned around and caught up to her. "Can I join you?" she asked. "I'm feeling—I've been a little lonely."

"I'm not surprised," said Mrs. Hanlon.

"Why not?" asked Lily.

"It's that kind of place, isn't it? Not very warm. Father was the exception there. I never knew how he took it, all those years."

"Did you clean for him the whole time he was at St. Mary's?" Lily asked.

"Yes," said Mrs. Hanlon.

"By the way, do you know what's supposed to happen with his belongings? Some of the stuff is packed in boxes, but some's still hanging in the closet. It's strange."

"That wouldn't be my job," said Mrs. Hanlon, "disposing of Father's things. You'd have to ask one of them." She jerked her head back toward the church, as if to define the "them."

"I did," said Lily. "I just can't get any answers."

There was a pause in which Lily hoped Mrs. Hanlon would offer some other morsel about the parish—its inherent lack of safety, lack of warmth. But the woman remained silent.

"Had he been ill for a while, before he died? I wondered if—" Lily paused—what had she wondered?—then continued. "I wondered if his illness had kept him from being around over the last few years. You said the parish has changed, and I wondered if it had happened suddenly, or over time, maybe because of Mr. Barnes's absence, or—"

Mrs. Hanlon stopped short, set down one bag, and pushed a curl off her forehead. "He was a healthy man," she said. "He walked three miles every day." After which, she picked up the bag and continued.

Lily caught up to her. "Then he wasn't sick?"

"They're saying it was the diabetes that killed him, but he wasn't sickly. He kept tight control—knew exactly how much of his medicine he needed, ate carefully. So, no, he wasn't ill, no matter what you hear."

"Oh," said Lily. Then she walked in silence, sorting through what she had just heard.

As if she couldn't contain this last comment, Mrs. Hanlon added, "You should know the facts."

"Yes," said Lily. "I agree. But you're saying his heart attack wasn't caused by diabetes?"

"Insulin shock," said Mrs. Hanlon.

"So it *was* the diabetes?"

Mrs. Hanlon answered with a terse, "That's what they say."

In the brief silence, Lily heard laughter from a basement bar they passed. Finally she said, "I'm confused. You don't think—"

"I'm the one who found him, right there on the kitchen floor," said Mrs. Hanlon.

"Good Lord," said Lily, "that must have been . . . awful." She suddenly recalled the muggy July afternoon when her own father had collapsed at the kitchen sink; first he was rinsing out his tea cup, then he was on the floor.

"Mmmm," replied Mrs. Hanlon.

"And was he dead then, when you discovered him?"

"Mmmm."

"I'm sorry," said Lily.

They had reached the MTA stop. "I'll leave you here," Mrs. Hanlon said. "No use you making the climb for no reason." Then she walked rapidly toward the stairs that led to the elevated Charles Street station.

"Good night," Lily called to her, "see you Thursday."

"Yes," replied Mrs. Hanlon over her shoulder, and she began to make her way up. On the third step she stopped and looked down at Lily. "If you're going to work there," she said, "if you're going to stay, you should know the facts."

Lily watched as Mrs. Hanlon reached the top and struggled with the heavy door. She wanted to help, but her help wasn't wanted, so she turned back toward the church. Lily walked all the way down to Beacon, turned right, and right again onto Brimmer, taking the long way home, sorting through what Mrs. Hanlon had told her, and what she had not.

As she turned off Brimmer, Lily could see the graceful spire of St. Mary's rising above the church buildings on the corner of River and Lee. Lee Street was a single block of elegant private homes, their brick fronts facing directly onto the narrow lane. At the end of the street sat the church, a small gem in the crown of the diocese, famous for its intricately detailed stained-glass windows depicting the life of Mary and the side chapel with its miniature rose window. On the east side of the church was the courtyard, bounded by the parish hall and chancellery on the north and by the rectory on the east, facing the church wall.

Halfway down the street, Lily glanced ahead at the church and was surprised to see a dark figure standing just inside the portico. She thought at first the young man— slight, with a heavy jacket and a baseball cap—must be looking for a warm place to sleep. She opened her mouth to call out to him, but she stopped when she distinctly heard the heavy deadbolt slide into place. He had a key to the church door.

She picked up her pace and the sound of her cowboy boots against the pavement echoed loudly in the narrow lane. As she approached, the figure hurried down the portico steps and disappeared around the corner onto River Street. Lily started a slow trot past the church, but when she reached the corner, she found the side street empty. She walked back to the main door, discovered it locked, and returned slowly to the rectory.

For a few minutes she stood on the porch, breathing deeply. The figure hadn't been familiar, but only a few people had the key to that door, so it shouldn't be too hard to discover his identity. On the other hand, she couldn't think of anyone in that category who fit the description of the person she had just seen—if "seen" was exactly the right word to describe a quick glimpse from half a block away on a dark night.

Inside, the rectory—a lovely two-story house with mullioned windows and wainscoting—smelled pleasantly of wood soap. She would have been comfortable there except for the eerie, lingering presence of the Reverend Mr. Frederick Barnes. His tan raincoat and heavy winter overcoat hung in the hall closet, next to a peacoat and winter parka; two black umbrellas stood in the carved stand by the door, along with an elegant, silver-handled walking stick. Dishes—four of everything, all matching—waited neatly on the shelves in the small kitchen. The spices still stood meticulously alphabetized on the rack above the stove. In the bathroom was a tube of toothpaste, rolled from the bottom with a tiny silver attachment, and a whole shelf of immaculate shaving gear.

When she had asked John Neville, the senior warden, about plans for disposing of Barnes's personal effects, she had gotten a confusing response, a sort of stammered assurance, accompanied by blushing and a quick jerk of the chin, that it was "all being seen to." With no guess as to why, Lily felt she had embarrassed him or caught him off guard, and she hadn't forced the matter then.

Glancing into the study, Lily remembered that the desk here, like the one in the church office, had been emptied, cleaned out. The whole packing job seemed an odd combination of thoroughness and thoughtlessness, as if someone had begun the task and then lost heart. Or, as if someone had started packing and then found some reason to stop.

The parishioners' behavior, Mrs. Hanlon's indirect hints, the stripped desks amid the abandoned belongings, and a young stranger with a key to the church door—they were all pieces of a puzzle. And though Lily could see no pattern and had no idea what the pieces might yield, at least she had something specific to look for. She would find the young man. She felt sure his face would appear in the finished picture.

# chapter ❈ 4

At the end of Sunday morning services, Lily felt cheered by the comments from parishioners as they filed past her in the narthex. Their gratitude seemed genuine, their questions full of interest. She had kept her sermon simple, pastoral. That had seemed safest. But she wouldn't be able to mask her politics forever.

The gospel text had been Matthew 22:34–46, the two great commandments—that we love God with our hearts and souls and minds and that we love our neighbors as ourselves—the text at the center of her faith. But she hadn't been able to write a sermon about that faith, not to these people, not at this time.

The blessing had turned out to be the reading from Hebrew Scripture, Exodus 22:21–27, which begins: "You shall not wrong a stranger or oppress him, for you were strangers in the land of Egypt"—a commandment of compassion, conjuring the history of the Hebrew people and the hard-won wisdom of suffering. She had focused her meditation and research on this passage—poignantly resonant for her right now. What is it to be a stranger, and haven't we all been one at some time? It was a quick trip from there to a love of our neighbors.

After everyone had left, she stood for a moment in the door of the church, a spectator to the breezy autumn noon, filled with light and shadow. Lee Street was quiet. A few of the parish children played outside in the courtyard to her right; she could hear their cries and the voices of a couple of the parents.

Two young children came out of one of the houses across the street. The older child, a girl, began to teach a smaller boy how to draw a hopscotch pattern on the pavement. Lily saw that the older child signed as she spoke; the little boy was deaf. Something about the girl's patience and precision, the care with which she guided the boy's hand, filled Lily with a compassion that included even the hard-sell members of St. Mary's. This apparently unrelated scene, combined with the acceptance of her sermon, produced in her the happy notion that Charlie might be right. Maybe she was, after all, there for a reason.

Ten minutes later, all such thoughts had vanished. Just before the service, Cynthia Babcock had mentioned that there would be a brief emergency meeting for vestry members in the robing room during coffee hour; she had asked Lily to be there, at least for the last few minutes. As she hung up the surplice and cassock in the office closet, Lily wondered about calling a meeting at such short notice, but parish etiquette wasn't her strength or, in this case, her problem.

In the hallway, she could hear John Neville's voice, monotonous, querulous—and she almost turned around and ducked back into her office. But Cynthia had asked her, so she ought to go. She slipped in and leaned against the shelves to the right of the door. Neville stood across from her, and the five other vestry members who had been able to attend sat in folding chairs facing him, their backs to Lily.

". . . a full year," Neville said. "And that's just to get the search started. At least that's what he told me yesterday, but as far as I know, no one here has been consulted about this . . ." He glanced in Lily's direction and continued, somehow managing to convey that, though he had not expected her there and didn't much want her, it wasn't worth a scene. He was in his sixties, a widower, tall and thin, with tortoiseshell glasses and a long, oval face. He continued, slowly, the story of his meeting with Bishop Spencer, and her mind drifted away from the gloomy drone of his voice.

To the far right, Jo Leonard lounged in her folding chair—an elegant cat, sleek and neutral. Lily had a habit of studying women like Jo; she'd formed a theory that they had been given an additional gene, something that enabled them to buy shoes that matched their bags, jackets that matched their skirts, and scarves that tied the whole thing together—like the chocolate brown silk scarf with cream-colored roses draped around Jo's delicate neck. Jo maintained an air of the disinterested spectator, but Lily noticed that just below the surface Jo seemed watchful; she stared at her husband, Stanley, as if gauging his responses to Neville's monologue.

Stanley Leonard was not watching Jo. His level of nervous energy was notched up even higher than usual, one heel lightly drumming the floor, one hand playing a kind of arpeggio on the other leg. He was the music director and the unofficial keeper of the liturgical flame. Lily had never met anyone who knew more, or had more opinions, about the Anglo-Catholic liturgy. Because she knew less, and certainly cared less, she had decided right away to leave any crucial decisions on this subject to him.

"John, I'm sorry to interrupt, but I'm not sure we can make any decisions today with so few of us here. I'd hate to try to do this without Dan, at least." Cynthia Babcock's voice cut into John's monotone with refreshing briskness. Though the two were about the same age, Cynthia was Neville's opposite—short, stocky, and no-nonsense.

"Dan is especially busy right now," said Neville. He sounded like an ambassador sharing bad news with the court.

"Yes, I know; but still, we need—" began Cynthia, but Neville interrupted her.

"Please," he said, raising his palm. "We don't have much time, and we have a major item here: we need to develop a response to the diocese about this search issue. I want to petition for a shorter process—one we can start right away."

Cynthia's cheeks turned pink, her eyes widened. Lily thought the woman might be holding back tears.

Neville rolled on. "Also," he said, "we need to make some decisions about Diocesan Convention, which is just around the corner. But perhaps we should stick with the search issue right now and take up convention questions next time."

Jo Leonard leaned forward in her chair and caught Neville's attention. "I have to agree with Cynthia on this one. There's no point hashing this out again—either subject, really—if we're not all here. I can't imagine I'm the only one who's had all the frank and honest exchanges she can take for the moment on the subject of homosexual unions."

John Neville gave a sharp, short laugh, but no one else joined in. After a silence, Stanley raised his hand. Neville nodded in his direction with what looked like relief.

"If we could just return to the first topic, perhaps we could at least come to consensus on that. It doesn't seem too difficult—or too rash—to decide we need to hire a permanent rector within the year. A year's really a very, very long time," Stanley concluded.

"All right. Yes," said Neville. "I'm sorry I even brought up the convention. Can we just have five more minutes of discussion about the search question and then call a vote? It's quite straightforward, and I feel comfortable saying that both Dan and Elliot are very much behind the idea of moving ahead."

As soon as Neville paused, Lily cleared her throat and tried to catch his eye. When she saw he wasn't going to look at her, she spoke. "Could I just . . ." she began. Neville nodded reluctantly in her direction.

"I believe the idea behind the longer waiting period is to give the parish a chance to get used to Fred Barnes's absence before getting on with the business of self-study and search. Your priest of many years has just died and I imagine—"

But Neville interrupted again. "Yes, yes," he said. "I understand that, but the point here—"

"Good," said Lily, with more energy than she intended. "Because it's important that the vestry understand the process—that there has to be a period of mourning and assessment before you move ahead. This man has been important to all of you for a long time, and he's been a wonderful priest for this parish. You need to take time to appreciate that."

Was she imagining this or had the emotional temperature in the room dropped a degree or two?

"But," she continued, "he also made mistakes, because he was human, so you have to look at those. It can seem blasphemous, at first, or ungrateful. But over the years I've come to see how important it is for a parish to admit the ways their priest failed them. And . . ." Lily faltered. No one was looking at her. She hadn't imagined the chill. "You need some distance from the past. Then you can see what will be best for you in the future."

Another short silence followed, after which Stanley Leonard turned to John Neville and said, "I'm beginning to feel that Cynthia may be right. It's going to work much better with the entire body present."

The two other members in the room, a young man whose name Lily could not remember and a tall, quiet, white-haired woman named Frieda Klass, voiced agreement. Cynthia raised her hand to speak, but Neville ignored her and gave a little sigh. "Fine," he said, his eyes closed in defeat. "Someone move to adjourn."

Afterward, Lily visited the meeting room in the basement. Almost everyone had left the coffee hour by then, except the vestry members, who had arrived late to begin with. Frieda Klass talked with her for a few minutes—she wanted to let Lily know she would be gone through the holidays, staying with her family in Austria, an annual event.

"I'm sorry," said Lily and felt surprised by her response. "I mean, I'm not sorry you're going, but I am sorry you won't be here. I look forward to getting to know you."

"And I, you," she responded. "I know it's not—what's the polite way to say it?—a very welcoming place. If you should need anything, have any questions, I'm sure John or Cynthia can answer them. But, in any case, if I can be of help, you should write. My address is on the master list in the office."

"I do have a question now, as a matter of fact. Do you mind?" asked Lily.

"Not at all."

"Since you're a vestry member, you might know who has keys to the church door on Lee Street. I'm trying to get that sorted out."

"Yes," said Klass, "I do. At least, I know who is supposed to have them. As with so many things, it was an issue." She raised her eyebrows slightly and emphasized the last word. "After a few minor acts of vandalism last spring, we voted for a new lock and five keys only." She held out her right hand—Lily noticed how rough and elegant it was, with large knuckles and blue veins—and counted on her fingers. "One for Fred—I assume you have that now—one for the cleaning woman, one for the sexton, and one apiece for the music director and senior warden."

"So there are only those five keys around, then?" asked Lily.

"As far as I know. Ask John, though. He has the last word on all of this. And now, I hate to rush, but as I am leaving tomorrow, I have too much to do." She held out her hand to Lily, who took it warmly and wished her a good trip.

"Do write," she said once again. "If I can ever be of service."

Lily stayed for a few more minutes and listened to Cynthia's long description of the afflictions of her elderly golden retriever—a horrible tumor in his mouth, keeping him from eating, making his breath unbearable. Lily tried to look pastoral; it was the best she could do.

At one o'clock, she left the church building and crossed the courtyard to the rectory. At least she now knew her visitor hadn't been anyone who was supposed to have a key. And she knew something else, too: Whatever mistakes Fred Barnes had made, they must have been real beauties.

Inside, she changed into her jeans, boots, and plaid flannel shirt. As she reached into the hall closet for her parka, she saw Barnes's navy peacoat and was tempted to try it on. She thought she deserved some perks for tolerating the shaving gear on the bathroom shelves and Neville's oppressive leadership. She took it off the hanger, feeling petty and rebellious, like a bad teenager.

The coat fit perfectly and Lily had a brief wrestle with her conscience. Obviously, it didn't belong to her. But who would know? She grabbed her keys and stuck them in the right-hand pocket, but it was an old coat and the lining felt thin. She searched for an inside pocket and found one on the left, just at her heart. When she checked the lining she discovered the pocket wasn't empty. She drew out a tiny narrow slip of paper covered with exceedingly neat writing.

The scrap was the corner of a page, with smooth edges on two sides and carefully torn edges on the opposite two. The letters and numbers appeared to have been written by a draftsman, squeezed into the meager space with precision; she guessed, for obvious reasons, they had been written by the late Reverend Mr. Barnes. They read:

> RT31
> 2941
> 4267
> SAFE

Safe. That was Mrs. Hanlon's word, she thought. And then she tried to make sense of the contents. Was it a route number, a telephone number, some kind of combination for a lock? There was no way to know. And no way to know whether or not it mattered.

Lily replaced the slip of paper, put the keys in her jeans pocket, and walked out onto the porch. The day had changed, was changing, to a cool afternoon with high gray clouds and a brisk wind. She buttoned the coat and stood for a moment, watching the door from the church offices into the courtyard.

She remained aware of the note in her pocket. After the vestry meeting today, Lily felt sure the parish was hiding, or hiding from, something. The "something" had to do with Barnes, and, judging from Mrs. Hanlon's remarks, it had to do with his death. As did this odd-looking note—she was certain. For an instant she felt exhilarated, released. She knew if she threw herself into finding the truth, she could avoid the grim sadness always in her heart these days—and all in the name of helping others.

Throughout the following week she dreamed vividly, in bursts of color and high drama. Lily had mixed feelings about her dreams. To begin with, she loved to sleep, and when she dreamed this kind of attention-getting saga she found it impossible not to wake up excited, sometimes panicked, and equally impossible to get back to sleep afterward. Also, though she never talked about it with anyone, she regularly dreamed small slivers of events that only made sense later, in the context of her daytime life.

She dreamed of Mrs. Hanlon trudging down Charles Street, trying to get a wheelchair up the steps to the MTA station. In one dream, Charlie kneeled on the floor in front of her, hemming her vestments; Mrs. Hanlon assisted him. There was the figure in the church portico, this time a little boy, or a boy with his father, searching for a place to sleep. The father turned out to be the young Hispanic man selling *Spare Change* in the rain. And she dreamed of another man writing the careful, square letters of the note in the pocket—Father Barnes, who looked something like her own father, but with a great, bulky coat and a clerical collar, driving the back roads outside her hometown in Texas, looking for safety.

# chapter ❈ 5

Mrs. Hanlon's presence in her dreams gave Lily the odd sense that the two had spent more time together than they had. When the older woman appeared at the office door on the following Thursday, Lily felt a warm familiarity toward her, as if the nighttime visits had been shared by them both. After greeting her, Lily asked if Mrs. Hanlon could continue to clean the church through the holiday season.

"It's up to the vestry, I think, to find someone else, but nothing's been done," said Lily, not adding that nothing had been done because she hadn't spoken to anyone about doing anything. "And I could talk with your priest, if you like."

"No, no," said Mrs. Hanlon, "the decision's mine. Father Bill doesn't like telling people what to do, though he's a good listener, and full of his own opinions." She tacked on the last part, as if she were afraid Lily might think less of a man who trusted his parishioners without check.

"Obviously, you can leave whenever you want," said Lily. "But I'm still having a hard time getting to know the place, and it would be helpful to have someone around who could talk a little about what's going on right now— someone with a different perspective."

"I have that," said Mrs. Hanlon.

"Exactly," said Lily, persisting. "I don't like to force people to talk about Fred Barnes—"

"No," said Mrs. Hanlon. "They wouldn't want to, not some of them, anyway."

"Why's that?" asked Lily.

The older woman didn't respond. She stared through the window onto the courtyard. Lily followed her gaze and saw Cynthia Babcock at the gate on Lee Street, her arms full of folded choir robes. Cynthia tried to balance the robes in one arm and manage the gate latch with her free hand. There was something charming and comical about the scene until John Neville appeared.

To Lily, his few seconds of silent observation were eerie; he reached out no hand to help and offered no greeting. At last he must have spoken, for Cynthia Babcock startled, dropped one of the robes, and wheeled around. Of course, Lily didn't know what they were saying, but it was a painful moment, and she felt indecent for having witnessed it. As Cynthia bent down to retrieve the robe, Neville turned and left.

"So there," said Mrs. Hanlon, under her breath.

"What?" asked Lily.

"Those two used to be Jack and Jill." She held up two fingers of her right hand and squeezed them together. "Like this," she said. "Never apart."

"What happened?"

"I don't know," said Mrs. Hanlon. "But it's happened since Father's death. Ask her about it sometime. You'll never get anything out of him."

Cynthia Babcock entered the hall from the courtyard and appeared in the office doorway with a hearty "hello." Her face was red and her voice was pitched a note or two higher than usual, but other than that, there was no hint she had just had a set-to with a fellow parishioner.

"I came to pick up messages for the Pastoral Care and

Concerns Committee," said Cynthia, "and to return these—refurbished for Advent." She held out the robes for Lily's inspection. "I'm doing a little work for the altar guild, too. They're short-handed these days, but who isn't?"

"Great," said Lily, noting a faint smudge of brown dirt on the top robe. Then she asked, "Are you all right?"

"Me? Yes. Fine," said Cynthia. She turned, straightened her shoulders, and headed for the robing room.

Lily stepped out into the hall and called to her.

"While you're here, Cynthia, I wonder if I could ask you about Fred Barnes's things," she said. "I talked with John Neville, and he said something would be done, but it's all just as it was."

"You mean his clothes?" asked Cynthia.

"His clothes, his shoes, his mouthwash, his books—"

"Oh no. What a mess. And not much of a welcome for you, is it?" Cynthia paused, began to speak, thought better of it, shifted the robes in her arms, and finally said, "I'd love to offer to help, but it's not really my territory."

"Any ideas about what I should do next?" Lily asked.

Cynthia glanced at Mrs. Hanlon, standing just inside the office door. She paused before she answered, then seemed to get an idea. "Why not talk to Dan?" Cynthia asked. "He's the one that gets things done. Isn't it always the case? Like wives and secretaries—the person in charge is never the person who actually gets things done."

Lily took a moment to catch up with the thinking. Dan Talbot was the junior warden, the second in command on the vestry. "So in this case I ask the junior warden, not the senior warden," she said. "That makes sense."

"Good," said Cynthia. "I'm glad to be of help."

As Cynthia turned away once more, Roger Frye, the sexton, the man in charge of keeping the church buildings in working order, opened the door from the courtyard. He walked through the group of women in the hall without a word. He was in his forties, with close-cropped ginger-colored hair and a pale, flat face; Lily had never seen him in anything other than Marine fatigues. Frye had a reputation as a man with a temper, but there was a patronizing acceptance of him among the parishioners. Before reaching the basement stairs, he turned to Lily and asked, "Can I talk to you?"

"Yes," said Lily, in a kind of gasp. "Now?"

"No," he said and looked at the other two women. "Later."

"Sure," said Lily. "I'm here all day today. Anytime." She thought her enthusiasm sounded overdone, but Frye didn't seem to notice. He nodded to her, then trudged down the stairs to the basement.

Cynthia's eyes narrowed, and she shook her head in a kind of marmish disapproval. Then she walked into the robing room, leaving the two women in the hallway. Lily caught Mrs. Hanlon's eye; the older woman raised her eyebrows as if to signal surprise, amusement—? Lily wasn't sure, and yet it was a moment of complicity, a moment Lily had craved since she arrived at this parish.

"I'll get on here, then," said Mrs. Hanlon, after which she picked up her bags and headed for the stairs.

Back in her office, Lily left two messages for Dan Talbot, one with his secretary and one on his answering machine at home. Then she hung up to call Charlie. She dialed the number of the monastery and settled in for the long process of getting him on the phone, but to her surprise he answered with a clipped "Hello?"

"Hello?" she said, imitating him. "You're not much of a receptionist. You should go back to the greenhouse where you belong."

"Oh, it's you." He sounded fed up and angry.

"What's wrong?" she asked.

"Wrong?" he said. "I don't know that anything's wrong."

"Something's definitely wrong," said Lily.

"You mean besides the fact that I spent the entire morning at a committee meeting?"

"Which committee?"

"The Diocesan Committee on Human Sexuality," said Charlie. "I mean think about it, think about the name."

"Yes," she said. "You don't really want to hear the words 'committee' and 'sexuality' in the same sentence."

"No kidding."

"And what's the agenda now?" she asked.

"Nothing too grand. Just an answer to the twin questions of the ordination of gay and lesbian priests and the blessing of gay and lesbian unions. I mean, it's dressed up as issues about human sexuality and marital fidelity, but we all know what we're talking about."

"How can you stand it?"

"I'm not sure I can anymore. What really bothers me the most is that this is supposed to be a process of discernment. But there's no discernment going on here. I'm as guilty as anyone. We all knew what we thought when we arrived—maybe not all, now that I think of it. There are some people really struggling. And I find I have more patience than I ever imagined, especially with the struggle. But the others—if you could hear the paranoid, homophobic drivel I listen to . . ."

Lily waited for her friend to catch his breath and finish his sentence. "I'm really sorry," she said. "Can you get out of doing it?"

"No. I told Spencer I'd stay until we get this settled. Of course, I didn't know it was going to be a lifelong commitment."

"Have you tried praying for the other members?" she asked.

"Day and night, sweetheart, day and night. But this isn't why you called."

"I don't mind listening," she said.

"Thanks. I know. But I don't want to hear myself anymore. What's up?"

"I'm thinking about taking off more time from work."

"You mean from the Women's Center?" asked Charlie.

"Yeah," she said. "I was going to start half-time again next month, but this interim job is so—"

"Absorbing?"

"That's one way to put it," she said. "The position's supposed to be half-time, but I spend less than that doing

the actual work, but more than that—what?—trying to figure out what the work is."

"Is it okay at the center—for you to be gone that long?"

"Yes and no. They need the help. As usual, though, they
don't really have the money to pay me. What do you
think?"

"I think it's probably a good idea," said Charlie.

"Why?"

"A couple of reasons," he said. "First of all, the stuff
you do at the center—the race and class and gender
groups—that's really draining, and takes a lot of the same
energy you need for parish work."

"And second?"

"Second, I think you ought to leave some time for yourself."

"I knew you'd say that," she said. "But that's fine. I
need someone to tell me I'm doing the right thing."

"Then you're doing the right thing, definitely," said
Charlie. "And we'll have more time to hang out."

Lily thought of "hanging out" with the brothers in the
spare, gray monastery chapel, cigarettes dangling from the
corners of their mouths, baseball caps backwards, sneak-
ers untied beneath their cassocks. "Yes," she said, smiling
to herself, "that's one of the best parts." Then she added,
"Maybe you could take a few deep breaths before you
hang up."

"Deep breaths?" said Charlie.

"I was hoping for a sort of hyperventilating effect," she
said, "a sort of meditation as carbon-dioxide narcosis."

Charlie laughed and said, "It feels like a year since I've
done that."

"Hyperventilated?" asked Lily.

"No, laughed."

"I know the feeling," she said, then was surprised to
hear what sounded like angry voices from downstairs in
the church basement. She rolled the desk chair across the
thin carpet until she could reach the door and shut it.
"Charlie," she began, interrupting him as he started to

speak. "Something's happening here. I think I'd better go."

"Are you okay?" asked Charlie.

"I'm fine. But somebody's yelling at someone in the basement."

"Call me later," said Charlie. "We can compare notes."

As Lily hung up, a red-faced Roger Frye banged once on the office door and swung it open.

"I don't answer to her," he said loudly. "I answer to you and Mr. Neville."

"Are you talking about Mrs. Hanlon?" she asked him.

"I am. I'll talk to you about the reverend's things. But I'm not talking to her."

"What about the reverend's things?" asked Lily.

Roger glanced over his shoulder into the hallway, then turned back to Lily. "It's not just about his things," he said. His voice dropped slightly.

"What is it about?" asked Lily.

He paused for a moment and stared at her, then he shook his head, said, "Forget it," and stormed out the door into the courtyard.

Lily watched him walk down the path and bang the gate closed behind him. Then she went to the stair railing, leaned over, and looked down into Mrs. Hanlon's face peering up at her from the stairwell.

"I wouldn't worry about him," said Mrs. Hanlon. "He'll go out and have a few beers and be fine this afternoon. I'll be over to the rectory by then, anyway." Her face disappeared.

Curiouser and curiouser, thought Lily, as she turned back toward her office. Cynthia Babcock was standing at the door of the choir room, a heavy brass candlestick in one hand, a polishing rag in the other, and a look of desperate confusion on her face.

"What happened?" she asked Lily.

"I'm not quite sure," Lily said. "Evidently Mrs. Hanlon and Roger had a disagreement. Roger wanted to talk with me about Barnes's belongings—at least in part. It's hard to know. But I've been told everything will be fine, so I'm going with that for now."

Lily walked back into her office, sat in the leather desk chair, placed both her feet flat on the floor, and focused on the thick branches of the giant fir tree in the courtyard. From the basement she could hear the sounds of Mrs. Hanlon opening the door to Frye's work area. And from nearby, just across the hall, she heard what she thought must be the sniffling of Cynthia Babcock, crying in private.

# chapter �֎ 6

The next morning Lily tried to work in the rectory study but found it hard to keep her mind on next Sunday's sermon. She read the Gospel passage a few times, then set out for a walk to help her think. The weather was wintry—grim, damp, bitter—and Lily loved it. Growing up in Texas, she had felt something was missing, something about the climate. When she came East to seminary and discovered a world with four seasons, she had known immediately that this was what she had longed for all that time.

She crossed Beacon Street and entered the Public Garden. When she reached the bridge that spanned the narrow waist of the pond, she stopped halfway across. The water was dark and still, the boats in storage, the children in school, and the gardens almost deserted. But she could not view the scene without adding an overlay—like the plastic transparencies in an encyclopedia—of spring tulips and daffodils, swan boats, picnickers on the grass, solitary spectators on the green benches. For now, though, she preferred the landscape just as it was.

She leaned on the railing of the bridge and tried to reflect on the Gospel for All Saints' Day. Last week, Lily had persuaded Stanley Leonard to use the second set of readings—Luke's version of the Beatitudes and a passage from Ecclesiasticus: "Accept whatever is brought upon you, and in changes that humble you, be patient. For gold is tested in the fire, and acceptable men in the furnace of humiliation."

When she had first read it, she'd been struck by the universal truth of the words. But she hadn't thought much about how they applied to her. In this moment of stillness on the bridge, Lily recognized their particular, private truth.

At some point in those nights in Texas, awake in the old leather lounger she had dragged into her father's room, her life had stopped making sense. There was no rational process involved. She had just stopped trusting God.

She still *believed* in prayer, in the Holy Spirit's power to move and change her. But now her beliefs made no difference; they only existed in her head. She had become the object of her own scorn—a priest without faith—and she was humiliated. She was in the furnace.

Impatient, restless, she crossed the bridge and headed toward the Common. In four weeks they would be stringing lights on the bare tree limbs. It would be Advent, her favorite season in the church. And she would be spending that time in a parish where she felt like an outcast.

When she reached the Common, she headed up and across, toward the Cathedral of St. Michael and All Angels on Tremont. She had begun to feel a little desperate. Maybe this was the day for that talk with the bishop.

Lily had never liked the cathedral. The building was square and graceless on the outside and uninspiring on the inside. The gray walls and salmon-colored cushions struck a note of false luxury, like a cut-rate hotel lobby aspiring to better things.

She walked down the center aisle, bowed to the altar, and went through a door on the back wall, through the robing room, down the stairs and into the offices of the diocese. The hallway was quiet, but as she approached the reception area she heard the Right Reverend Lamont Spencer's unmistakable bass voice saying, "Good-bye." As suffragan bishop of the diocese, Spencer was second in command. An ardent civil-rights activist for the past forty years, Spencer now served under a moderate bishop, Greg Lewis, whose main goal was to bring the diocese back in line with the more moderate national church. The result at the moment was a kind of stalemated tug-of-war in which two powerful forces pulled in opposite directions with equal strength.

As she entered the lobby, she saw Spencer standing with his back to her, waving out the door toward the bookstore. When Lily was first getting to know him, he had confided to her that he saw his very existence as a kind of test. "You know," he had said, "Episcopalians see this big, black man in a fancy priest suit, and a lot of them don't know what to make of me. I can see the battle going on inside some of them—do they see me as a black man or a bishop? Or *both?*" After she'd gotten over her surprise at his honesty, she had felt a flood of gratitude. And she'd recognized an ally in the diocesan offices.

As he turned to the receptionist, the bishop saw Lily and smiled with a look of welcome and surprise. He appeared older, his short hair grayer, his face more drawn than it had been six months earlier. But the energy in his tall, broad body, which Lily connected with his powerful faith, was just as evident.

"This is great," he said. "I've been thinking about you. I've wanted to see you. Do you have a minute now?"

Lily shook his outstretched hand. "I think that's my line," she said. "I'm the supplicant here."

He laughed. "That's not a role I really picture you in," he said. "A supplicant—no, that's not how I see you."

The bishop turned to the receptionist, a young black man in a gray turtleneck.

"Can you do me a favor?" Spencer asked him. "Can you call upstairs so I can see what I have next?"

"Sure," he answered, picked up the phone, pressed two buttons, and handed the phone to Spencer.

Spencer asked about his next appointment, then listened for a moment and muttered, "Oh, Lord." He added, "Stall him just a few minutes. We won't be long. Tell him it's a crisis of faith."

Finally, Spencer opened a metal fire door and led Lily down a flight of concrete stairs to a small basement room with a Coke machine, a Ping-Pong table, and a matching set of folding card table and chairs. He took some change from his pocket and looked at Lily.

"Do you drink Coke?" he asked. "I don't remember." She nodded, and he continued. "I didn't for a long time— South African holdings. But that's what machine we had here, so that's what I drink. I tried to get it changed, but no clout. Power corrupts—that's what they say. I think that's true, but you know what corrupts as much, maybe more?" He was still looking at her, "Powerlessness."

Lily laughed. "You're right," she said. "I hadn't thought of it. Maybe that's what's happening to me."

"How so?" he asked and turned to put money in the machine.

"I'm not really sure," Lily told him.

He turned back to her, handed her a Coke, got his own, sat at the table, and motioned for her to join him.

"I am sure part of it's me, what I've been through with my father," she said. "But, still, everything's not as it should be at St. Mary's."

"How do you know?" he asked.

"I know," she said. "I've done this before, a few times, and pretty successfully, if you recall. Here I try to plan a coffee hour, and nobody calls me back. Or they call me back, but they can't do anything. And when I go to meetings they plan, it's worse. No one can look at me, much less listen to me—especially if I mention Barnes. They're more like a parish that's been burned, you know, whose rector has betrayed them."

He nodded but didn't comment.

"It reminds me a little of St. James's," she said. "After McNamara got caught messing around with what was essentially the soprano section of the choir. This group feels more like that. You remember how they tried to keep the whole thing under wraps—the worst of it, at least? And I kept telling you they were hiding something."

"Yes, yes, and I didn't believe you. I remember."

"This feels similar somehow, even though the details are so different. St. James's was a wonderful parish. This place is a spiritual wasteland."

"That's pretty damning," said Spencer.

"If you like them so much, you be their rector."

"I don't like or not like them. But I'm not ready to divest them of the Spirit," said Spencer. "I find it a very challenging place." He paused, then added, "Rich people have problems, too."

"Yes," said Lily, "but I have problems with rich people."

"But you come from money yourself, don't you? Didn't someone in your family have a lot of money?"

"My mother did. My mother's family. Not *my* family." She hoped her clipped tone would signal the end of the subject. But Spencer was impervious.

"And you're not in touch with her anymore, are you, or with anyone on that side? Maybe there's some connection there—you think?" He raised his eyebrows and nodded, as if to underscore the obvious.

"Most likely," said Lily, staring back at him. When she was first considering ordination, she had told Spencer the story of her childhood—of her mother's disappearance from their hometown when Lily was four; of her father's silence on the subject for the first year; of the annulment and of her own ensuing miserable childhood summers, traveling with her mother and a variety of drunk companions. Lily had told him once, but she had never talked with him about it again, and she certainly didn't want to talk about it now. She averted her eyes and asked, "So why did you send me there?"

"I heard you needed a place to live," he said, and smiled.

"Thanks," said Lily, "but I would have preferred the Y."

"All right, then. I probably don't even know all the reasons, but here are some of them. I know you're a confirmed tentmaker—and for you that's an especially apt term."

"What do you mean?"

"I think you like the image of the spiritual nomad," said Spencer, "not being tied to any particular parish or liturgy. Maybe it's the cowboy in your blood."

"Yeah—I'm a real yahoo," said Lily. "For six years I lived in the same apartment on Commonwealth, rode the bus to the Women's Center, went to Tuesday night eucharist with the boys at the monastery. There's no tying me down."

"I said *spiritual* nomad. In any case, you've been one of our best interim priests, and you're experienced working with tough cases—St. James's for one. You can make it all the way through a sung liturgy. And you've got a rare combination of compassion and common sense that can really help a parish in this kind of troubled time. The problem is that your own work at the Women's Center—the anti-bias stuff, the activism—takes you so far from the mainstream that I worry you're losing the common sense part, and the compassion, too, for that matter."

Lily opened her mouth to object, but he raised his hand, a request to go on uninterrupted.

"You're a good pastor, but you've got to practice. And," he continued, "this is a tough call, this parish."

Lily looked at him, head to one side, a pained expression on her face. "So, if I stay, will you help me?"

"How?"

"Find out what you can about them, about Barnes. Was there trouble between them before he died? Why is there so much tension on the vestry over there? And, by the way, how come both the desks were totally empty, cleaned out, but I've still got his shaving stuff in the john?"

"Is that all you need to know?" he asked.

"No," she said. "See if there are any younger members, guys, maybe teenagers, maybe young adult, twenty at the oldest—family members, whatever—who are in trouble."

"Why?"

"I'll tell you when I know more. But I promise I won't

make a big deal about anything until I have more information."

"Fine, then," said Spencer. "But let me say this. The vestry—Neville, Talbot, Babcock—they deal directly with Greg Lewis whenever possible. Greg and Talbot have known each other for years, and—though you'll no doubt find this hard to believe—they're more compatible—how should I put this—politically."

"I'm stunned," she said, flat-voiced.

"Yes, well, the point is, I'll try to find out what I can. But Greg can be quite protective of your new parish. It's an important resource, in many ways, for him."

"I understand that," said Lily.

Spencer glanced at his watch, then leaned back in his chair and stared up at the ceiling, his hands folded in his lap. After a moment of silence, he said, "I have a feeling, and so do you, I think, that this parish is in trouble. There aren't a lot of people who would bother to go any deeper than absolutely necessary, but you will. We would never have known the whole story on McNamara if you hadn't been their interim. I think this is a similar situation—I don't mean that Barnes was sleeping with the choir—I hope not, anyway."

Lily thought of the kitchen shelves—the alphabetized spices and matching dishes. "I don't think so," she said.

"Me neither," said Spencer. "He was a nice man, really. We didn't agree on anything, but he was a nice, honest guy. And he took his job seriously." He paused again, then asked her, "Did you know him?"

"No. I'd seen him around, at Diocesan Convention. But I never spoke with him."

Spencer looked down at the Coke can in his large hands, then tipped it, as if to see what was left. "I'll let you know what I find out. That's the best I can do for now."

Lily smiled a tired, resigned smile and nodded.

"Meanwhile," said Spencer, "You find out what you can, too. Get to know them. You're a good priest. You can help out over there, if you decide to do it."

"Okay," she said.

"It's a bewildered group of people—that's what I think—and I want them to have a strong soul with them now."

Lily winced; this was not the assessment of herself she'd come up with on the bridge.

But he didn't seem to notice. "The church is changing, you know that. And it's very scary for a lot of mainline Episcopalians. We don't give them much to hold on to—no dress code, no strict rules, no do's and don'ts."

He looked at his watch and then at her.

"Don't be too hard on me for this," he said. "I got you into this thing, and I won't abandon you there. I have a lot of faith in you, Lily, and that's nice for me, because there's so little I can say that about these days."

He stood and held out his left hand, a gesture of comradeship, of comfort. She took it in her right hand and clung, she noticed, for a moment, before letting go and standing up herself.

# chapter ✳ 7

she stopped in the cathedral bookstore on her way out, thinking a browse in a bookstore, any bookstore, usually cheered her up. Today, even this failed her. She saw a book by a seminary friend who had stayed in graduate school, gotten her doctorate, and gone on to publish an important study on the role of the modern church in anti-Semitism, Lily's own field. The woman's second book examined the church's responsibility for its imagery and treatment of people of color. She should buy it, she knew, but she couldn't bring herself to contribute to the success of the book by adding to the number of hardcover sales. As she turned away she thought, I've reached the bottom—I can't get lower than this.

She left hurriedly, crossed the street to the corner delicatessen, bought a pastrami sandwich, and took her tray to a table by the window. She watched a group of Hasidic Jews pass by, four young men who simultaneously burst into gleeful laughter as they reached the corner. Orthodox religions offered clear guidelines for behavior: honoring the Sabbath, keeping kosher, or the comfort of confession and penance. But the Episcopal Church was a church of inquiry and reflection—scripture, tradition, and reason—which was one of the things that had attracted her in the first place.

At Catholic school, Lily had assumed she would become a nun. She had in mind the most self-sacrificial and romantic version—working with the poor someplace dangerous. But as she got older, the vision became more practical. She saw who had the power in her church—the priests.

Her vision of service became more practical, too. During her college years in Boston she worked in the soup kitchen at the nearby Episcopal church. She loved it, but she didn't want to be serving soup forever. She wanted to make a world in which soup kitchens were obsolete. And she felt that was the church's job. But there was no place in the Catholic Church—or at her Catholic college, for that matter—for a woman who wanted to be a politically active Catholic priest.

Then one evening after work in the kitchen, she'd gone upstairs with a friend to an Episcopal Evensong service, and the deacon had been presiding—an ordained woman. The next day Lily had met with her and had her first taste of the elasticity of Episcopal doctrine, the story of women's ordination. Two months later, she had begun confirmation classes.

But this didn't make her a spiritual nomad. What made that true (and she admitted to herself it was true) was her restless inability to accept the church as it was: flawed, self-serving, and limited. At seminary, she had studied Judaism, Islam, Hinduism, Buddhism, and her faith now contained elements from all of those religions. So she had ended up as an ordained Episcopal minister who worked for a nonprofit women's center teaching the acceptance of all religions, all beliefs, all people. Then, once in a while she stepped in and worked for the church as an interim priest. That's when her nomadic attitudes became most obvious.

She picked up half the sandwich, looked at it, and smiled. The answer here was to stick to the task at hand. Eat the sandwich, drink the tea, and do her job at St. Mary's. Spencer had said "find out more about them," so she would, whether they liked it or not.

Dan Talbot was the logical place to start for many reasons. First of all, as junior warden of the vestry he was the second most powerful layperson at St. Mary's. Talbot had done most of the early interviews and negotiations for her interim post. He had been businesslike but affable and, unlike so many people active in the church, seemed to understand the concept of privacy, for her and for himself. He hadn't needed to tell her his life story, or anyone else's, for that matter.

Mostly, though, starting with Talbot seemed a good idea because his offices were on the corner of Temple and Tremont, half a block away from the deli, and a cold drizzle had started up. Talbot's place would be a handy stopping point where she could wait out the rain. And then, of course, there remained the problem of Fred Barnes's belongings. Cynthia had said to see Dan, so she would.

But, half an hour later, seated in the reception area on the top floor of his office building, she wasn't sure this was such a good idea after all. She suddenly felt inappropriate and ridiculous, showing up without an appointment in her parka, cowboy boots, pullover, and clerical collar. The offices were ten floors above the main store of the chain Talbot owned and operated—SDT Discount Services, large discount stores with everything from garden shops to pharmacies. Because of the location and the type of store it was, Lily had expected a more modest, worklike setting. Here, the carpets were thick, the tones were beige, the lighting recessed, and the furniture leather.

The receptionist, a handsome woman in her late fifties, dressed to match her surroundings in an off-white knit suit and a short string of pearls, had responded at once to Lily's clerical collar, appearing eager to help. But as soon as Lily said she hoped to see Talbot, the woman—Mrs. Hennessey, according to the nameplate on her desk—had been firm about the impossibility of granting that particular request.

According to Mrs. Hennessey, Mr. Talbot was in a meeting then, would be in a meeting later, and was leaving for a meeting in Chicago that night.

"It won't take long," said Lily. "Really I just stopped by to say hello. I'm the interim at St. Mary's, Mr. Talbot's church, and I'm trying to get to know the members of the parish a little better. And I need some help from Mr. Talbot on a couple of things—you know, consulting with the powers-that-be."

Lily thought maybe the word "powers" softened Mrs. Hennessey. She told Lily she could certainly wait if she wanted to—there was no telling how long they would be in there—maybe there would be a few minutes between meetings in which she could just nip in and steal a second of his time.

"Great," said Lily, sounding more cheerful than she felt. She sat down next to an end table stocked with current issues of *Life, Forbes,* and *U.S. News & World Report.* Through the plateglass wall behind the reception desk Lily saw that the drizzle had turned into steady rain. And though the place was making her uncomfortable and she suddenly felt unsure of her purpose, she thought she might as well stay.

Halfway into the second set of articles about who ran the White House, Lily heard a heavy door open, then a chorus of hearty male voices wishing each other well. She recognized the unmistakable ring of self-congratulations. The meeting had gone swimmingly. Someone was making money.

Briefly, a woman's voice joined the chorus, then three men appeared from around the corner behind the desk. Mrs. Hennessey stood up, told them good-bye, walked past them, consulted with someone, sat back down, and never once looked at Lily. The men, with a few furtive glances at the woman priest in the jeans, got on the elevator, leaving the waiting area silent.

After another minute, a buzzer sounded on Mrs. Hennessey's desk. She picked up the phone, said a few words, hung up, and turned to speak to Lily. At the same moment, Dan Talbot appeared, smiling, his hand outstretched.

For an instant, she imagined him as a little boy dressed up like a businessman. He was short, at least an inch shorter than she, with rounded corners and no angles. His blond hair had been neatly cut, and his cheeks looked bright and pink, as if he had just come in from the snow. There was a brightness to his eyes, too, but it was a shrewd brightness, and Lily had no doubt that whatever had just happened in his office, he had, somehow, come out ahead.

Talbot seemed gracious but reserved. He spoke to Mrs. Hennessey, introduced Lily to his assistant—a young woman with cropped blond hair and wearing a black suit—then showed Lily into his office and began to point out landmarks in the view from his plateglass windows. Lily worried that their time together would be consumed by an aerial tour of downtown Boston. Finally, he offered her a seat in a leather swivel chair by the window and took the one facing her.

"So, what can I do for you?" he asked.

It took Lily a second to catch up. She felt unsure of herself, like a woman visiting a specialist, seeking help for a vague, suspicious complaint of fatigue.

"This was pretty spur-of-the-moment," she began. "I was next-door, at the cathedral"—something told her to leave Spencer out of this—"and thought I'd stop by. Also, you've been on my mind, you and your family."

"Really?" he asked. "In what way?"

"A few ways, actually. First of all, I haven't seen you much around the church. I'm not in the habit of taking attendance, but I think John mentioned you were especially busy. Something in his tone made me think maybe you were busy with not entirely pleasant business."

Talbot nodded and smiled noncommittally. "And the other ways?" he asked.

"I just worry that people—that you and Sally—might be staying away out of your sadness about Fred Barnes. I wish—" she paused, then decided to tell the flat truth. "I wish I could be more help there—that I understood more about what went on with Barnes."

He nodded, as if to say he sympathized, as if to say she might be right. But he waited a few seconds before answering. "It has been hard to be there since his death. We were very close, all of us—" He broke off here, and when he spoke next his voice had shifted to a lower, less relaxed register. "I miss him. We all miss him." He looked out the window. Lily looked, too, at the rain blowing diagonally across the glass.

"My family's going through a rough patch right now. My son—he's a teenager, you know?" he added, with a wry smile.

Lily's heart gave a small jump; she nodded calmly. "Just let me know if I can do anything," she said.

"Right," he answered. "I don't think we're ready to talk about it yet, with anyone outside the family."

"That's fine," she said quickly. "But if that changes, I'm here."

"Thanks," he said. "Anything else? Vestry stuff? Schedules? Stewardship campaign? I'm better at that."

"There are some specific things I need to know about," she said. "Like who's in charge of Barnes's belongings." She thought she sensed in him a withdrawal, as if from a chronic, familiar pain.

"I thought John was handling that," he said.

"So did I, but nothing's happened. It's not that important, but . . ."

"Don't apologize. It should have been done weeks ago. I'll talk to him. Everyone's so scattered by all of this— still, I'm sorry."

"Don't *you* apologize," said Lily.

"It's a deal," he said. After a pause, he pointed out the window, across the Common, toward Charles Street and the church. "You can see it from here," he said, "the tip of St. Mary's spire. See?"

Lily looked in the same direction. "I think I can," she said, but she wasn't sure. The rain obscured the distant scenery.

"Practice," said Talbot. "I've been looking at it for, oh, almost fifteen years."

She heard a quiet knock on the door. Talbot's assistant, the young blonde, opened it slightly, nodded at him, and closed it. He stood and offered his hand to Lily.

"I'm glad you came by," he said. "I'll sort through this confusion about the rectory. As for the rest, give it time . . ." He waved his hand in the air, vaguely, implying some topic beyond words, somewhere in the direction of St. Mary of the Garden.

In Lily's experience, if you asked enough people enough questions, you would eventually get some answers. It wasn't an elegant method, and it wasn't very efficient either. Waiting was as much a part of the work as asking. But she believed she would get information, in time.

She had not learned much today—except that the Talbots had a teenage son. This, of course, could mean nothing. Surely there was more than one teenage son in the congregation, even though she had not seen any at church.

Even with her hood up, the tiny drops stung her cheeks and blurred her vision; it was raining sideways. When she crossed Charles Street, a car skidded through the red light just as she reached the sidewalk. The image of the driver's terrified face stayed with her through the evening, long after she turned off the bedside light and lay awake, listening to the sounds of the old house in the darkness.

# chapter ✳ 8

"First person born in the Western hemisphere to be canonized by the Roman Catholic Church," said Lily.

"Oh, it's that woman you like so much . . . the one born in Peru . . ." answered Charlie.

"We need the correct name, please," she said in the officious voice of a game show host. "You have twenty seconds left, and you must put your answer in the form of a question."

"Wait, wait," said Charlie, "I know, the Rose of Peru."

Lily laughed out loud and said, "That sounds like a movie in the Combat Zone." Then she added, "Not 'the Rose of Peru'—'St. Rose of Lima.' One of the earliest liberation theologians."

The river shone in the cold, bright light of November. Three weeks had passed since Lily's visits to Bishop Spencer and Dan Talbot. So far she had gotten no answers, at least nothing she recognized as an answer, to the questions she had asked in October.

This year's Diocesan Convention had come and gone, the contingent from St. Mary of the Garden voting against anything having to do with gay men and lesbians and any increase in the budget for outreach and mission work. The vestry had begun the self-study that precedes the search for a new rector, having reached a compromise with the bishops over the length of waiting time. After these weeks of relative calm, Lily even wondered if she had made too much of her own discomfort. Maybe the only thing wrong at St. Mary's was a bad match between interim priest and congregation. Still, the image of the young man running from her on the dark street remained vivid, and not only in her dreams.

A jogger passed Lily and Charlie as they walked together along the path, arm in arm. They were playing a game they had invented while studying for their ordination exams—Jesuit Jeopardy.

"Your turn," said Lily.

"First Catholic liturgy for same-sex marriages."

"What is the forty-fifth century," said Lily, "A.D.?"

"Wrong. We now have evidence that there was a liturgy for same-sex unions in the early Church, maybe as early as the eighth century. What do you think of that?"

"Who's 'we'?" asked Lily. "You and Barney Frank?"

"As a matter of fact, it's from a professor at Yale, so there's some credibility to the findings," said Charlie. "Now, who's ahead?"

"Charlie, I stopped keeping score a long time ago, since you had that tantrum about one of the Thirty-nine Articles. No one's ahead. On the other hand, if I *were* keeping score, *I'd* be ahead."

"That's convenient."

"Let's turn around," said Lily. "I'm cold. And today's Thursday. If we're lucky, we can get Mrs. Hanlon to have tea with us. She thinks you're swell."

For the past three weeks, Charlie had visited Lily on Thursdays; he and the older woman had struck up an immediate friendship. Unfortunately, Charlie's presence diverted them from talk of the parish. But Lily told herself to be patient. When Mrs. Hanlon was willing to tell her story, she would.

"I know she likes me," Charlie said after a moment, "but I'm not sure why."

"Maybe it's because the two of you seem to know half the Catholic families in South Boston. You think?"

"Could be. But she still can't quite figure out exactly what I am. I doubt that she's ever heard of an Episcopalian monk."

"I hate to tell you this," said Lily, "but not many people have. There's something oxymoronic about the term— like an Evangelical Unitarian."

They crossed the footbridge over Storrow Drive to Arlington Street, then turned up Beacon in the direction of St. Mary's. Charlie was silent; Lily decided she'd hurt his feelings. After a moment, she reached out and took his hand.

"I'm sorry," she said. "I'm angry half the time these days, and I'm not used to it, so I just take it out on the closest vertical object. Last night I knocked over the coat tree."

"At least I'm in good company," said Charlie, and they walked to River Street in a more comfortable silence.

Mrs. Hanlon was indeed still at the rectory, and she appeared glad to see them. In fact, Lily felt surprised by the enthusiasm with which they were greeted.

"Officer Casey from the police department called you," she said to Lily. "I wrote his number down by the phone."

"Thanks," said Lily, even more surprised, "but you don't have to answer the phone when I'm not here. And who in the world is Officer Casey?"

"Definitely," said Charlie, ignoring the question. "Lily doesn't answer it when she *is* here. No need to break the pattern."

"I do answer it," said Lily, "some."

"So I'll put on water for tea," said Mrs. Hanlon, "and you can return your call."

"Anyway, people can always leave a message at the office," continued Lily defensively. "But why would—"

"Go ahead then," said Mrs. Hanlon, interrupting her. "Make your call."

"Wait a minute," said Lily, louder now. "Why are the police calling me?"

"It so happens Tom Casey's mother is an old friend of mine," said Mrs. Hanlon. "And he has an interest in this case."

"What case?" asked Lily.

"Father's death," said Mrs. Hanlon.

"I'm lost," said Charlie.

"So you had this guy call me to talk about Barnes's death?" Lily asked. "But I don't know anything about it."

"Exactly," said Mrs. Hanlon. "But Tommy does. Because I've been speaking with him about this for a while now, and he looked into a few things for me."

"But I still don't—" Lily began.

"Lily," said Charlie calmly. "Call the guy back. Mrs. Hanlon thinks it would be a good idea."

Mrs. Hanlon took Lily into the study and spoke to her in a low voice. "Something's going on here—I think you know that's true. I've wanted to talk with you about it for a while now, but I needed to be sure you were the right person—the right people, you and Charles. I needed to make sure you would listen. And Tom will only help if you call and invite him. He doesn't want to overstep his bounds."

After a moment, Lily said, "All you had to do was ask."

"I thought so," said Mrs. Hanlon. "But I couldn't be sure. These things can take time. You know that."

Then Mrs. Hanlon squeezed Lily's hand and left the room, leading Charlie out of the hall and into the kitchen with her. Lily turned to the desk and dialed the number written down on the pad. When a child answered she assumed she had made a mistake.

"Sorry," she said, "I've got the wrong number."

"Who do you want to talk to?" asked the child, word by word, repeating a learned sentence.

"I was looking for Officer Casey, but . . ."

"I'll get him," came the reply.

While Lily waited, she heard a woman's voice and, in the distance, a baby's loud screech, more playful than distressed. This is some police station, she thought. Then she heard a man's voice on the other end of the line.

"Casey here," he said.

"Is this Tom Casey?" she asked.

"Yeah. What can I do for you?"

"You left a message for me to call you back, I think. I'm Lily Connor."

"Oh, yeah, yeah," he said. Lily heard recognition in his voice, and something else—discomfort, confusion? "You're the priest, right?"

"Yes," said Lily, "among other things."

"I've been told there are some loose ends to tie up about your predecessor."

"Look. As you know, Mrs. Hanlon's here, so she's explained what this is about, more or less. She wants you to come over now if you can. And so do I."

There was a brief pause, during which Lily heard the woman's voice, the sound of a slamming door, then silence.

"Okay," he said.

"Do you know how to get here?" asked Lily.

"Oh, yeah," he said. "I've driven her over there before. No problem. See you in, say, about half an hour?"

"Fine," said Lily and hung up.

When she reached the kitchen door, Mrs. Hanlon smiled up at her. "He's a lovely boy," she said. "I've known him since before he was born."

"Yes," said Lily, "I had that impression."

"He's smart," said Mrs. Hanlon. "And he's been on the force for a long time. He's not actually a policeman anymore," she added, sounding mildly confused herself.

"What does that mean?" asked Lily.

"He's more of a photographer. He takes pictures, of dead people. He was a policeman, but now he . . ."

"Takes pictures of dead people. I see," said Lily.

"This sounds interesting," said Charlie. "I assume I can stay."

"Please do," said Mrs. Hanlon before Lily could answer him. "I'll make more tea."

Lily's first thought when she opened the front door and met Tom Casey was that he didn't look like a policeman. He was slight but solid, about her height, with thick brown hair, a bit too long on the collar, and hazel eyes; he looked more like a rookie reporter, someone fueled by the easy curiosity of the innocent. Lily guessed he was her age or a little younger, early to mid-thirties.

Once Mrs. Hanlon gave Casey tea, they began to chat about their neighborhood. The talk made Lily feel like an impatient child at a long dinner, wondering when the grown-ups would finish. Lily became sure she would spend the rest of her life trapped at the kitchen table hearing the story of the neighbors' new wolfhound.

Finally, she said, "I'm sorry to interrupt, but I've got work to do."

"Lily," said Charlie. "Don't be rude."

"No, no, no," said Casey, interrupting, "she's right. And I've got to get going anyway."

Now three pairs of eyes looked at Mrs. Hanlon.

"Well?" said Lily.

"Well," began Mrs. Hanlon, "you asked me, so I'll tell you. From the beginning . . ."

In truth, Lily was not entirely sure why she felt as jumpy as she did; some of it had to do with having the information sprung on her like this, but some of it had to do with Casey. He appeared relaxed and straightforward; Lily could tell he was very fond of Mrs. Hanlon. There was nothing special about him, Lily thought, but she found herself too observant of his movements, his expressions, too eager to interpret his most casual gesture, too conscious of his hands. Once she became aware of what was happening to her, she sat back, ready to listen.

"Tommy," said Mrs. Hanlon, "you've heard all this before, so don't get fidgety." Then she turned to Lily. "I'm the one who found him, I told you that. It was a Thursday, and when I arrived he wasn't in the church office where he usually was. But I didn't like to bother him. He had said the day before, on the phone, that he had something, maybe a little flu or some kind of infection—'Not that bad,' he said to me, I remember. He'd done his hospital visits that morning so he was going to take it easy that evening. I thought he had just stayed home.

"Anyway, I cleaned the church and I still hadn't heard anything from him, and it didn't seem right. I decided to call, to see if he needed anything, and to make sure he still wanted me to clean over here in the afternoon."

At this point, Mrs. Hanlon took a deep breath, then continued. "I called him but I didn't get any answer, and that's not like him either. He always answered the phone, day or night," she said, with a meaningful glance at Lily. "Day or night," she repeated. "Then I felt worried for certain. I took my key and knocked on the rectory door on and off for five minutes maybe, but I got no answer again, so I used the key and came in."

Mrs. Hanlon sipped her tea. Tom Casey leaned back in his chair, eyes closed, listening.

"He was here in the kitchen," said Mrs. Hanlon, with a small shrug, as if to shake off the memory. "There was broken glass, juice, you know, he was going for the juice—his eyes were wide open. And blood, some blood, not much, down the front of his pajamas. The test strips were out on the table, the insulin, the syringe. It was an awful mess—"

"Test strips? I'm confused," said Charlie.

"Barnes was a diabetic," said Casey.

"So he was testing his blood levels?" asked Charlie. "But what happened?"

"Every evening, before dinner, he took down his test strips, tested his blood sugar, then took out his two bottles of insulin, his shot, all the things he needed," said Mrs. Hanlon. She stood, opened the refrigerator door, and pointed to the meat drawer. "He kept most of it right here. He used this drawer for his insulin." Then she closed the refrigerator and sat down.

"So what was it that actually killed him? A seizure?" asked Charlie.

"Yeah," said Casey, "insulin shock with seizures followed by cardiac arrest. He had probably given himself too much insulin. And if he was sick, he might not have been eating—no one knows for sure. I checked the coroner's report. No autopsy. It's not *that* unusual. I mean, it happens."

"That's what you think, Tommy," said Mrs. Hanlon, "and I don't blame you. But I'm telling you again that Fred Barnes would not have made a mistake with his insulin."

"He wouldn't have had to, necessarily," said Casey. "He might have felt bad, not eaten enough, gotten disoriented. It can happen pretty fast."

"But he didn't, because he wouldn't have," Mrs. Hanlon said, her voice becoming strained. "He kept tight control, that's what he called it. He knew exactly what he could eat and couldn't."

After a pause, Tom Casey spoke quietly. "Tell the rest," he said.

"Someone else was here," said Mrs. Hanlon.

"How do you know?" Lily asked.

"There were dishes."

"Dishes?" asked Lily.

"In the drainer—not where he would have put them. A plate and a glass, washed and wiped but left in the drainer. Where he never left a glass sitting, or anything else for that matter. He washed, wiped, and put away."

"So someone else put them there. I guess I don't see—" said Charlie.

"Of course they did. I've never washed, dried, or put away a dish in this house as long as I've worked here—over ten years. No matter who visited, or how many, or how late. He washed, dried, and put away. Always. There's no better way to get to know a person's habits than to clean his house. And when you know a person's habits like I knew his, you know what's his business and what's other people's."

For an instant, Lily had a vivid memory of her father lying in his own bed, a hydrating solution drip in one arm, and the window air conditioner rattling in the far corner. Sweat was streaming down the sides of his face, into his ears, his hair, onto the pillow. She couldn't keep him dry. She shut her eyes and forced the memory away. Then a new thought occurred to her. "Wouldn't he—let's say he ate dinner and left his plate in the drainer, for whatever reason—"

Mrs. Hanlon started to interrupt, but Lily stopped her. "Let me finish. When did you say he usually did his insulin?"

Mrs. Hanlon turned her head to the side slightly, then said, "He usually did it—early evening, before dinner." She turned back to Lily, her eyes wide. "So if he'd already had dinner, and used those plates, why was he getting the insulin out?"

"That's what I wondered," said Lily. "Of course, it could have been breakfast dishes, I guess, or lunch."

"He ate lunch out that day, he told me, at the hospital, with Mrs. Grant. Her daughter was in surgery for hours," said Mrs. Hanlon. "Besides, how many times can I say it? I have never seen a plate in that drainer." She pointed emphatically toward the green plastic dish drainer on the matching mat by the sink. "Never."

Mrs. Hanlon lowered her hand. "There's something else," she said. "I know it doesn't make sense to anyone else, but he was barefoot, and in his pajamas," she raised her eyes to Lily's, then continued. "It's just not, I don't know how to say it, he just never would have . . ." Her voice trailed off. "When he was sick at home, he wore his slippers, pajamas, and robe. And there were his slippers right by the bed, side by side. I checked. He had gotten into the bed, in the early evening, very strange. Then come back down, like that, no robe—after dinner?—to do the insulin."

Lily nodded. She glanced at the kitchen shelves, the orderly matching dishes. And she thought of the shelves upstairs in the bathroom, the methodically rolled toothpaste tube.

"I'm not through either," said Mrs. Hanlon. "There was

a bottle of some kind of pills, called Ceclor—I wrote it down before I forgot—by his bed when I went up later, after they'd all left. And then when I came back the next day, it was gone. Nowhere in the house."

"So who would have moved them?" asked Lily.

"Maybe the EMTs?" asked Charlie.

Tom Casey shook his head. "Nobody's got them. It seemed pretty straightforward at the time. I don't think anybody thought to check around here."

"Did you find out what Ceclor is?" asked Lily.

"It's antibiotics," said Casey. "He felt lousy, he thought he had an infection, he called his doctor—you know."

"But the tranquilizers," said Mrs. Hanlon to Casey.

"Did you bring them?" asked Casey.

"Yes." She walked out into the hall and came back with a small, brown prescription bottle. The pills, Xanax, were issued to Frederick Barnes, to be taken as prescribed. The bottle was half full, and the prescription was dated early August.

"What's unusual about them?" asked Lily.

"He didn't take tranquilizers," said Mrs. Hanlon. "He wouldn't in a million years. And I've never seen the bottle before, either."

"Where did you find them?" asked Lily.

"In the medicine chest, when I was looking for the other ones, the antibiotics."

"Listen," said Charlie, "I can see I'm missing something here. But, really, why in the world would someone want to hurt a man like Fred Barnes? Even if there was anything convincing to indicate someone *had* tried . . ." He paused, then added, "It's just too far-fetched. I feel very uneasy about all this."

"I don't know exactly why, but I know there was a reason, or maybe a few reasons," said Mrs. Hanlon.

No one spoke.

"Last summer he was very, very worried," she continued. "He doubted himself. He said he'd let someone down . . ." Mrs. Hanlon closed her eyes and tipped her head back, as if she were doing a sort of conjuring trick, trying to capture the dead man's exact words and tone. "I'm disgusted with myself, I can't think of the words he used. But he said something like he was going through a dark night of the soul, and that he'd never fully appreciated the power of a secret, or maybe it was when people in power have secrets—I can't think. Of course, he wouldn't use names."

She opened her eyes and looked at Lily, adding, "Now I see that from the first minute I got to the church and found him missing, I was afraid right away, because of the feel of the place. Nothing had been right for a good while."

"And it still isn't," said Lily.

"No, it's not, is it?" replied Mrs. Hanlon. "And it won't be until somebody finds the truth and puts it right."

The two women looked at one another, acknowledging their certainty. Then Lily glanced at Charlie and caught him watching both of them, Mrs. Hanlon and herself, a pained expression on his face.

Tom Casey cleared his throat and said, "I guess I'm somewhere in the middle on all this. There's not much to work with." He spoke slowly, which drove Lily wild. "On the other hand," he continued, "I think maybe there's enough to make it worth our while to look around again, a little more carefully."

"Around where?" asked Lily. "Here?"

"Can we do that?" asked Charlie.

"I don't see why not," said Casey. "It's your house now. As long as it's real clear I'm not official." He looked at Lily and added, "And as long as it's okay with you."

Color flooded her face. "Let me think," she said. "What's your role in this actually going to be?" she asked Casey.

"Look, this isn't a case," he answered. "We'd have to find something a lot more interesting than what we've got now to make anybody from the department look at it again. I already tried once. But this is my day off, so I could help get you guys started. Past that, I don't know. Maybe nothing."

Lily turned to Mrs. Hanlon and asked, "Do you want

to do that, look around a little, see if we find anything else?"

"Yes. Yes, I would," said Mrs. Hanlon. She appeared relieved. "But I can't stay long. Mr. H. likes his meals on time."

"So?" Lily asked Charlie.

"Right," he said. "I'm really going to say 'no' at this point. Okay. I'm in."

Lily wasn't sure what she felt at that moment, but she thought maybe there was a tinge of disappointment. Maybe she wanted Charlie to go home. She didn't want his skepticism around, and it was too much for her to be dealing with him and Casey at the same time. Charlie's wariness made him less a participant and more a witness. And maybe, for whatever reasons, she didn't want any witnesses.

# chapter ✳ 9

The following Tuesday morning, Lily arrived in the church office to find a message from Bishop Spencer on the answering machine, asking her to call him, saying he had a couple of different kinds of information.

She called him back and was put through right away.

"You're a hard woman to get hold of," he said. "Where do you spend all your time?"

"I have a very active social life," said Lily, thinking of her weekend spent weeding through the last of Barnes's belongings.

"So I gather," said the Bishop. "Listen, we have a few things to talk about. Why don't I take you to lunch somewhere?"

"Why does this bode so ill?" she asked him.

"I have no idea," said Spencer. "You asked me to forage for you. Do you have a guilty conscience?"

"I do," said Lily. She had already decided not to fill Spencer in on Mrs. Hanlon's story and their search through Barnes's possessions on Thursday afternoon. She didn't want to lose control of the information, and she certainly didn't want to be told to stop looking.

For Lily, the most interesting thing they found was a box of books by contemporary theologians and church historians—Daly, Spong, Ruether, Gutierrez, Atkinson—books Lily herself had read and studied, books that had helped shape her own faith and practice. Most of these writers were interested in the church, the Bible, and the power of faith as sources for social change, change toward a more just world. And the issues they addressed—Christian anti-Semitism, religion and homophobia, the role of women in the church—didn't mesh with Lily's original picture of Barnes's interests and attitudes.

Once again, she had to revise that picture in light of new information. In order to learn more about what Barnes had read and what he thought of it, Lily decided to thumb through a few of the books, looking for notes and underlining, looking for some idea of what the man had been after. She put a stack of them by her bed, hoping to get to them over the next few weeks.

"We can talk about your conscience over lunch," Spencer was saying. "How about noon?"

"Today?" she asked, surprised.

"Definitely," said Spencer. "I look forward to it."

They planned to meet in a small restaurant near the church, located in the basement of an old brownstone, with a modest entrance and a barely noticeable sign. It was just the kind of establishment Spencer would know, she thought, and she was sure the food would be very good indeed, much better than what they might have gotten in one of the better-known cafés just around the corner on Charles. Good food was one of the bishop's specialties.

Once she entered, ducking her head to avoid the quaintly low cornice, she saw at once that the bishop wasn't there, so she chose to wait outside. The wait could be a considerable one—Spencer was not known for his punctuality—and she didn't want to have to appear absorbed by the menu for the next half hour.

November was holding clear and warm, for Boston, with temperatures still in the fifties during the bittersweet afternoons. Lily sat on a stoop next to the restaurant and leaned her back against the steps, eyes closed, face raised to the sun. Her mind wavered somewhere between tranquility and edginess.

The warmth and quiet were about to win out when she felt a shadow fall between her and the sun. She opened her eyes and raised a hand to shield her face from the bright aureole outlining the dark figure standing above her. At first, she thought it was someone wanting to use the steps, although she couldn't understand why he didn't just go around her. Then she realized he was staring down at her.

She jumped to her feet and stood facing Stanley Leonard. It took Lily a moment to catch her breath and speak.

"Stanley," she said, "you startled me."

"So I see," said Leonard. "Guilty conscience?"

Lily didn't like the echo from her earlier conversation with Spencer, and she began to get the angry rush that often follows fear.

"Not particularly," she said. "What's on your mind?"

"Nothing special," he said. "I was on my way to the church to practice the postlude and there you were, basking in the sunlight. It was irresistible."

"What was?" asked Lily.

"Stopping to watch, I suppose," said Stanley, his right eyebrow arched. "No sin in that, is there?"

"I don't know. I'll look it up when I get back to the office," said Lily.

He laughed, a short barklike noise, more of a loud snicker. Lily felt determined to get along with Stanley, who appeared to be the force that kept the services moving smoothly in the wake of Barnes's death. So far, it had not been hard—Lily was glad enough to hand over decisions about hymn choices and liturgical details. But she could see how easily the boat could be rocked. Stanley Leonard seemed to be a proud, sensitive man, not someone she would choose as an enemy.

"Actually," said Leonard, "I've been thinking about you—and about the parish."

"How so?" she asked.

"I know John can be difficult, and Dan has been scarce—which is very bad form on his part. I'm afraid we've been less than welcoming."

Lily proceeded cautiously. "It's been difficult for everyone involved," she said.

Leonard was dressed in a long, black coat, almost to his ankles, and his dark hair was slicked back; she suddenly pictured him as Dracula.

"Yes," he said. "I'd like to offer myself as a kind of liaison, if you would find that helpful. And I do have one or two ideas—I don't know if this is what you want to hear . . ."

Lily smiled at him—encouragingly, she hoped.

"It's simply this," he said. "Since you are temporary, and I assume you'll be continuing your other work elsewhere, I would hate to see you spend too much time and energy on us."

She nodded, though she felt lost.

"We've all been around one another so long," he continued. "It's a bit Gothic, entangled, over there. And, then, we were so very close to Fred. I think it might be best for everyone involved to have a more formal relationship with our priest, at least for now. Perhaps it would help us in the future, encourage us to become healthier as a congregation, less dependent."

Lily glanced down the street, hoping Bishop Spencer's arrival would save her from having to answer. But the sidewalk remained empty. Finally, she said, "Thanks, Stanley. I'm not sure what that would look like—a more formal relationship, I mean. But I'll think about it."

"I'd be glad to talk details with you. Will you be returning to the church this afternoon?"

"Probably," she said. "But right now I'm meeting a friend for lunch. So, I'll just go on in. Maybe later . . ."

"At your bidding," he said and then made an irritating

court bow, which happened to coincide with the bishop's appearance at the end of the street.

"Ah," said Stanley, catching sight of Spencer, "I see you're dining with royalty. I'll leave you to it." Then he turned and walked away from the approaching bishop.

"Good Lord," said Bishop Spencer, "what was that?"

"That was my organist, choir director, and active vestry member," said Lily. "Stanley Leonard."

"Oh, was that Stanley?" asked Spencer. "He looks like Dracula."

"I know," said Lily. "I think he just told me to buzz off. He's worried it might be a waste of my time to get involved with the more intimate details of the parish. What do you think?"

"I think that's an odd thing to suggest to an interim priest. It's too bad, too, because he could be helpful. He knows more about the church than God."

"So maybe I'll try to find out what he meant, what was behind all that. Any suggestions?"

"Don't mention women's ordination," said the bishop, smiling.

"That's terrific," said Lily.

"We'll think better when we've ordered lunch," said Spencer. "Let's go in."

Everyone knew him. He was not a forgettable presence, and his love of food had earned him a place in the owner-cum-chef's heart.

"I have come out to tell you that we have cassoulet," said the large, red-faced man in a white apron. "You want it?"

"I do," said Spencer. Then he looked at Lily and asked, "Have you ever had it?"

"I don't think so," she said.

"French soul food," said the bishop, smiling. "Are you willing to gamble?"

"It depends," she said.

"Do you like garlic?" asked the owner. "Do you like onions? Do you like white beans? Do you like duck?"

"Yes," said Lily.

"Good, then you will like it. I'll bring you two. And salad?" he asked Spencer, who nodded agreement. "And wine?"

Spencer looked at Lily. "No wine for you, right?"

"Right," said Lily.

"A glass of Burgundy for me, then, with the cassoulet, and a bottle of mineral water, and"—Bishop Spencer looked at Lily—"anything else?"

"I have no idea," she said.

Spencer laughed. The owner left for the kitchen. Lily smiled at the bishop across the table.

"How's the drinking going?" he asked her after a brief silence.

"It's going great," she said. "I don't do it anymore."

"Do you miss it?"

"Sometimes," she said. "Not often. Not right now."

After the mineral water was served and poured and they had both buttered pieces of the warm, fresh French bread, Spencer asked her, "Did you know Charlie was on the Diocesan Committee on Human Sexuality?"

"I've been hearing about it. Nothing confidential—well, maybe a little confidential—but mostly just general frustrations."

"And you've kept up with the fate of the two resolutions from this last Diocesan Convention?" he asked.

"Sure. I know that the church is divided, and that there are, as usual around here, lots of warring factions."

"Excellent analysis. I've seen the church wrestle with plenty of angels—I mean, I've been one of the wrestlers, you know that—but I'm not sure I've ever seen people so hysterical. Don't quote me."

"That's what Charlie says," said Lily. "That he's impressed with the effect this subject has on otherwise rational people."

"I'm not sure I'd agree with the description of the folks involved, but Charlie's always been a generous person. Anyway, I brought this up for a reason. I found out something about your parish. It seems that Barnes had done a one-eighty on this particular question. You know what the parish's take on the subject has been and still is, I assume. But Barnes had begun lobbying openly in favor of the two resolutions."

"I don't get it," she said.

"There's more," said Spencer. "It appears—and this is hearsay—that the vestry, probably Neville, talked with the big bishop about getting rid of him. He felt Barnes could no longer represent their point of view."

"What do you mean 'hearsay'?" Lily asked skeptically. "If you live in the diocesan office, how come you end up with 'hearsay' from the diocesan office?"

Spencer looked out the narrow window at street level before he answered. "You would probably be impressed by the number of things that go on in that set of rooms that I know nothing about. That's not an excuse, understand—just an explanation."

Lily nodded. She did understand. One of their closest bonds was that as a liberal, activist woman and a black activist man they remained, vestigially, outsiders in the Episcopal church. "So he had this change of heart," she said, thinking that this explained the books piled by her bed. "Then what? Why didn't he resign?"

"I don't know, and I don't know if anyone else knows either," said Spencer. "That is to say, Bishop Lewis seems confused, though not about to say so to me."

Lily shook her head. "I'll never get used to the way this church operates, or doesn't, as the case may be. If Bishop Lewis is so close to everyone over there, how can he not know what went on with Barnes?"

Spencer shrugged, buttered a thick piece of bread, took a bite, and leaned back in his chair. After he was done, he said, "Sometimes people like you—people with a lust for the absolute truth—are a pain in the neck. Or, really, people like you are always a pain in the neck to someone. But it takes your brand of absolutism—the whole truth and nothing but the truth, right makes might, you know the rest—to get some things done. Most people don't share that—what?—that passion."

"You believe in the truth," Lily said defensively.

"I believe in the truth, but I'm older than you, and I have a wife and kids, and some battles don't seem worth it to me, or they don't seem worth my fighting them."

"Oh," she said. "But they do seem worth *my* fighting them."

"Absolutely," said the bishop. "Are you going to do it?"

"I don't even know what *it* is," she said. "I'm there, so I'm going to stay there because I said I would, and if serving them means getting to the bottom of this stuff, then I'll do that, too. If that's what you mean."

"That's just what I mean. Now let me give you the bad news before the food comes. Last week Bishop Lewis came into my office for a chat. This is pretty rare. It turned out that John Neville had complained to him about your—I think he used the word 'aggressive'—presence. According to him, you attended some vestry meeting uninvited—"

"But I was invi—" Lily began.

Spencer raised his hand, palm out, to stop her. "I assumed as much," he said. "Neville also said something about a visit to Talbot, at the office, is that right?"

Lily shrugged and nodded.

"He said you bypassed him and went to Dan. That Dan's got a lot on his plate. That you already knew that. Need I go on?"

"This is such bullshit," said Lily. Then she added, "Sorry."

"Quite all right," said Spencer.

"Look," said Lily. "You told me to get to know them better. I was next door to Talbot's office. I stopped and had a chat."

"And?" asked the Bishop.

"And what?"

"Did you get to know him better?"

"Yes. No. I don't know," she said. "He's a nice man. He's worried about his son—did you know he had a son?"

Spencer paused, then shook his head. "I don't remember knowing it. What else?"

"He loves St. Mary's. He was very polite. Somehow, I

don't think he would have complained. I think it was Neville—he couldn't stand the idea that I reported how lousy he's been at his duties lately."

"Yes," said Spencer. "That could be. But take it easy, okay? You can't find out anything if they replace you. And it wouldn't help your reputation as an interim either."

"That's not much of a threat at this point," said Lily, watching their waiter approach with two steaming cassoulet dishes.

After he returned with Spencer's glass of wine, there was a brief exchange about fresh pepper, during which Lily looked at her meal in dismay.

When they were alone again, she said, "I can't possibly eat this."

"Why not?" asked Spencer, visibly upset.

"Because I'm so angry I can hardly swallow my own spit," she said. "Why didn't Neville just come to me?"

"That's not how it works," said Spencer. "You know that. These guys have a chain of command. He tells the main man, who tells the second man, who passes it on to you discreetly so Neville doesn't have to do any dirty work and . . ."

She tried to interrupt him, but he held up his hand again to stop her, then he concluded, "And you feel humiliated. That's the point."

"That's the point, huh?" she asked.

He nodded.

"I knew that," she said. "What a son of a bitch."

"True," said Spencer, glancing around the restaurant which was more than half full, "but let's finish this conversation so we can enjoy ourselves. I hate to think of an astonishing meal being spoiled by pettiness. And I don't think anything's going to come of it."

Lily took a deep breath to calm herself and caught the aroma of garlic and tomatoes and duck.

"Boy, this does smell good," she said.

Spencer beamed at her. "I knew you could do it," he said, raising his glass to her.

For a moment they ate in silence. Then Lily glanced up

and caught him watching her. He leaned across the table and touched her hand.

"I want you to know that whatever is going on here, and whatever happens out of all of this, and no matter what you decide to do about it, I admire you. And I wish we had many more priests like you in this diocese."

"Wouldn't that make your job a whole lot harder?" she asked him.

"Yes, probably, and a whole lot more interesting. But, no, more than interesting, it would be . . ." He paused, then continued. "What everyone seems to forget when we talk about 'apostolic succession' and ordination is that we're talking about sending people out into the world to heal. 'And he gave them power and authority over all demons, and to cure diseases' it says, 'to preach the kingdom of God, and to *heal.*' To heal." He took a deep breath, then added, "Most people don't know that."

"And I do?" she asked him.

"I think so. I think you do. Don't you, honestly?"

She looked at the pale sunshine slanting through the glass, then turned back to him and said, "Yes, I think I do. But that doesn't mean I do a very good job of it."

"Oh," Spencer exclaimed, laughing slightly and waving his right hand in dismissal, "none of us does a very good job of it. There's just a handful of people in history who have let God's love shine right through them, who have gotten so good at it they could just, just *be* God's love. But that's not the point. The point is to do it badly, humanly, to keep doing it in spite of how badly we do it."

"That's the point?" she asked him again, smiling this time.

"That's it," he said. "That's it. That's all there is to it."

"I think I've got the 'badly' part down at least," said Lily.

"Can you please do one thing for me though?" asked Spencer.

"I don't know," she said, wary at once. "What is it?"

"Eat," he said. "Could you please just eat?"

•   •   •

It was not until coffee was served that Lily was willing to talk business again. She was still angry, but after the crème brûlée, nothing seemed quite as dire.

"Tell me more about Barnes," she said, "about the changes."

"The changes are puzzling," said Spencer. "Basically, it's what I've said: Evidently, Barnes, after years of middle-to-right-of-middle Anglican cakewalking, suddenly began pushing hard for the parish delegates to support the two resolutions."

"At Diocesan Convention?"

"Yes, and he started to badger the parish about outreach, about sharing their space, and profits, with Episcopal City Mission, Urban Caucus—you know, the radicals."

"Who told you all this?" she asked him.

"An ecclesiastical Deep Throat," said Spencer.

"A reliable Deep Throat?" asked Lily.

"A few reliable ones, actually. But it's not what I would call public."

"I understand that. But obviously the parish knows this part of it. I mean, they were there. And doesn't that explain what's going on now? You remember I told you it felt like they'd been burned, that somehow Barnes had betrayed them?"

"I don't know who knows what," said Spencer, "and it's my impression that not everyone knows everything. Probably the vestry tried to keep this to themselves, as much as possible. Something tells me there's more to it, too, but that's not even from my Deep Throat. That's just venerable instinct. After all," he added, eyebrows raised, "what makes a man change like that?"

"Generally it's something like being struck blind on the road to your next persecution event," said Lily. "What do you think?"

"I have no idea," said Spencer, "but I would be interested to know, wouldn't you?"

"And why do you think this powerful vestry didn't kick him out, if that's what they wanted?" asked Lily.

"They didn't have to, did they?"
"Right."

Outside the day had turned colder. Though the sun still shone, there was no warmth in it. Lily suddenly felt chilled and very much alone. When she and Spencer shook hands, she wanted, again, to hang on.

Once he disappeared around the corner, she grew angry all over again. She dreaded returning to St. Mary's, and talking with Stanley seemed a waste of time. The last thing she needed was a list of ways in which to distance herself further.

She noticed that her enthusiasm for getting Barnes's belongings out of the rectory had disappeared. Ever since Thursday afternoon, when they had searched through boxes and drawers and shelves, she had felt that his possessions belonged there with her. That feeling focused especially on the tiny note in the pocket of the peacoat. She told herself she had forgotten to mention it last Thursday, but she knew there was more to it than that. The rectory was her house now—her world, her story. She would hoard her discoveries as she made them; that way she would remain in charge.

If she planned to talk with Stanley, she needed to go. But she thought she probably would walk down to Cambridge Street and see a movie. She smiled to herself, knowing this lapse in professionalism was partly out of a desire for revenge on them all—petty and sure to backfire—and partly out of a need for simple pleasure, an only slightly more dependable motive, but worth the gamble.

Arriving back at St. Mary's at dusk, Lily was so lost in the world of the movie—a woman's lover dies suddenly, but he reappears as a ghost, or a guardian angel, when the woman's grief keeps her from continuing with her own life—that on her return to St. Mary's she almost didn't notice the light in the church office. As she climbed the steps to the rectory, she glanced back over her shoulder and noticed the yellow gleam from behind the hedge. It must be the desk lamp, she thought, yet she was sure she hadn't turned it on that morning.

She walked to the side door of the church and found it open, another surprise. Was there a study group meeting tonight? She didn't think so. In the hallway she called out— a quiet "hello?"—then walked to the landing and called out again into the basement. There was no response, but the light was on down there as well. Maybe the lights and the unlocked door were another side of Stanley—in the rapture of organ practice he became a warmer, messier person.

But when she got to her desk in the office, there was a brief note from him that reconfirmed all her original impressions: "Waited until 3:00. S. Leonard." The letters were so neat, so square and perfect, that they could not have been written by someone who rapturously left lights on and doors unlocked. In fact, they looked identical to the tiny block letters and numbers she had found in Barnes's coat pocket.

With her eyes still on the note before her, Lily reached over to play the tape on the answering machine. Then, in the instant before she pressed the button, she was sure she heard a noise from downstairs, a weird, shuffling sound, like a cat batting a paper ball. But there was no cat, and she was alone in the building, or at least she had thought she was. Although if someone were downstairs, that would explain the door being left unlocked.

Once again she walked to the landing and peered down into the stairwell. Silence. Then the rustling sound. Then silence.

"Hello?" called Lily, again, keeping her voice calm.

Nothing.

She switched on the light above the stairs and stood on the first step. Then she walked quietly into the robing room where the altar guild kept its supplies. From the top shelf, she took down the heavy, brass candlestick she had seen Cynthia polishing weeks ago. She held it by its top half and felt the heft of the base, a good five inches of solid metal. Finally, she dropped her hand, holding the candlestick casually by her side, just in case an oblivious parishioner appeared, having been straightening up in the kitchen.

At the top of the stairs she paused again and listened. Still nothing. Had she imagined the sounds, or were they from the furnace? Lily walked slowly down the steps, aware of every creak. On the landing, she leaned over to look into the parish meeting room on the right. All was quiet. Then she walked to the other side of the landing, knelt down, and peered through the balusters.

To the left, the door was open onto a short flight of steps that led down into the cellar workroom. On the bottom step, Lily could see the lug sole of a heavy boot. Suddenly it moved, a kind of crazy twitch that lifted the boot off the stair and caused it to knock into a shopping bag hanging on the nearby newel post of the banister. The bag swung wildly back and forth for a few seconds, then stopped. And the boot was perfectly still.

For one instant, Lily felt relief. So *that's* the noise, she thought.

Then the scene came into full focus, and she saw the pant cuff, the crumpled sock, the white, veined ankle. The hall light illuminated the rest of the pant leg, olive drab army pants, to the knee.

Later, when she would describe it to Charlie, Lily would recall that she had also smelled whiskey and urine and heard a low, almost human moan.

# chapter ❋ 10

After Lily made sure she couldn't revive Roger Frye herself, she called 911. She had just propped open the door to the courtyard when the EMT truck pulled up onto the sidewalk, its red light flashing in the silent street.

The EMTs were a surprising pair: a tiny, almost child-size woman with long, thick, black hair worn loose around her pale face; and a tall black man, dark-skinned, with a shaved head. The Mutt and Jeff team came rapidly up the courtyard path, rolling the stretcher between them.

When they reached the steps, he asked, "Is he in there?" and nodded toward the church building.

"Yes," Lily said. "He's down in the basement. It looks like he's fallen on the stairs . . ."

The man glanced back at his partner, whose lovely, doe-eyed face remained immobile. "Shit," he said to her, under his breath. "Sorry," he said to Lily, glancing at her collar.

"Did you see him fall?" the partner asked.

"No," said Lily. "I just found him, and he looks pretty bad, his breathing is raspy, you know, hard . . ."

The man interrupted her and turned back to his partner.

"Okay. We'll take the stretcher to the top of the stairs," he said, "bring the oxygen down, check him out, then I'll come back for the board."

The young woman nodded. Italian, Lily thought, as she led them down to the basement. Roger Frye lay sprawled on his stomach, his head resting on the concrete floor, his legs against the stairs.

"We'll need your help," the woman said to Lily when she saw Frye. "Are you okay?"

She nodded at her and noted that while everything was actually moving very fast, her own internal sense of time had not so much slowed as expanded to include the rush of events along with a steady flow of her own internal commentary. For instance, she kept noticing how well these two worked together, how well they communicated, and she reflected on how much they must have had to figure out in order to get where they were.

The two EMTs were kneeling beside Roger Frye, attaching an oxygen mask to his face. The man disappeared back upstairs and the girl, as Lily couldn't help thinking of her, showed her how to help roll Frye onto the spine board once the man returned. The instructions were clear and precise, and this small, dark-haired person suddenly appeared much older, entirely adult. Lily could see now that there were fine lines at the corners of her eyes, and a disturbing, yellowish, faded bruise just below her right cheekbone.

Lily stared at the bruise for a moment. Then she asked, "What's wrong, with him I mean? Is he just drunk?"

"Looks like he's in some kind of shock. Was he taking anything—drugs, medicine?"

"No," said Lily. "I mean, I wouldn't know if he was. I . . ." She stopped when the man appeared in the doorway.

Together, the three of them rolled Roger onto the spine board and carried him up the stairs. At the top landing, Lily stepped aside while the two EMTs attached the board and oxygen tank to the rolling stretcher. Then she followed them as they wheeled him out the door and down the path to the ambulance.

"You coming?" the young woman asked her.

Lily thought for a moment. She wanted to climb into the ambulance but not just because of Roger Frye; she also didn't want to lose her sense of teamwork, of membership in something that worked. "Where are you taking him?" she asked.

"Mass General," the man called over his shoulder as they lifted the stretcher into the waiting ambulance. The hospital was only a few blocks away, across from the Charles Street T-station.

"I might come later," she said. "I've got to make some calls, find out about next of kin. I don't really know him very well . . ."

The man looked at her from inside the back of the van. "That's fine," he said. "This guy won't know what's going on for a while anyway. Thanks for the help."

"Oh, thank *you,*" said Lily emphatically.

He climbed into the front of the ambulance while the woman hooked up the oxygen to a larger tank. "Take care," she said, absentmindedly, over her shoulder. Inside the dark cave of the van, the bruise was invisible.

After they pulled away from the curb, Lily crossed the courtyard to the side doors, still propped open, spilling light onto the lawn. As she reached the stairs, she glanced at her watch and thought it had stopped. Fewer than fifteen minutes had passed since she made the call. She stood in the cold air, noticing the hazily shrouded stars and the silence.

It was then Lily heard Casey unlatching the gate behind her. She hadn't seen him yet, but she knew who it was.

"What brings you out?" she turned and asked him.

"It's a long story. Let's just say news travels fast over there," he said, nodding in the direction of police headquarters at the other end of Tremont. He had gotten a haircut; it made him seem younger, more sincere. He had on a black parka, cable-knit sweater, jeans, and he looked more like a college student than a guy who took pictures of dead people.

"I didn't know the police were even involved in this one," she said.

He glanced back down the path, then said, "I had just talked with a friend about Barnes. She was on duty the morning Mrs. H. found him. And she was on duty tonight. When she saw the ambulance out front she let me know. What's up?"

"It was Roger Frye, the sexton," Lily said, pointing toward the building, "custodian of the church."

He nodded.

"I came in this evening, heard something downstairs, went to see what it was, and found him lying facedown in his own vomit."

"Nice," said Casey.

"Very," she said. Then she looked at him and asked, "Do you think it's a coincidence?"

"What with what?"

"Frye and Barnes. Two medical disasters so close together. It's kind of weird, isn't it?"

"You know that saying, 'Lightning never strikes the same tree twice,' or whatever it is?"

"Yes," said Lily, "that's close enough."

"When you're in this business you see what a crock *that* is. I've actually started to think it's *more* likely to strike the same tree twice. Karma." He said the last word with an ironic glint, as if he had said "voodoo."

"You don't believe in karma?" asked Lily.

He hesitated, then said, "I'm not sure I know what it means."

"You used it right," she said. "It's as if this place is sending out some kind of signal that attracts medical emergencies."

"Yeah, and death," said Casey.

"I don't think Roger's going to die," said Lily.

"That's good," he said, "or they might have to haul you in."

Lily gave him a weak smile. "Let's go inside," she said. "I'm cold."

They went up the steps and into the hall in silence. Lily

closed and locked both doors, then walked ahead of him into her office. She sat in the leather desk chair, putting her elbows on the desk and her head in her hands.

She rubbed her eyes and said, "I feel really, really bad about this. I'm so lousy at this job . . ."

He watched from the door for a couple of seconds, then asked, "Look, have you eaten?"

"No," said Lily, her head still resting in her hand. "No," she said again. "I haven't. I guess I should." She sat up and looked at him. "You want to go get something?"

He nodded. "Just let me make a phone call."

Right, the crying baby, she thought, the bright little voice answering the phone. "Actually," she said, "I've got about a million things to do here. I've got to let somebody know, see if Roger has any family that I need to contact. I'm just so . . ."

"What?" asked Casey.

"Disgusted," said Lily. "I'm just so disgusted with everything. I think maybe I better just do my job here and crawl into bed."

"Okay," he said. "Is there anyone else you could call? It may not be such a great time to be alone."

"No, that's fine. It's how I usually crawl into bed," said Lily. She had unsettled him. He blushed, laughed self-consciously, and stood up straighter.

After a short silence, he said, "Maybe you should go on over to the house."

"Right," said Lily, briskly, "right. Good idea. I think I will. Let me just play these messages back, straighten a couple of things here, clean up downstairs."

"I'll tell you the truth," said Casey. "I don't feel right about leaving you here. It's not that I think anything would happen. It's just . . . Why don't you do what you need to do upstairs, I'll get started downstairs, and you can help me when you're done. Okay?"

"You haven't seen downstairs," said Lily.

"Whatever it is, I've seen a lot worse," he said, then disappeared around the corner.

Lily leaned back in the chair, breathed deeply, and tried

to order her thoughts. She noticed how much she didn't want to think about what was happening—about Frye, about Barnes, about Tom Casey. She wished she could walk out and go to another movie, or maybe even the same one again. But she was the adult in charge now. She needed to make the necessary phone calls, alert John Neville, maybe Dan Talbot, maybe Cynthia Babcock, about Roger's accident.

Before she picked up the receiver, she reached over to play the tape on the answering machine. There had been three calls, one from Charlie, one from Cynthia Babcock, and one from Sally Talbot. Charlie was calling to say hi, and Cynthia was calling to see if she could make an appointment with Lily for later in the week. But it was Sally Talbot's call that got her attention.

"Dan and I were hoping you could come for dinner this week. He just had a change of plans and tomorrow night opened up, so he called from Chicago to ask . . ." There was a long pause, then she finished by saying, "to ask if you could come tomorrow night. I know it's not much notice but, anyway . . ." Her speech was slow, almost slurred. "Call back when you can."

If I didn't know better, I'd guess she was stoned, thought Lily. She wrote down a list of the messages, then looked up Neville's home number and dialed. No one picked up, and there was no machine. Now what? she thought, acutely aware of her isolation in this job. She decided to try the Talbots; at least they had invited her to dinner. Sally would know how to get in touch with Dan in Chicago, and Dan would know whether or not Roger had family—or so she hoped.

When Sally answered, she didn't seem to know who Lily was for the first few seconds. Finally she perked up some, after Lily accepted the dinner invitation. Lily had only talked with the woman two or three times, at coffee hours and a dreary vestry dinner, and had not formed a clear impression of her. Sally was small—a little shorter than Dan—but where Dan was short and stocky, Sally was delicate and fine-boned. She had thick, dark hair and pale skin. Lily had no trouble imagining her as a debutante, glimmery in a white dress. But she found it harder to locate an identity for Sally in the present—warm enough, friendly enough, but more like a porcelain on a mantelpiece than a grown woman.

"I'm afraid I've got some unpleasant news," Lily told the other woman once dinner plans were settled. "Roger Frye's had an accident here, down in the basement. He's just been taken to Mass General. I can't get hold of John, and I need to find out about Roger's family or friends. Could you give me Dan's number in Chicago?"

The silence lengthened. Lily finally asked, "Sally, are you still there?"

"Yes," said Sally, "I'm just trying to . . . I'm not sure what to do really. I hate to bother Dan."

Lily suppressed a rush of irritation. She took a deep breath, then asked, "Do you know where he's staying?"

"Yes. I mean, I've got the name of his hotel. You know, he's there on business."

"But I'm sure he would want to know," said Lily.

"Let's see," said Sally. Lily heard what sounded like Sally's shuffling papers. "The Bradley," she said, after a few moments. "Could that be it?"

"I don't know," said Lily.

"That's where he's always stayed before," said Sally. "I think that's where he is now."

"Great," said Lily, writing down the name. "Do you have the number?"

"No," said Sally, accompanied by more shuffling sounds. "I don't think so. I don't see it."

"That's okay," said Lily. "I'll call information. And thanks for the help, and the invitation."

"Certainly," said Sally, now on firmer ground. "I look forward to seeing you."

A few moments later, Lily was talking with the operator at the Bradley Hotel in Chicago, asking for Talbot's room. But the operator had no listing for Talbot and couldn't tell Lily whether or not he had been registered earlier that week. "Would you like to speak to the concierge?" she asked.

"Yes, please," said Lily.

As it turned out, the concierge, an Episcopalian himself, was pleased to give Mr. Talbot's priest that information. He was quite sure Mr. Talbot was still in the hotel. The operator had made an error. No, he did not know his room number, but he would be happy to give Mr. Talbot her message when he saw him that evening, as he would surely do.

Exasperated, tired, lonelier than ever, Lily hung up and called the hospital. Roger Frye had arrived, was being treated in the Emergency Room, and would not be in any shape to have visitors before tomorrow. Good, thought Lily. Now I can go down, help Tom clean up the puke, and drag myself to the rectory. But she couldn't stand up, at least not right that minute. She switched off the light on the desk and sat in the darkness, willing herself out of the chair but staying seated.

When she heard footsteps on the stairs, it was as if she had slipped into a sort of reverie. She stood quickly and Tom Casey arrived in the doorway.

"All done," he said, then rolled his eyes.

"Really a mess, right?" she asked.

"Not as bad as a corpse in a dumpster in August," he said with a half smile. "What are you doing here in the dark?"

"I was on my way down to help," she said weakly, feeling guilty.

"Nice timing," he said.

"Thank you," she said. "I mean thank you for cleaning up. I really appreciate it."

"You've got your own messes to clean up, right?" he asked, nodding in the direction of the desk. "I'd rather work the mop."

Lily laughed. "With good reason," she said.

They walked to the door together. Lily switched off the hall lights, and they headed out into the cold darkness.

•　•　•

The next morning Lily returned Cynthia Babcock's call and told her about Frye. As far as Cynthia knew, Roger Frye had no family, at least not in the immediate area, but, she added, Lily should talk with Dan about it because he knew the man better than anyone else, now that Fred was gone. Then she assured Lily that someone from the Pastoral Care and Concerns Committee would visit Roger later that day. Cynthia also suggested that she and Lily wait to schedule their appointment "until after we get this sorted out with Roger." At first Lily objected to the delay, but Cynthia sounded happy to have an excuse to avoid the meeting, at least temporarily. Well you called *me*, thought Lily.

Then she dialed the hospital. The nurse on duty in the sixth-floor Intensive Care Area said Frye had woken a couple of times that morning, was sedated, might or might not recognize her if she visited. After Lily hung up, she walked across to the rectory for a quick cup of tea, then started off down Charles Street to visit Roger Frye at Mass General.

In the Intensive Care Area—a small, four-bed unit, the next stop after the ICU—Roger was the only patient. Lily sat by him in silence; watching his chest rise and fall; watching his face, in repose, for once; watching the monitor record the beat of his heart. He seemed fragile, infantlike, entirely dependent on other people and machines. Slowly, as the moments passed, she began to feel protective of him. She now believed there existed something—destructive, disguised—from which he and others in the parish needed protection.

At the end of the day, after a visit to the Women's Center, she found herself strolling again down Charles Street, this time in the fading pink light of the November evening toward the Talbots' home. They lived on Mt. Vernon, only a few blocks from the church. Their house was on the right, halfway up the steep street, and though it matched the surrounding townhouses in most respects—black iron railings, faded bricks, ivory-colored trim—it looked somehow newer, spiffier. Lily saw that the black door had been recently painted, and the brass knocker shone in the glow of the nearby streetlight.

She pressed the doorbell. After a wait, during which no one appeared and she heard no answering motion inside, she pressed again, harder and longer. This time she heard voices—she thought they were both female—then brisk footsteps. Sally Talbot came to the door looking flushed and oddly wide-eyed, as if she were holding her eyelids open by an act of will.

"I'm *so* sorry," she said to Lily, taking her hand and drawing her through the vestibule, through the second door, and into the foyer. "I was upstairs getting dressed, and I thought Florence would hear you, but she didn't. She says she doesn't play music in there," Sally added under her breath. "But I know she does because if you touch the radio after she leaves, it's still hot."

For an instant, Lily had an eerie sensation she had arrived at the wrong place. She had never seen Sally this animated or this off-putting. Her small, oval face looked as if it had been hit with a flying makeup kit—pink lips, pink cheeks, and two dramatic swoops of green eyeshadow. Dressed in gray wool slacks, high heels, and a sheer, white silk blouse, she reminded Lily of a little girl playing madam of the house. Lily became aware that half of her mind was searching desperately for something to say, while the second half studied the other woman carefully, wondering what drug had produced Sally's drowsy elation.

Her pupils were dilated, her motions erratic, and her speech cheerfully sloppy, full of little slips and slides over words and phrases. Sally reached out a limp, elegant hand toward Lily's parka and said in a kind of East Coast drawl, "Here, let me have that." As Lily took off her coat, Sally tipped back her head and called out, *"Florence,"* in a booming voice. Lily felt as if she were witnessing a scene from *The Exorcist.*

A middle-aged Latina woman appeared in the hall. She glanced at Lily's clerical collar once, then twice, then looked directly at Sally. "Yes?" she said.

"Ms. Connor would like a drink," Sally said to her, "and

so would I. What do you want?" she asked Lily, who still stood holding her own coat.

"Nothing," said Lily. "Water maybe. Water would be good, thanks." She tried to make eye contact with Florence, but it was impossible. Florence kept her eyes on Sally, almost warily, as if watching for her next move.

"We have champagne," said Sally in a hurt tone. "I can't open a bottle just for me."

No one said anything. After what seemed to Lily a long silence, Sally turned to Florence and said peevishly, "All right, then. Just bring me a glass of wine."

After Florence returned to the kitchen, Sally glanced into the living room and walked away. Lily watched her wander into the room and sit down in a chintz-covered chair next to the fire.

Lily hung her coat in the hall closet and followed Sally into a square, high-ceilinged space with one set of French doors looking out onto Mt. Vernon and another set opening onto a tiny, lighted courtyard with a black wrought-iron table and matching chairs. The room was beautiful, the windows draped in sheer fabric that filtered the glow of the street lamp and the sound of passers-by walking home in the dusk. The walls were off-white, and on the space between the front windows hung a huge canvas of blues, greens, lavenders, what looked like a contemporary version of Monet's water lilies. The fabrics of the sofa, the pillows, the chair in which Sally now lounged, all echoed the tones of the canvas.

Florence appeared at the door with two glasses on a small, silver tray. She walked first to Lily and presented the tray to her so she could take the glass of water.

"Thanks," said Lily. Still no eye contact.

Florence walked across the room and put the wine on a white, plaster pedestal that served as a side table. Sally never stirred. On her way out, Florence looked directly at Lily and gave her a barely perceptible, questioning shrug. Then she was gone. Something about the woman's presence, her self-possession, made Lily suspect she had been a college president or structural engineer in her native country.

"This is a wonderful room," Lily said.

Sally sat up and turned toward Lily. "Do you think so?" she asked. "I can't tell anymore."

"I do," said Lily, "and I love this painting. Who did it?"

"I did," said Sally. She reached for the glass of wine, almost full to the top, and took a long drink.

"You're kidding," said Lily, much too loudly.

"I know," said Sally sadly. "That's just how I feel about it. It was a hundred years ago, just before Roy was born. I was still painting, still hopeful." She studied the painting for a moment, then leaned back in her chair again, drink in hand.

Lily walked over to an end table near the sofa and put down her own glass on a blue coaster. "Roy's your son?" Lily asked.

Sally nodded but didn't speak.

"Is he here now? I'd love to—"

"No. He doesn't live here."

"Is he away at school?" asked Lily.

There was no answer. Lily looked at the other woman. As she watched, Sally put her head against the padded backrest and closed her eyes.

There was no point in bullying Sally into conversation. She took this chance to wander around the room, noticing the collection of delicate china boxes on a miniature antique writing desk, the generous spray of coral beach grass in a pale blue vase.

In the far corner of the room stood a black baby grand, its back lid closed. The surface was covered with framed photographs of what Lily assumed were family members and friends. As she approached the piano, she saw that most were beautifully composed, more like portraits than snapshots, capturing a certain look on the subject's face or a telling moment of affection. She found pictures of Dan Talbot, some as much as twenty years old, she thought. There were a few portraits of an older couple; the woman looked remarkably like Sally and had the same distant, glazed look Lily had seen tonight. But the most frequent subject was a boy, their son, Roy, Lily assumed, at every possible stage of life and in every possible mood, from grinning infant to sulking adolescent.

On the far corner of the lid she found a photograph of Dan and Roy, sitting in wicker chairs, gazing through open French doors at a brilliant view of the seashore. The picture had been taken from behind them, into the bright light of the view. The chairs had been turned slightly toward each other, so that all one could see of the father and son were two dark profiles, silhouetted against the white glow of the sky.

Lily reached over and picked up the photograph, then walked to a floor lamp near the piano bench. She had never met Roy Talbot; she felt sure of that. She studied the picture, holding it under the light for a better look. Yet she knew the profile, the silhouette of a teenage boy seen dimly, from a distance.

As Lily stood with the photograph in her hand, she heard the front door open, then heard Dan Talbot call out, "Hello?" She set the picture back on the piano and turned to greet him. Lily could tell from the look on Dan's face as he stood in the doorway, still wearing his coat, still holding his briefcase, that Sally had remained slumped in the chair by the fire.

Lily walked toward Dan quickly, speaking softly to him as she went. "Sally doesn't seem well," she said.

He stood staring at his wife, then raised his left hand to his eyes and rubbed them halfheartedly. When he took his hand away Lily saw tears, though whether they were from the rubbing or from some pool of collected disappointment, she didn't know. He gave Lily an apologetic glance, then turned back into the hall without a word. She stood in the doorway watching while he set his briefcase inside the closet and hung up his coat and scarf. Then he walked through the dim dining room to the kitchen door and disappeared inside.

There was a moment in which Lily stood alone in the

marble foyer, between Sally asleep in the chair by the fire and the slightly swinging kitchen door, framed in bright light at its edges. She felt suspended in time, or out of time, caught in an instant of distortion in which she was witnessing the most private darkness of these peoples' lives.

The door swung open again and Talbot emerged, followed by Florence. This time he offered her his right hand as a belated gesture of greeting. "I'm sorry about all this," he said. "She's been on some new medication, and, obviously, it's not right. You must think we're . . ."

Lily waited for him to finish his sentence. Then she took her hand from his and said, "I think maybe you need some help."

Florence stood behind Talbot, just inside the dining room.

"We'll handle it all right, won't we?" he asked and turned to include Florence. She inclined her head to him.

Lily felt certain he had deliberately misunderstood her offer of help, and she hesitated, unsure about whether to explain or to wait for a better, less fraught moment. The man deserved privacy, she decided. He needed to attend to his wife.

"I'm going to go then, unless you want me to stay," she said.

"No, I don't think so." He smiled and walked to the closet. "Let's do this another time, soon. We'll get this straightened out with Sally. It won't be . . . it will be just a matter of . . ." He opened the closet door and stared inside, then turned to her and asked, "What does your coat look like, anyway?" His tone sounded plaintive, almost peeved, and Lily saw how carefully he was holding himself together.

"I'll get it," she said. She put on her parka, then added, "If you want to talk later, just call."

"I appreciate it. Thanks. Thanks a lot."

He saw her to the door, held it for her, opened the street door, then stood watching as she walked down Mt. Vernon. A fine, powdery snow was just beginning to fall; she could see the flakes in the glow of the street lamps.

• • •

Back in her bedroom at the rectory, having said the Evening Office, Lily sat on the mat in her meditation corner, noticing her in-breath, noticing her out-breath, watching images float into consciousness: her anxious waking at dawn; Roger Frye's oddly angelic face against the white pillow; Sally's slack-faced figure in the easy chair; the giant canvas of lilies; the picture of a man and a boy, profiled against a summer sky; the dim portico of the church, the profile of a young man, someone running into the dark.

# chapter ❋ 11

over the years, Lily had come to believe that most hospital patients, even the apparently unconscious or uncaring, could use another human presence, especially if the presence wasn't asking anything of the patient. So she arrived at Roger Frye's room the next morning with one of the books she had found among Barnes's boxed belongings, *Rescuing the Bible from Fundamentalism*, by Episcopal Bishop John Spong. She had already decided to spend at least half an hour with Frye, reading and being quiet, if that's what he wanted.

He had been moved to a small observation room directly across from the nurse's station. The only window looked out onto the large, U-shaped station desk and the busy hallway. With the curtains open, being in the room was like being on view in a human aquarium.

Lily sat in an orange armchair beside the bed and opened the book. Roger was lying on his side, his back to Lily. Against the background of nurses and orderlies rushing past the window, the room seemed dim and quiet. Idly, she thumbed through the pages, her mind on Roger and the scene in the church basement two nights ago. Then she sat up straighter and stared at the blank back page: there was a narrow rectangle of paper missing, carefully torn from the right-hand corner.

At that moment, the duty nurse came in, wheeling a set of monitors. She nodded at Lily, then leaned down to speak to her patient. "Roger," she said in a quiet voice, "you're in Mass General. You came in here the night before last. Today is Thursday. Can you lie on your back for me, just for a minute?" He responded by rolling onto his back. Then she studied him closely, placing one hand on his shoulder and looking directly at his chest. She took his wrist and gauged the pulse against her watch.

Lily's thoughts traveled back and forth between the activity in the room and her discovery. Was the missing corner of the page and the list of letters and numbers in the peacoat pocket part of Barnes's secret? Was Roger Frye's collapse connected to Barnes's death? To the list?

The nurse took Roger's temperature, checked his blood pressure, and attached what looked like a red plastic clothespin to the tip of his index finger. Finally, she turned away to inspect the IV drip and the two monitors on the portable unit. When she turned back from the screens, she said, "Hello," smiled at Lily, and asked her if the day had warmed up any since that morning.

"No," said Lily, "it's pretty dreary, but I kind of like it. I like all kinds of weather."

"Yuck," said the nurse, "not me. I keep saying I'm going to Florida, but you know how that goes."

Lily nodded, even though the thought of moving to Florida made her feel queasy. She began to study the woman in front of her, who stood looking down at Roger, one hand again resting on his left shoulder. She was powerful-looking, with straight, gray hair, a round face, and bright, expressive eyes. The name tag on her uniform pocket said "LENA, R.N."

After a moment she looked up, caught Lily staring at her, and said, "I'm glad you're here. He hasn't had any other visitors." Then she leaned down to Roger and said in a completely different voice, evidently reserved for patients, "Let me know if you need anything, okay? Just ring the bell. You remember where it is?"

Lily thought she saw a slight movement of the man's head, but she wasn't sure.

Lena seemed satisfied. "Great," she said and patted his shoulder. When she straightened up, she caught Lily's eye and indicated, with a nod toward the door, that she wanted to talk with her outside the room.

Lily stood and followed Lena into the hallway.

"How well do you know him?" Lena asked.

"Not well," said Lily. "He's the custodian at the church where I'm the temporary priest. I don't really know any of them very well."

"Has anyone told you anything about this?" She indicated the room behind them where Frye lay, awake and docile.

"No," said Lily. "I haven't seen a doctor, yet. I guess I assumed it was garden-variety alcoholism, that he just passed out. I know he drinks. But one of the EMTs said it looked like shock, so . . ."

Lena was nodding her head as she listened. Lily could see the nurse had more to tell, so she stopped speaking mid-sentence.

"You'd think so, wouldn't you?" asked Lena. "I mean, that's what it looks like, and he's an alcoholic, for sure. You should see the size of his liver. Look, I don't usually tell priests anything, but no one else is here for this guy, and since you're a woman, well, here's the deal. It looks like he was taking Antabuse. You know what that is?"

"Yes," said Lily.

"He's never talked to you about his drinking?" asked Lena. "Or about trying to stop?"

"No," said Lily, shaking her head, recalling Mrs. Hanlon's description of Roger's likely agenda on the day of their quarrel. "Of course, there's no reason I would have known, necessarily, but I'm surprised. I just never had the impression he was trying to stop."

"Right," said Lena, still watching Lily closely. "I'm not

sure he was. I think he's totally blown away by this. No one's bothered to ask him yet, because he's still pretty wiped out, but I mentioned the Antabuse to him this morning, and he didn't seem to know what I was talking about. He was a little perkier then. We've got him sedated for withdrawal, so he might have just forgotten. I don't know though . . . he's not, like, guilty or ashamed. He's just sort of . . . blown away and afraid."

"But there was Antabuse in his system?" Lily asked her, confused.

"Yeah," said Lena. "They found it in the tox screen. He lucked out and got an intern who had just come on duty, so she was still awake." Lena paused and drew a deep breath, then exhaled upward, ruffling her bangs, as if she were hot or just fed up. Lily had the feeling that the woman had once been a heavy smoker, the kind that would take a very deep drag at dramatic moments, like this one. "Anyway," Lena continued, "don't get me started on *that.* So, this intern's good, too, in general. She, like, *gets* it, you know?" Lena looked straight into Lily's eyes, and Lily nodded vigorously. She didn't want to seem like one of the ones who *didn't* get it.

"She saw he was in some kind of shock," Lena continued, "that he'd been drinking, so she had them screen for Antabuse. And he had a good dose of alcohol in there, too, which is kind of weird. Antabuse usually works fast— usually they're sick in five or ten minutes, so when did he have time to drink that much? Though, you can't ever tell, actually. I've seen someone—a guy I knew—finish a fifth of Jack Daniels while he was on Antabuse. He said it got him higher."

"You know a lot about this," Lily said to her. "Is this your specialty?"

"Yeah, I specialized for years," said Lena with a slight, ironic smile. "First few visits here I was a patient, in worse shape than our friend in there. Now I'm a nurse. An improvement, right?"

"Congratulations," Lily said.

"Thanks," said Lena. "Anyway, I'm glad you're here.

The ones who have visitors do a whole lot better. Makes sense."

"Definitely," said Lily. "Can I ask you something?"

Lena shrugged and nodded.

"What were you doing in there, when you put your hand on him, on his shoulder?"

Lena studied her, as if sizing her up, then shrugged once more and said, "I just figure a lot of these people never get touched, except to have something poked into them or pulled out of them. So I try to touch them every once in a while, for no reason, you know."

"I thought that's what it was," said Lily admiringly. "Look, thanks for the information. I'll see what I can find out from him, or someone else, although I don't think anyone really knows him very well."

"That figures," said Lena. "It would be nice to know who put him on the Antabuse, though. Not a great call."

"Not a great call because . . . ?" asked Lily.

"Mainly because it almost killed him," said Lena. "Look, the whole Antabuse thing is a joke. You think an addict is going to stop taking drugs because they make him sick? Alcohol has been making this guy sick for years. It doesn't make sense to me, but then a lot of things doctors do don't make sense to me. Don't get me started. Anyway, I've got to get going here, but I'll see you around."

And she vanished into the room across from Roger's. Lily could hear Lena's special voice for patients—gentle and soothing—beneath the intercom calls for "keys to the desk," the clatter of trays, the distant laugh of someone near the elevators.

When Lily returned to Frye's room, he was lying on his back, staring at the ceiling. His hands were clasped together on his chest, which rose and fell steadily, and his eyes were opened wide. He looked completely awake.

Lily stood by the armchair for a moment watching him, then picked up the book from the seat and sat down. Before she could find her place, she was interrupted by the sound of Frye's voice.

"I wasn't taking that drug," he said. "I don't do drugs anymore."

He lay still, staring ahead, then he closed his eyes and took a deep breath. Lily waited to see if he would say anything else. She studied him for a moment to be sure he hadn't fallen asleep.

"Roger," she said, "do you know why you're here?"

There was silence, and then he said, without opening his eyes, "Is this a test?"

Lily laughed out loud. Roger kept his eyes closed but smiled slightly.

"No," said Lily. "It's a real question. I really want to know."

The next silence lasted for what seemed a long time. Lily sat still and watched. Then tears started to run down his face. He never opened his eyes, and he made no noises. Lily moved to the bed and took his hand. She stood next to him like that for at least ten minutes, maybe more, until the tears stopped.

A little over an hour later, after visiting another parishioner—Mr. Latham, now recovering from the uneventful removal of a cyst in his chin—Lily walked slowly down Charles Street, soaking in what was available of the wan sunlight just breaking through the clouds. She noticed her hunger, her sadness for Roger Frye, and her confusion. The first one was not so hard to remedy. She stopped at an upscale deli on the corner of Charles and Mt. Vernon, bought a turkey sandwich named after a town in France, and walked back out into the cold light.

She could not do much about feeling sad for Frye, Lily reflected. At least, the sadness was tinged with hope. Frye appeared to be a broken man—a good thing to be. Lily believed in brokenness; she believed faith was all about brokenness, about getting broken, having pride and illusions of power taken away so that people could start all over again. Or at least that's what she used to believe; she found now that she liked theories about humility a lot more than she liked the experience of being humbled.

Across from the church, on River Street, was an antiques store. She paused and looked in the window, in which the display of expensive furniture and whimsical knickknacks seemed to change almost weekly. On a small, mahogany rolltop desk sat a miniature triptych, its center panel a scene of the Annunciation. Looking closely, Lily could see that Mary appeared anything but glad to hear the angel's message. The Holy Mother-to-be looked not at the winged messenger but out an open window, her tiny, dark face touched with longing, her childlike hands held up as if to stop the words before they reached her. And the angel didn't look much more cheerful herself.

The young owner—they had met a few times, briefly, on the sidewalk—tapped on the window. Lily reluctantly shifted her gaze from the sullen angel to the face of the smiling blond man behind the glass. They waved, a little idiotically, the way people do to pantomime pleasure, then Lily turned and crossed the street to the church. The image of Mary's face stayed with her. Talk about being *humbled,* she thought.

Moments later, standing on the rectory porch, she knew instinctively there was someone inside the house. Her pulse quickened, then she remembered it was Thursday, so Mrs. Hanlon would be inside, and probably Charlie, for his now regular weekly visit. He actually comes to see *her*, thought Lily, surprised by how much she cared.

When Lily opened the outer door, Charlie's youthful face peered around the corner from the kitchen. He grinned idiotically when he saw her through the window in the inner door, reminding her exactly of the antiques dealer on River Street.

"Here she is," she heard Charlie call out. Then he walked toward her, waving happily. Lily laughed. This is why people have dogs, she thought.

"Where have you been?" he asked as he opened the door wide for her.

"It's a long story," said Lily. "I hope you've got all day."

"As a matter of fact, I do . . . or most of it anyway," said Charlie, looking suddenly serious. "Are you okay?"

"I have no idea," said Lily, putting her book and the paper bag containing her sandwich on the hall table. She took off her parka and hung it on the hook of the closet door, then picked up the deli bag.

"You want some tea?" Charlie asked her.

"I do," said Lily, and they walked together into the kitchen. Mrs. Hanlon was standing at the stove, talking over her shoulder to Tom Casey. He sat behind her, at the table, his fingers drumming a soft tattoo on the checkered tablecloth.

After Lily had caught them up on the events of the last two days, eaten her lunch, and drunk two cups of very strong tea, she felt better. The act of telling the unreal saga—seeing the light in the window, hearing the noise, finding Frye's body, calling 911, visiting the hospital, talking with Lena—brought the images all back into the realm of daily life. She even included the antiques store—the triptych, the faces of Mary and the wistful angel, a simple version of her thoughts on humility.

"Oh Lord," she said, after a brief silence. "I just remembered I told Stanley that I'd see him today if I missed him Tuesday."

"He's there practicing, as always," said Mrs. Hanlon. "When I go out, he goes in. The man's like clockwork, Tuesdays and Thursdays. But I think you've made enough visits for one day."

Lily gave her a grateful look and relaxed.

"So what's the story with Frye?" asked Casey. "Do you think this nurse is right, that he didn't know about the Antabuse?"

Lily considered for a moment. "Yes, I do." She paused, then added, "I think she knows what she's talking about."

"I'd be very surprised to hear that Mr. Frye was on a no-more-drinking program," said Mrs. Hanlon.

"What does *he* say?" asked Casey.

"Not much," said Lily. "He's not in good enough shape

to answer questions. But I think he's frightened by what happened to him, whatever it was."

"I've been thinking," said Casey, looking at Lily, "since we talked last night, how much alike these two things seem—the stuff with these two men, Frye and Barnes."

"I think so too, Tommy," said Mrs. Hanlon. "And I also thought—what if Roger knew the same thing that Father knew?"

Lily remembered her discovery of the missing corner of the blank page. It was one thing to hoard secrets when no one else was affected. But now Roger Frye had been affected, or might have been.

She got up and walked out into the hall. When she came back, all three were watching her. She sat down and put the slip of paper in the middle of the table. Charlie reached out and took it. He studied the note for a minute, then passed it to Mrs. Hanlon, who held the scrap at arm's length and squinted. She shook her head and passed it on to Tom Casey.

"So what's this?" Charlie asked.

"I don't know," said Lily. "I found it in the inside pocket of Barnes's old peacoat."

Casey passed the scrap back to Mrs. Hanlon.

"This is his handwriting, all right," she said.

"You mean Barnes's, right?" asked Lily, remembering Stanley's note from Tuesday evening.

"Yes," said Mrs. Hanlon. "But what could he mean? Maybe that's a license plate number on top, but not enough digits. Unless it's one of those vanity things."

"Or a route number," said Lily. "But what's *safe?*"

Casey took the paper from Mrs. Hanlon. "How about letting me take this with me?" he asked Lily. "I could run a couple of searches on our computers with these numbers, see if I come up with anything."

"Is that legal?" she asked him.

He thought for a moment, then said, "It's probably legal—maybe not kosher, but legal. Do you mind?"

Lily laughed out loud, in surprise. *"I* don't mind," she said. "I thought maybe your boss might mind."

"Yes, Tommy," said Mrs. Hanlon. "Don't get in trouble for us. Your mother would never forgive me."

"I wouldn't put it in the category of police corruption," Casey said and smiled.

She felt her heart tighten, just for an instant, then relax. So he has a great smile, she thought. He's young, he's Catholic, he's married. This is not a healthy future I see in front of me.

"Sure, go on," she said, sounding much more cavalier than she felt. It was unreasonably hard to part with the note. She felt suddenly bereft and anxious. "But let me have it back when you're through," she added. "I think I know where it came from—that scrap."

"Where?" asked Charlie.

"A book Barnes was reading. You know it—*Rescuing the Bible.*"

"So he was reading the batch of radicals you found," said Charlie. "But why?"

"I'm trying to figure that out. And I need to ask something," Lily said to Mrs. Hanlon. "But it can't . . . I can't answer any questions about my question, if you know what I mean. And no one else can know I asked you. Okay?"

Mrs. Hanlon nodded.

"What do you know about Dan and Sally Talbot's son, Roy?" Lily asked, turning again to Mrs. Hanlon.

"Why?" Mrs. Hanlon responded.

"I can't answer that, remember?" Lily said.

"I don't know him, you understand," said the woman. "But I know he and Father were awfully close. Until the boy left last summer."

"What do you mean 'left'?" asked Lily.

"I'm not sure. I think it was in June he left town altogether. I thought you knew. I thought that's why you were asking me," said Mrs. Hanlon.

"No," said Lily, shaking her head.

"I don't know much. Except now, as you ask me, I see it was just after the beginning of the mess here. Father was troubled in the spring, I told you that. Then, early summer, he mentioned to me that the Talbot boy was gone. I think

I'd asked him about the family. They've always been nicer than some."

"So you think Roy Talbot was one of the things Barnes felt bad about?" asked Casey.

"Yes," said Mrs. Hanlon. "Father never said anything at the time. But now I see it. The boy's leaving was definitely part of the trouble here."

That night in the rectory, Lily was irritated to find herself tensing up at every stray noise: the radiator pipes clanging in the study corner; the scurry of mice between the floor and ceiling overhead; a sudden, deep creaking somewhere in the frame of the old building. These were familiar noises, common enough, but tonight they sounded amplified and portentous.

Twice she got out of bed and walked through the whole house, turning on lights and looking into corners, chastising herself throughout. Before he left that afternoon, Charlie had suggested she make a retreat at the monastery. Lily had dismissed the idea, but now she began to wonder. Maybe she needed to be somewhere else for a few days. Maybe the place itself was part of the problem.

Finally she made a cup of herb tea and went back upstairs for what she promised herself would be the last time. She opened the Spong book to the section she had been scanning at the hospital, studying Barnes's neat, minimalist pencil strokes in the margins. Judging by the faint exclamation points and fainter question marks, there was a lot that had puzzled or surprised the priest.

Throughout the section in which Spong speculates about "the real man Paul," so troubled by his divided self, Barnes had begun joining the two hieroglyphs, making an exclamation point followed by a question mark. In that chapter, Spong hypothesized that Paul was, perhaps, homosexual. The speculation itself had gotten a lot of airplay when the book first appeared. Remembering that, Lily wondered why the older man had chosen to read the book at all.

Near the end, she found what appeared to have been the most important chapter for Barnes. He had underlined whole sections in which Spong writes about the "barrier-free love" witnessed in the life of Jesus and about people's inability to live with such a love. "We build churches to house the righteous while relegating the sinners to the ranks of the rejected. . . ." writes Spong, beside which Barnes had drawn two solid lines and a pair of exclamation points.

Five pages past the passage she had just read, Lily discovered a folded piece of white notepaper. On the top, embossed in black ink, was:

### Frederick J. Barnes
### St. Mary of the Garden

Below this, on the page, was the draft of a note, incomplete, lines crossed out, written in square, neat, familiar letters:

Dear Roy,
This is a difficult letter to write, in part because I have so much to say and it seems so very important to me to get it right. There is the terrible awareness of the harm I have done. That awareness makes me afraid I will fail you again.
~~I ask that you read this through to the end~~
~~I do not ask anything of you. I only hope you will hear me out.~~
I write for two reasons: First, I must ask for your forgiveness. Over the past few months I have been given a great gift, the gift of sight—or, perhaps, two great gifts, the gift of sight and a second chance to act on what I now can see. You are not the only one who has suffered from my blindness. Please forgive me.
I also write to ask you to come home. I think I can understand your anger, and your fear, but I believe in my heart—perhaps I have to believe this in order to go on—that with God's love and forgiveness, and our own courage and patience,

we can amend the past by living faithfully in the present.

~~I have not spoken with your father, but I believe that he too can be helped~~

~~God bless you~~

Please be careful

"Amen," Lily whispered to herself when she had read it through a second time. But not until after the third reading did she begin to understand exactly what she had found.

# chapter ✳ 12

The upstairs hall of the monastery guest house was empty and silent on Sunday evening. To the left, a row of identical oak doors opened onto narrow rooms, each with a bed, a desk, a closet, and a small kneeling bench. Lily stood with her hand on the doorknob of her room, nearest the top of the stairs at the end of the hall, and listened for any sounds that might indicate other people were around. She heard nothing, which indicated nothing—napping and praying were both silent activities.

The morning after finding Barnes's letter, she had decided to take Charlie's advice. When she had called to arrange a brief retreat, she had not asked Brother Samuel, the host of the guest house, if she would be alone upstairs. Asking seemed indiscreet, but she wasn't sure why. Probably because of Brother Samuel, a very discreet man—small, white-haired, with polished lace-up shoes shining from beneath his cassock. He had been at the Brattle Street monastery longer than any of the other brothers—through women's ordination and the revisions of the prayer book, through Pike and Hines, *Situation Ethics* and *Honest to God*.

Charlie revered him, but Lily never knew exactly why. To her he seemed fussy and overly practical, much too interested in the number of towels in the linen closet. But Charlie said Samuel had a sense of history and proportion—those were his own words—that most of the newer brothers lacked. He also said Brother Samuel was a truly spiritual person, which didn't jibe, for Lily, with his obsessive interest in towels. "God is in the details," said Charlie. Yes, but which details, she always thought.

The back stairs across from her door led to a similar first-floor hallway of small offices where the brothers met with people seeking spiritual counseling. At the end of that hall was the chapel. Beyond that lay the brothers' wing of the monastery, the refectory, kitchen, living quarters, a lush yet orderly greenhouse, and the common rooms, two all-purpose meeting rooms, one with a small television tucked into a corner of the bookshelves. Lily had only visited the brothers' territory, beyond the refectory, once, when Charlie was just home from the hospital after a bout of pneumonia, and that wing still held a fascination for her—it seemed both safe and mystical.

From the chapel, a small bell sounded eight times, somewhere between tinny and silvery, announcing Evensong. It was a good service here. There were a few brothers with fine voices and near-perfect pitch, so the chants were full-bodied, not the anemic warbling you get in most parishes.

There was only one light on in the lower hall. Lily made her way in the dusk. She could hear the sounds of closing doors and soft footsteps as the brothers came together in the chapel. Almost everyone was assembled by the time she slipped into the corner of a back pew, nearest the door that led from the guest wing. The pews lined the walls in rows of three, facing out across the nave, so rather than looking at the altar and crucifix, congregants saw one another.

Three fellow retreatants were already there, one in the pew in front of her—a tall, heavyset man with a shaved head and a tiny gold hoop in his right ear—and two in the pews across the way, facing her—one middle-aged woman with thick glasses and a receding chin, and a slight round-shouldered man with a goatee.

The brothers sat in the pews in the two back corners of the chapel, next to the grillwork that separated the nave from the narthex, the outside world from the inside. Lily saw everyone but Charlie and Brother Samuel. As she opened the black binder that held the Daily Office, the two men arrived together, clearly having hurried, although now they moved down the aisle and took their places in the back pews.

"Hail Mary, full of grace . . ." one of the brothers began. "The Lord is with you . . ."

Did Charlie look funny? Lily wondered. Why was she so sure that his lateness had something to do with her?

"And blessed is the Fruit of thy womb, Jesus," the group continued—Lily along with them. Her breathing began to slow.

The Advent wreath stood just in front of her—a lush circle of pine boughs woven with purple ribbon and holding five thick candles. Only one candle was lit for this first week of the season; she watched the flame burn, flickering slightly in downdrafts from the vaulted ceiling. "Holy Mary, Mother of God . . ." they prayed in unison.

The altar was a table of gray marble, with a graceful marble canopy resting on four slender columns, like the canopy in the Giotto painting of the child Jesus being presented in the temple. Through the arched space between the two closest columns, Lily could see the crucifix and, above that, a faint haze of incense against the stained-glass windows.

"Pray for us sinners, now and at the hour of our death," intoned Lily. And peace, for an instant, came to her, the peace of call and response, of knowing what comes next, the peace of faith and ritual.

The refectory tables each held two smaller versions of the Advent wreath, one wreath at either end of the long tables, and each wreath with one candle lit. The room smelled of juniper and fresh bread. At dinner one of the younger brothers, she thought it might be Thomas, read from *The Gospel According to Jesus,* by Stephen Mitchell—an unorthodox rewriting of the story of Jesus's life based on the author's research into the historical Jesus and Mitchell's own practice of Buddhism. Lily had given Charlie the book for Christmas last year. She felt surprised when she recognized the text, and she gave Charlie a raised eyebrow across the room.

As she stood washing her plate and cup in the kitchen sink, Charlie came up behind her and whispered, "There's someone who wants to talk with you, or, at least, he's willing to talk with you."

Lily turned to face him and mouthed, "Who?" although she already knew who, and what she really meant was, "Why?"

Charlie pointed toward the hallway that led to the guest wing, and Lily felt a moment of disappointment. She had thought she was going to get to enter the brothers' quarters, the wing of closeted sanctuary.

Instead, after she had put her dishes in the drainer, Charlie led her back to the lower hallway beneath her room. He opened the door of his own office, offered her a seat in a small, blue armchair, then said, "Wait here," and left.

Lily scanned the books on the shelves. They looked like books Charlie had chosen to impress his counselees, titles meant to reassure them he was qualified to be doing this work: *The Wounded Healer, Pastoral Care and Counseling, Stages of Faith.* The whole idea made her feel bone tired.

Charlie opened the door, stood back, and ushered in Brother Samuel.

"You two know each other," Charlie said, standing in the doorway. He glanced from one to the other of them, waiting for acknowledgment.

"You know we do." Her voice carried some of the tiredness she had just felt.

"Sit down, sit down," Charlie said to Samuel, then added,

"I appreciate your doing this." He gave Lily a kind of pleading glance, a "Be nice, okay?" glance, and shut the door.

Lily turned to Brother Samuel, but he stood where Charlie had left him, staring at the wall above her head. Finally, he shifted his gaze to her.

"I'm not sure where to begin, with this, with our talk . . ." he said, as if testing each word to see if it would bear up under the weight of his intentions.

"Maybe you could start by—" began Lily. She planned to say "sitting down," but Brother Samuel began speaking again.

"Charles has told me you are now the interim priest at St. Mary of the Garden. That interests me, because of my history, my connection with that parish, a connection of many years." He was looking at the books on the shelves to Lily's left. "Perhaps you know about this, perhaps you have already spoken with someone . . ." he said. It didn't sound exactly like a question, but the pitch of his voice rose at the end.

Lily raced into the gap. "Why don't you sit down?" she asked him.

He looked down at the chair, then nodded.

When he sat, Lily began to answer him. "I'm not sure what—" but Brother Samuel continued exactly where he had left off.

". . . about our friendship, although, really, I'm not sure who would have known to speak with you about it, and, then, why would anyone." The pitch rose again, but Lily couldn't be fooled this time. Clearly, he was reflecting on all this in some weird, rhetorical isolation. This must be how pets feel, she thought.

While she half-listened to his explanation of his interest in St. Mary's, having to do with its history as an Anglo-Catholic parish that had descended, over the years, to the mid-ranks of liturgy and practice, she studied the man. He was small and square and, as he spoke, very still. He wore thick glasses with black frames that almost filled the top half of his face. She felt as though she were sitting with a character out of a storybook, an old owl, a sorcerer. Then, the next thing he said snapped her out of her dreamy audience trance.

". . . whatever was on Fred's mind weighed on him . . ."

"Fred Barnes?" asked Lily. She felt as if she had shouted the name into the room.

Brother Samuel looked at her, and a deep frown began to wrinkle his forehead. "I am not very adept at talking with people. I can say what I need to say, but it takes me a long time."

The pitch rose. She nodded.

"But because you are interested in Fred Barnes, I want to talk with you, or to you," he corrected himself, with a slight smile. "You are interested in Fred Barnes, is that right?"

When she realized he had asked her a direct question, she cleared her throat. "Yes," she said, nodding her head, making her eyes wide.

He shifted in the blue chair, putting his hands on the armrests, fixing his eyes on the wall above her head, and continued. "Fred Barnes and I were best friends from seminary, and throughout our lives," he said.

"Yes," she said again, "I see."

"We were very much alike, in some ways, and very different, in others. He wanted to be out among people. I think—I suspect—he felt I had taken the easy way out, when I took Holy Vows. But he would never say so. He was a kind man."

Brother Samuel stopped talking and took a deep breath. "I have been—I still miss his company. He was a true friend, a true friend, and a Christian, although we may mean different things by that, you and I."

He seemed to expect a response this time.

"I don't know," Lily said, "but I think there would be similarities. After all, there's Charlie."

The monk nodded at her. "Yes. That's a good point." This time he shifted his gaze to the narrow leaded window above the desk. "But then Charles is an unusual figure, an unusual monastic. For instance, he is able to have for friends a man like me and a woman like you." He leaned back in his chair for the first time and closed his eyes.

"Fred and I were ordained before all of this took hold— liturgical renewal, social action. We took the church at face value, so to speak." Another pause. "But we were both committed, and we found ways to help each other through the changes. He was most helpful to me many, many times. And I, I would like to believe, to him."

During the long silence that followed, Lily was not sure if she actually gritted her teeth or if she just imagined herself doing it. But she knew better than to try to start another sentence.

"Charles is an important voice here, you know," he said. "He is able to give words to knotty, difficult questions. I think he may be superior here eventually. I hope so." He stopped abruptly, as if catching himself in a gaffe. "Perhaps you won't mention that to him, that I think that. It's only my opinion."

"No, I won't," said Lily.

"This fall," he said, "Fred was wrestling with an angel. Those were his words. He wouldn't talk about it. I don't think he would have told anyone anything, if he didn't tell me. Perhaps Frieda . . ." he murmured at the end.

"Frieda?" she asked, startled.

"Frieda Klass," he said. "Is she no longer a parishioner at St. Mary of the Garden? Because when we last spoke I believe she was on the vestry . . ."

"Frieda Klass?" echoed Lily, dumbfounded, conjuring the tall, austere woman who had sat silent through that vestry meeting, who had gone to Austria to visit her family, who had offered twice to help Lily.

"Yes," he said. "I see I have surprised you. Frieda was at school with us. The only woman at the seminary at that time—some sort of special student, they called her. She and Fred and I have always kept in close touch. Have you spoken with her yourself?"

"Yes, briefly," she said. "I had no idea."

"He seemed," Brother Samuel continued, "Fred seemed

almost tortured by this thing—a combination of things, really."

Another pause here lengthened unendurably. "A secret he had been told, about someone in his parish, I believe. His own failure in his vocation, though I still doubt that very much. And what had been done to someone else, a young person."

She thought he had finished. But staring at the floor he added, "Fred wanted this young person, a young man, to come stay here with us—possibly for an extended period. He needed sanctuary, that was the word Fred used. And I made a mistake that I now regret. I advised him against that course, primarily because it seemed inconvenient to me at the time." He looked at Lily and said, "I'm sorry, now, I did that."

She nodded at him. He looked away after a moment. The silence between them grew and became almost another presence in the room.

Finally he said to her, "If you know this young man— Charles thought you might know him, or know who he was. Do you know him?"

Lily was startled. "I think I might," she said. "That is, I think I might know who he is, at least."

"I believe you and I should help him, if it's still appropriate, if it isn't too late."

Lily woke in the small, spare guest room before dawn on Monday with a sense that she had dreamed one long dream for the past six hours. What was oddest about it was that the two main characters, Fred Barnes and Roy Talbot, were so vibrantly present, even though she had never met either of them. At some point, Roy Talbot and Roger Frye were working with elaborate tools—one looked like a pool skimmer, a metal rod with a net on one end—to take down a door. In the dream, Lily knew that opening the door would be a disaster, but she wanted them to do it anyway. Fred Barnes stood behind the door, looking sunken and pale, and maybe Brother Samuel. Then the room turned out to be the monastery chapel in which, in the darkest corner, stood not Brother Samuel or Fred Barnes but Stanley Leonard and Roy Talbot. And everyone, crowds of people, struggling to see what they were up to, because they were up to something . . .

She had just shoved the Advent wreath toward the corner, lighting the scene, making it almost visible, when she came out of the dream, soaked with sweat. She got up, dressed, and made her way as quietly as possible past the row of oak doors, down the front stairs, and out into the walled courtyard. The sky was beginning to glow faintly in the east, but the air was night air, bitter cold and motionless.

Brattle Street was empty—no cars, no people, no stray dogs, no paper truck on its route. By the time she crossed Memorial Drive, behind the Kennedy Memorial, the river was already reflecting the silver pink of the sky. She turned toward the city and walked as fast as she could on the narrow bike path that ran along the water's edge, past the Harvard dorms on her left, past the boathouse on her right, toward the brightening sky and skyline of Boston. Joggers appeared, and then, on the river, a single skull skimming past her, leaving a perfect V-shaped wake.

She was hot beneath the wool watch cap she wore, so she pulled it off and her thick, dark hair tumbled free to her shoulders. An older man in a warm-up suit ran past, taking a long look at her. She felt a flash of irritation, but then realized it had little to do with the jogger. As she walked, her mind cleared, and the jumble of troubling images from the night before fell into place. It was not so much irritation as fear; she didn't like what she was thinking.

There was a note on her door when she returned: "Find me. I'm in the greenhouse this a.m. I'll meet you in the guest kitchen. Charlie." After she had hung up her coat, braided her hair, said her prayers, and made her bed, she went down to the office and asked the receptionist, a tall, thin young man with blonde hair and a clipped mustache, how to get a message to Charlie. He suggested that she name a place to meet, and he would have Charlie find her there.

"The guest kitchen," said Lily, her stomach rumbling on cue.

"Sounds like a good idea," said the young man.

Lily walked through the lower hall, then decided to stop off in the chapel. She had missed Morning Prayer, and now she hoped to recover a small bit of the peace she had found during Evensong last night. Someone else was kneeling in front of the altar in the Lady Chapel, one of the brothers—then Lily saw that it was Samuel. She sat with her back to him and read the Morning Office in the dim light from the high windows, but no peace returned. Brother Samuel's presence was too much a reminder of the world beyond the wrought-iron gate of the chapel. After a moment of silence, she crossed herself, got up, bowed to the altar, and left through the opposite door, leaving Brother Samuel alone again.

When she reached the refectory, Charlie was already there.

"Where were you this morning?" he asked her. "You want some tea?"

"I want more than that," said Lily. "I just walked to the B.U. bridge and back. I'm starving."

Charlie pointed to the counter, where there stood a wooden salad bowl of pears and apples, two hunks of cheddar cheese under a glass bell, and half a loaf of homemade raisin bread wrapped in a clean damp dish towel. "Help yourself," he said and made a slight bow toward the food.

He watched silently while she took a plate from the shelf above the sink and made herself a breakfast of the food on the counter. Then they walked together into the dining room, Charlie carrying their mugs of tea.

When they were seated at a corner of the table closest to the kitchen, he asked her, "So, how did it go?"

She eyed him speculatively, her mouth full of bread and cheese. She raised her hand to stop him from asking again, took a sip of tea, and leaned back. "Me first," she said.

"How did the subject of Fred Barnes come up between you two?"

"Let's see," said Charlie. "After you decided to come, I explained a little of the situation to Samuel, and he asked if he could talk to me later, alone. So that night he told me the story of their friendship—the same stuff he told you, I guess. Maybe I shouldn't have said anything. I just had a feeling."

"You were right," said Lily.

He smiled. "Does this mean I'm forgiven?"

"I'm not blaming anyone for anything at the moment," said Lily.

"That's a nice change," said Charlie.

She ignored him. "I'm just trying to put this all together. In your terms, I would say that my conversation with Brother Samuel last night was meant to be, was part of the plan. In my terms . . ." she began, then paused, looking down at her plate. She thought she felt like crying, but couldn't. "I don't know what my terms are anymore."

"Isn't that what faith is," asked Charlie, "at least partly—walking blind?"

"Probably," said Lily. "Anyway, I might as well tell you, I don't like what I'm thinking, and I don't like the effect it's going to have if what I'm thinking—oh hell . . ." she said.

"Why don't you just tell me?"

"I've got a story with a young man, or boy, who spent a lot of time at church. He was really close with the priest, a single, older man. Then this boy—lots of money, decent family—suddenly runs way from home. I find a letter from the priest asking the boy to forgive him. Do you want me to go on?" she asked.

"I think I get it," said Charlie. "But what about Samuel's story? Why would Barnes be looking for a safe place for the boy to stay?"

"I'm not sure," she said. "Maybe someplace where no one knew the boy—where he couldn't tell anyone what happened?"

"That doesn't seem likely, somehow," said Charlie. "Besides, Barnes told Samuel the boy needed sanctuary—from what?"

"I don't know. And I don't know what I'm supposed to do with all this anyway." She glanced up at the light coming through the high windows. Then she said quietly, as if beaten, "I've always been so sure about what my faith meant in my life and about where it led me. I feel like I'm starting all over again."

"Good," said Charlie. "That's just the right place to be."

Lily gave him a pained, skeptical look. "Charlie, don't you ever get tired of being a cheerleader?"

Charlie beamed at her, leaned forward, and whispered, "You've just hit on one of my secret ambitions."

Lily spent the rest of the day following the schedule of the order, attending Noonday Prayer (". . . send your Holy Spirit into our hearts, to direct and rule us according to your will . . ."); Evensong ("I will bless the Lord who gives me counsel; my heart teaches me, night after night"); and Compline ("For God shall give the angels charge over you, to keep you in all your ways . . ."). The next morning, reluctantly, she packed her clothes, stripped the bed, and stuffed her books into her backpack. Maybe she'd learned what she came to learn, though she couldn't have known what that was before the visit. And the lessons were not only about the recent history of St. Mary of the Garden.

Among other things, Lily had never realized how much she begrudged Charlie his safe harbor, that somewhere in her she thought he was taking the easy way out, that *real* faith called us out into the world. And now Charlie and Brother Samuel got to retreat to the fragrant silence in their wing of the walled building, while she schlepped her heavy backpack down the steep escalator of the Harvard Square station and returned to St. Mary of the Garden to finish whatever she had blindly, faithfully started.

# chapter ✳ 13

The Charles River shone brilliantly blue-cold and choppy. Though the Red Line back into Boston seemed busy for mid-morning, Lily had found a window seat with an empty space beside her for her backpack. She gazed out at the water uninterrupted by her fellow passengers.

Since the Charles Street stop was directly across the street from Mass General, she decided to visit Roger Frye on her way home. She felt guilty for neglecting him during her stay in the monastery. Technically, this wasn't her job. Visiting the sick fell to the committee Cynthia Babcock chaired—Pastoral Care and Concerns—but Lily had taken on some of the visits as a way to get to know parishioners. Also, having found Frye in the basement, having loaded him into the ambulance and held his hand while he cried, Lily felt responsible for him. And she admitted to herself that she had a second, less pastoral reason for seeing him right away: She hoped he would be a source of information about the parish and about the Talbot family, especially their son.

When she stepped off the train, the wind on the platform hit her with a fierce blast. As she negotiated the door to the landing, she had a clear memory of Mrs. Hanlon, struggling with the door, hands filled with shopping bags, heading the opposite direction—could that have been only six weeks ago? Remembering the scene felt like watching actors playing, but not very well, Mrs. Hanlon and Lily Connor, pale, one-dimensional versions of the people they had now become. Of course, with Mrs. Hanlon, the difference was that Lily had hardly known her then. But Lily could not be so sure about the difference between the two versions of herself.

The wind blew just as fiercely down on the sidewalk and whipped up a small flock of pieces of trash that swirled in the traffic circle beneath the T-stop. Lily trudged with her pack across Cambridge Street and approached the main entrance of Mass General. When she reached the large bank of glass doors, she pushed her way inside, found a quiet corner near the elevators, and set down her pack in order to take off her coat and scarf.

Chance caused her to look up a moment later and see John Neville emerging from an elevator at the far end of the short hallway. He wound his scarf around his neck, managing, while he did so, a large red shopping bag with the calendar of December printed on both sides. The bag looked full and heavy. Lily started to call out to him, but his hurried, watchful manner stopped her. She would ask Roger if he had had company that day.

When Lily neared Roger Frye's room, she thought she heard singing—a soulful, lyrical voice crooning the old Hank Williams song "I'm So Lonesome I Could Cry." "The moon just went behind a cloud," sang the voice. Sang Roger, Lily could now see. He sat cross-legged on the hospital bed. To Lily, he looked like a skinny, white Buddha—eyes closed, head tipped back. He sang from the soul, singing as if his own heart would break, just like Hank.

Lily stood frozen in the doorway, uncertain what to do next, and reflected on what an unlikely connection this was with Roger Frye—country music. Where was Roger from?

she wondered, watching him from across the room. She had never thought to ask.

An orderly walked by, a young Asian man in a green, gauze shower cap. He glanced through the door at Frye, then looked at Lily and said, "He's better than most. At least he can carry a tune."

"Do you think I should interrupt?" she asked him.

"I don't think you can," said the orderly, continuing down the hall. "They've been trying to shut him off since yesterday. But good luck." He disappeared around the corner.

Lily leaned against the door frame and felt deeply disappointed. Roger Frye was not going to be much of a source of information for anything but the Hit Parade. "I've never seen a night so long . . ." he sang, mournfully.

Lily closed her eyes. Her nights of dream-packed sleep at the monastery had been useful but not restful. The smell and noises took her back to the hospital in Houston, to the hallway outside the room in which her father had died. But she couldn't think about that now. She opened her eyes and turned away from the door to find Cynthia Babcock standing just behind her, looking confused, concerned, and put-out, all at once.

"I didn't know Roger could sing," said Cynthia. Her voice sounded aggrieved, as if Frye had kept something from her all these years, something that might have benefited the parish.

Cynthia had on a pair of black zip-up snow boots with synthetic fur peeking out of the top, heavy black tights, a plaid kilt, and a bright red parka with countless pockets, gussets, and drawstrings, the kind you might wear if you were about to trek in the Himalayas. "We clearly can't do anything here," she said to Lily. "Let's get some coffee and talk." It sounded more like an order than an invitation, but Lily could hardly object since this was exactly what she had hoped would happen. Who could be a better source of information than the chair of the Pastoral Care and Concerns Committee?

Lily nodded agreement and stepped into Roger's room.

She walked to the bedside, took one of Roger's hands, held it for a moment, and spoke loudly, above the singing. "Roger, I'll be here again tomorrow, okay?" What she had not heard in his voice was the constant force of panic she now saw in his eyes, in his strained face, in the clenched fist resting on his skinny knee.

He faltered in the lyrics, "The silence of a purple . . . the silence of a falling star . . ." Then he pulled his hand away from Lily's and sang, louder now, "lights up a purple sky . . ."

Lily patted his shoulder, for lack of a better gesture, then turned around to join Cynthia in the hall. They walked toward the elevators, and as Lily pressed the red "Down" button, she could still hear Roger's voice, a faint echo in the bright corridor, "And as I wonder where you are . . ."

When they stepped out onto the sidewalk, a gust of chill wind held them both motionless.

"Good grief," shouted Cynthia over the bluster. "Where should we go?"

"Someplace close, and warm," yelled Lily.

Cynthia nodded and started off. Lily trudged along one step behind, feeling like a child being taken to tea by a dreaded aunt. Or worse, thought Lily, studying Cynthia's back: she had pulled the parka hood up and reminded Lily, now, of du Maurier's *Don't Look Now,* of the manic, misshapen figure who ran around Venice with a meat cleaver slaughtering tourists and natives alike. There was just a hint of the manic about Cynthia Babcock, Lily thought—a woman with a mission.

They made their way across the complicated rotary beneath the elevated T-station, then headed down Charles Street with the wind pushing from behind. I wish she'd just turn and look at me, Lily thought, at which moment Cynthia turned, pointed to a coffee shop a few doors down and yelled, "We're here." She then picked up the pace and entered the small shop.

Lily followed her. Once inside, she took off her backpack and joined Cynthia at a table for two in the bay window facing the street. The waitress, a short, wiry, white-haired woman, sauntered to the table, filled both their cups with coffee, and set down the menus.

"Oh," said Lily, raising her palm to stop the woman, but too late. "I don't drink coffee."

The waitress shrugged, picked up the cup and saucer, and disappeared into the kitchen.

Lily glanced across at Cynthia, who stared at her menu like a scholar studying a runic text. Finally Cynthia breathed a sigh, looked up at Lily, and flashed a small grin that faded almost instantly.

"We must seem like quite an odd bunch to you," she said, folding her menu and placing it on the table.

"Why?" asked Lily.

"I don't know," said Cynthia. "It just feels like everything's fallen apart since Fred died."

Lily felt insulted, then ashamed to have felt insulted. "That doesn't seem so surprising," she said.

"True," said Cynthia. The waitress returned to take their orders. Lily realized she had never looked at her menu; she hurriedly ordered tea and an English muffin. Cynthia ordered a full breakfast—eggs, bacon, white toast—in a defiant voice, daring someone to mention her health. Lily expected her to whip out a Gauloise and start puffing on it aggressively, but Cynthia only gazed out at the empty, wind-torn street, seeming to have forgotten what she wanted to say.

"What's up, Cynthia?" Lily asked after a pause.

"I'm not sure where to start," she said, then took a deep breath. "I feel bad about this, but I can't be on the vestry anymore. In fact, I may be taking a few months off from church. I haven't found my way, I guess, after Fred's death. Nothing works. Nothing has turned out the way it should. Oh," she finally exclaimed in self-disgust, "I have no idea what I'm saying."

"Take your time," said Lily. "I'm in no rush."

They chatted for a while about the cold, the wind, and arrangements for Advent. When breakfast arrived, Cynthia attacked her food with seriousness, buttering toast, digging jam out of the plastic containers, salting and peppering eggs. Lily's English muffin looked anemic by comparison. She waited until Cynthia was settled, then asked, "Is there a specific problem at the parish?"

"What?" asked Cynthia.

"That makes you feel like you need time off."

Instead of answering, Cynthia took a bite of toast, shrugged her shoulders, and pointed to her mouth.

"Does this have anything to do with John Neville?" asked Lily.

Cynthia's cheeks went pink. Lily thought the woman might cry, but then the moment was over and Cynthia took a long sip of coffee. "Yes, it does," she said.

Lily nodded.

"We are, we . . ." Cynthia stopped and looked out at the street again. "Things have become complicated," she finished.

"Do you want to tell me?" asked Lily.

"I'm not sure. I hadn't intended to go into it. The matter's private, of course, and most of it doesn't have anything to do with the parish."

"It's up to you," said Lily.

"I'm not sure," said Cynthia. "Fred wasn't much of a pastor, at least not for me. He was a decent man—" Another quick twinge of color in Cynthia's cheeks betrayed some feeling—confusion, shame—then she went on. "But I would never in a million years have thought of talking with him about anything personal."

"Did everyone feel that way?" asked Lily.

"No, no," said Cynthia, thoughtfully. "Some people did talk with him. I think some of the families found him helpful. The Leonards, the Graffs, the Talbots—" She paused, then rushed forward—or was Lily imagining the rush? "And Frieda Klass, of course; they're old friends. But with Fred and me it was always business."

"What about the younger members of the parish?" asked Lily. "The teenagers?"

"We don't have very many—as you've noticed. They aren't too interested in church at that age."

"What about Roy, the Talbots' son? Wasn't he around a lot for a while?" asked Lily.

Was there hesitation? Again, Lily couldn't be sure. "Yes, but, of course, Stanley was his organ teacher. He's a talented young man, the Talbot boy. Stanley and he are extremely close." As she spoke, she speared a bite of egg and a piece of bacon. After she was through chewing, she switched the subject. "I'm actually the person, or at least one of the people—since I'm a vestry member and chair of Pastoral Concerns—who should be filling you in on all of this. I'm sure it's part of the reason I need to take a break. I just don't feel I can do that," she said, then signaled the waitress for more coffee. "I'm worn out by the last few months. I'm afraid I don't feel very pastoral or concerned."

After Cynthia's cup was full, she suddenly seemed ready—in fact eager—to talk about her own problems at the parish. "John Neville and I have had a . . . relationship, I think that's the best way to describe it. We have been seeing one another for a few years; it's hardly romantic, in any real sense of that word. But we have been . . . companions. It began after his wife had been dead a good while."

She sipped her coffee, then glanced at Lily and continued. "I'm sure you've noticed that life at the parish has been tense. But I'm not sure—has anyone mentioned that the last few months before Fred died there was talk of his resigning?"

"Why?" Lily asked.

"So many things . . ." Cynthia said. "Or maybe just one main thing—at least it seemed like that at the time. He became dogged about these two resolutions that were to be voted on at the Diocesan Convention. He felt that we needed to vote in favor of them and, well, it was unthinkable. It was completely out of character for him, and it would have been equally out of character for us."

"Which two resolutions?" Lily asked.

"About homosexuals. Fred wanted us to do workshops and discussions. John—he couldn't stand it, couldn't stand the idea even. He and Fred had more than one out-and-out battle."

"What does John say on the topic?"

"For him it's clear," said Cynthia. "The Bible says homosexuality is a sin. And that's where the discussion ends. But he's quite angry about the whole subject, so where does the anger come from? If it's so cut and dried, why be angry?"

"And for you?"

"In the abstract, I think John's right. But when you apply the theory to real people . . . I don't know," she said. "It *doesn't* seem right. The whole impulse to exclude people seems—how can I say this?—antithetical to what the church is supposed to be."

"Yes," said Lily. "I know what you mean."

"Anyway," Cynthia continued in a much more businesslike tone, "John was all for going to the bishop about Fred, to try to get him removed. He said that Fred couldn't represent the parish anymore, since our views were so different. When Fred died, we were left with this awful mess. Although before that, John had, for some reason, backed off a lot. But there were still plenty of bad feelings, even though Fred had served the parish so well, so faithfully—" Cynthia's eyes filled with tears. She blinked and blew her nose on her napkin. "There ends the story," she said.

"So this has taken a toll on you, on the vestry," said Lily.

Cynthia nodded. "We all disagreed about so many things—and John and I disagree, have disagreed so much it's finally become impossible to be friends any longer."

"You disagreed about Fred Barnes?"

"Yes," said Cynthia. "You don't just throw someone out after all that time. I thought John was dead wrong on that one. I still do. He claimed to have other reasons."

"What other reasons?" asked Lily.

"He wouldn't say, not directly. He hinted at some kind of wrongdoing, but he knew I wasn't going to believe him. I may not have been as close to Fred as some of them, but I respected him, always, even when we didn't agree."

Cynthia's whole manner was so straightforward, it was impossible to think she was lying. And yet, Lily was fairly sure the woman wasn't telling everything she knew.

"You can't leave church business at the church?" asked Lily. She decided to let her off the hook for now.

"You'd think so, wouldn't you?" said Cynthia. "But one of the hard truths I've had to face was how much of our relationship was about the church. It's really what we talked about, and . . . I'm not sure there's much else there."

"But are the disagreements so deep?"

"They are very deep," said Cynthia. "I'm not sure I even know how deep they are."

With that, Cynthia closed the subject. She said it was too painful to talk about anymore. They had a short discussion about Roger, about who would visit him next, and then Cynthia signaled the waitress for the check. There followed a wrangle over whether or not Cynthia would pay for both meals. Lily found herself in the ridiculous position of insisting that Cynthia allow her to pay for her own food, then feeling she had insulted the woman with her insistence. So the meal ended on a note of resentment, with Cynthia shrugging her shoulders and admitting a kind of resigned defeat.

"Listen, Cynthia," said Lily, once they were out on the sidewalk. "I just want to say I'd be sorry if you left the vestry, and even sorrier if you left the parish. I don't know you that well, but I like working with you, and, anyway, it doesn't seem fair, does it, that you have to leave and John gets to stay?"

Cynthia chuckled. "No, it doesn't," she said. "I'll think about it. I've never been one to step aside—not gracefully."

They reached the corner of Charles and Mt. Vernon, where they stood for a moment in front of the bakery.

"If you want to talk again, about anything," said Lily, stressing the last word, "let me know. I mean it."

"Yes," said Cynthia, "I know you do. And I actually feel a little better. I'm beginning to rethink this woman-in-pulpit thing. I begin to see the point." She was half-joking, Lily thought, but only half.

•  •  •

After Lily had unpacked, she crossed the courtyard to the church building and found the side door unlocked. In the hall, she stood for a moment, listening. The buildings were silent, and she had convinced herself she was alone when she heard a sharp, grating sound from the sanctuary. Then the hall door opened behind her, and she gave a little gasp as she turned to see Stanley Leonard.

"Sorry," he said.

"That's okay," said Lily.

"I'm here practicing," he continued.

"I didn't hear the organ," said Lily.

"No? I was taking a rest. And now I'll return, if you don't mind." He disappeared, shutting the door behind him.

Almost immediately, he began to play. Lily recognized the music—Dvorak, she thought—but couldn't recall the name of the piece. It was simple, melodic, hymn-like.

She went into her study and sat at the desk. Then she took out the file of mailing lists and found Frieda Klass's address in Schrunz, Austria. Lily wrote the note three times before she finally decided to keep it simple, to refrain from long explanations and just ask what she needed to know. Frieda had offered to help, and she was a longtime friend of Fred Barnes. Maybe she could tell Lily what was behind his change of heart and mind.

When Lily had finished writing and addressed the envelope, she noticed Stanley had stopped playing. He must be packing up. She stood and headed back into the church.

The lamp attached to the organ shone dimly, and the pale December sun barely illuminated the southern windows. There was the silence after music, when the ghostly presence of the final chord lingers in the air. From the Advent wreath came the smell of pine. And beneath the silence, in the scented gloom, she could hear the wind, the creaks and groans of the building, the rattle of a loose tile on the roof.

She walked to the center aisle, bowed, then made her way through the choir stalls to the organ.

But he wasn't at the organ. When she turned around,

she saw him seated in a pew halfway back on the right, watching her.

"Stanley, I'm sorry. I didn't mean to interrupt again. I just wanted to catch you before you left."

"I've been caught," he said, then stood and walked toward her down the aisle. "What can I do for you?"

"Look, Stanley, I'm sorry we missed our chance to talk last week, but I'd still like to do that if you have time."

He walked past her to the organ, sat on the bench, and began to put the music into his briefcase.

"I don't have time right now, as it happens," he said. "But I'll be back tonight for choir practice. Maybe then . . . no, that won't work either. And I'm not here Thursday, as I usually am—dreaded faculty meeting. Why don't we talk at the first of next week and make a plan?" His voice was clipped, rushed.

"All right," said Lily, "but I . . ."

"I'm on a tight schedule here," he said, looking up at her quickly. "Sorry."

"No, I apologize for bothering you," said Lily. "Anyway, let's talk whenever you can."

"Good, we'll do that," said Stanley.

He stood and reached for his coat. After he had put it on, he turned to her. "Don't mind me," he said, his voice softer, more congenial. "Fred would often come sit in the back of the church while I practiced. When you came in— well, I miss him, that's all. But it's not your fault."

"No. But I do understand. If you ever want to—"

"Let's make a time for next week, shall we? Perhaps we can talk on Sunday. Good-bye, then," he added. He walked briskly toward the front door of the church, reached into his briefcase, pulled out a set of keys, then stopped. He held them in his hand for a moment before turning toward Lily. "I forgot I'm using the other door these days."

"I'll let you out if you want," said Lily, reaching into the pocket of her jeans for her own set.

"Never mind," he said. Then he shrugged his shoulders and added, "All right, then, fine, that would be good."

"I thought you had a key to this door," she said as casually as possible while turning the heavy metal lock.

"I did, I do, but I just sorted through this ridiculous collection," he said, holding up a large brass ring, "and I must have removed it by mistake. So I've been using the other door."

"Let me know if you don't find it," said Lily. "We don't want a lot of extra keys floating around."

"Yes," said Stanley. "I will."

She swung the wooden portal wide for him, and he walked through quickly. "Anyway, good night," he said and was gone without looking back.

# chapter ❈ 14

when Mrs. Hanlon arrived the following Thursday morning, Lily was on the phone to the hospital, checking on Roger Frye and a young parishioner who had just given birth to twins. The twins (a girl and a boy), mother, and father had fared well, and the hospital staff planned to move Roger to the VA detox center as soon as possible, probably tomorrow—Lily guessed they'd had it with the country swing. Lily called the new mother, wished her well, and decided to put off visiting Roger until he had been moved.

Advent was in full swing. The Festival of Lessons and Carols took place mid-December. (This was one of Stanley's specialties; the choir had been practicing for weeks.) Sign-up sheets had appeared on the bulletin board in the hall for the greening of the church (the fourth week of the season) and for the Christmas Eve potluck supper following the ten o'clock service.

Lily took some small joy in the planning—she could not resist the business of Advent. And the regular business of parish life limped along, more and more in need of her assistance. So when Mrs. Hanlon stuck her head in the door to say hello, Lily just waved and smiled, her thoughts on Isaiah 40:1–11.

An hour later, as Lily sat consulting Gottwald on the Isaiah of the Exile, Mrs. Hanlon walked into the office without knocking, a faint but noticeable lapse in her usually formal manner. In her hand she held a small roll of bills, wrapped in a white piece of paper, and all of it bound by a rubber band. She held out her palm with the odd package in it.

"What do you think I've just found?" she asked.

"Money," said Lily.

"Yes, exactly."

"Where was it?"

Mrs. Hanlon sat down in the armchair next to the desk and began to roll the rubber band off the end of the paper. "I'm not sure," she said. "I was working in the side chapel. I don't clean the base of the statue regularly, but I did clean it today. When I was wiping the back of the pedestal I heard something fall on the floor. I bent down, and here's what I found."

She had worked the elastic off and began to flatten the money in her lap. "It's a lot of money," she said. "Here, you do this." She picked up the money and paper and handed it to Lily.

"Why?" said Lily. "You found it."

"I don't care. I don't want to handle it. This is church property now. You do it."

Lily took the bundle from Mrs. Hanlon and laid it on the desk. First, she counted the bills. "Five hundred dollars," she said. "What in the world—" Then she flattened and unfolded the piece of paper. The writing was square and precise, a draftman's work. The perfect capital letters read: CALL YOUR MOTHER AT ONCE.

Mrs. Hanlon rose and came to look over Lily's shoulder. "Good heavens," she said. Then her face went white and she steadied herself on the desk. "Father's."

"Do you think?" asked Lily. "And it's been there all these months?"

"Could have been. I so seldom get around to cleaning back there."

"But who would he have left money for?"

"Lord knows," said Mrs. Hanlon, under her breath. Then she added, "And a young person, too."

"Why young—oh, 'call your mother,' " said Lily. She stopped and looked down at the note then out the window onto the courtyard. Yesterday's blasts had left a still, frozen world, frozen not by ice or snow but by temperatures in the teens. Lily needed to tell someone what she knew, and what she suspected. Mrs. Hanlon was the ideal confidante, except that she wouldn't be able to bear bad news about Barnes.

So Lily told Mrs. Hanlon about the stranger she'd seen weeks earlier in the portico; she described Fred Barnes's letter to Roy Talbot; she reported a discreet version of her talk with Brother Samuel and an edited version of the information from Cynthia; she ended with her discovery of Stanley Leonard in the church two days before, seated in a pew directly across from the side chapel.

In the telling, Lily came up with a possible version of events that Mrs. Hanlon would be able to stomach. What if Fred Barnes had discovered something going on between Roy and someone else, someone with whom the boy was close, someone he saw all the time, his teacher? What if Barnes had ignored the evidence and failed to help Roy when he needed it most? That would explain his apology and his search for a sanctuary for the boy. And it would clear him of the worst of the guilt.

During their talk, Lily also got an idea, a way to find the person at the center of all these questions. She shared her plan with Mrs. Hanlon, but swore the woman to secrecy. No one else could be told that Lily was looking for Roy. She didn't know why, but she knew she was right.

The church was dark and cold at night. Lily's back had begun to ache and she had finished her thermos of tea. From her spot on a small, carved ushers' chair in the southeast corner, tucked out of sight behind the entryway, Lily could see only a part of the side chapel set into the opposite wall: the shadowy outline of Mary's left hand, her tilted head, her robes; the famous miniature rose window, illuminated by the street lamp on Lee Street. The colors looked rich and jewel-like, suggestive of royalty.

Of course, that's how the church liked to think of the Holy Family, as royalty—Mary, the Queen. For Lily, Mary was the young girl in the triptych, frightened and alone. Not queen material, exactly. And what about the baby?— born, as the neighbors all knew, fatherless.

Many years before, she and her own father had built a small crèche. At Woolworth's they had bought plastic figurines of the Holy Family, and Lily remembered now how the baby's arms had been stretched out, as if he were begging to be held. Looking at him, she had felt sad beyond words, so sad she had kept her sadness a secret. Later that night, she had snuck downstairs to rescue the baby from the dark drawer where her father had planned to store him until Christmas morning. Lily suspected that the plastic baby Jesus had formed a part of her faith—much more than the triumphal bearded Christ of the Easter pictures, sailing home on a beam of light.

She heard the sound of metal on metal nearby. Someone was trying to unlock the church door. Either the lock was sticking, or the person was very nervous; the key rattled and twisted, with little accomplished. Lily almost got up to help, but her fear of scaring him away altogether kept her still.

The bolt was drawn and the door opened. She thought she had blown it, that somehow he sensed her presence and wasn't coming in, but then she smelled cheap wine and old sweat and felt a weird, frantic energy, like a rat in a box, something cornered.

He never noticed her there, behind and to his left in the corner, but he crossed directly to the side chapel, walked to the statue, bent over, and disappeared. Lily and Mrs. Hanlon had returned the note and money to a small niche they had discovered in the base of the statue, near the spot Mrs. Hanlon had been cleaning earlier. They had guessed at the exact hiding place, and Lily hoped that they had been right. Now she waited for him to find the note and turn toward the door.

She heard sounds of movement and finally the rustle of money. When he came out into the side aisle, Lily stood and moved toward the arched entryway.

"Roy," she said, in a flat, calm voice.

"Mom?" he called out.

"No, I'm not your mother," said Lily. "I'm a friend . . ." she began, but he had already started to move away from her. "Look," said Lily, still low-voiced, "I think I can help you. I'm not trying—"

She broke off. He had turned and was walking, fast, to the side exit, struggling to open the heavy, locked wooden doors, then up the steps to the door behind the organ, trying it, shaking it.

Lily moved slowly down the center aisle. "Roy, listen," she said. "I'm the priest who took Fred Barnes's place. I found a letter to you, a letter he wrote you, and I know he wanted to help you, but he can't now, so I want to do that for him . . ."

He stood at the organ. Lily's eyes were well-adjusted to the dim glow of the streetlights through the stained glass, and she could see his outline against the rose window.

"I don't know what happened," continued Lily. "I don't even know why you need help, but I'll promise you this: If you talk to me, we don't have to tell anyone, or talk to anyone else. We can just—"

He sat on the organ bench, facing the altar. Then he turned, swung his legs over the bench, and began to finger the keys.

"The woman who cleans the church found the note and the money," she said. "We guessed about the rest, about you. No one told us."

"Mrs. Hanlon?" he asked. His voice sounded young, soft.

"Yes, Mrs. Hanlon. Do you know her?"

No answer. His head was bent over the organ keys.

"Do you want to play for a while?" asked Lily.

He raised his head. "Play what?"

"The organ," said Lily. "Do you want to practice?"

"Right," he said. He held out his hands toward her; even in the dusky light she could see them shaking.

"Can I go now?" he asked after a brief silence, his hands at his sides. "I promise I'll call my mom."

"Look, Roy, I don't care if you call your mother or not. I mean, I do care, eventually, but not now. I just want to know what I can do for you, what's going on. I'd like to help."

"Those aren't the same thing, you know."

"What do you mean?"

After a pause, during which he sat, his head bowed, staring at the keyboard, he looked at her and said, "Just let me go, okay?"

She had not had a good look at him before now. As he stared at her, she saw that he was beautiful, with a small, delicate face, large eyes, a slender neck—his mother's son. She felt the silence around them and remembered he had spoken to her. "What do you think I'm going to do, wrestle with you?"

He stood and walked to the steps, stopping a few feet in front of her, his hands clenched at his sides, then touching his baseball cap. "I don't know what you're going to do," he said, quietly, rationally, as if they had just settled a minor argument, "but you're definitely not going to help me. I've had about all the help from you guys I can take." He walked down the stairs toward her. As he came closer, she saw his face looked gray and flattened by hopelessness.

"Do me a favor," he said to her in a low, suddenly adult voice, "don't help me."

Lily stepped into the pew and sat.

He walked down the center aisle, passing next to her. She smelled the wine and sweat, and then she heard the heavy metal hinges of the door.

    •    •    •

As she entered the rectory, the phone began to ring. It was late, almost eleven, but she felt the need for another human voice. She hurried into the study and lifted the receiver.

"Sorry to call so late," said Tom Casey, "but I'm glad to hear your voice. I thought about coming over there to find you."

"And how would you explain that?" asked Lily.

"To who?"

"Well, whoever. Are you at home or at work?"

"I'm just finishing some prints in the darkroom. Anyway, Mrs. Hanlon told me to check on you. She said to tell you she didn't tell me anything else, and I'm not supposed to ask. I'd like you to notice I'm not asking. It's not easy."

Lily sat in the desk chair and put her head in her right hand. She felt glad to hear his voice. "I'm noticing," she said.

"Anyway, I wanted to let you know what we'd come up with for the stuff on that slip of paper—which is not too much, but there is something. For 'RT' we came up with 'route,' of course, for Route 31, but then the rest of the numbers don't make any sense. Or 'right,' which would imply the numbers are some kind of combination for a lock. That would explain the 'safe' part. But then where's the 'left'? We also thought of 'rice treats,' 'retired terrorist,' 'real time,' 'rapid tran—' "

"Wait," said Lily.

"What?"

"I think I know what Barnes did right after he got the numbers. He wrote—or tried to write—a letter."

"Yeah," said Tom. "And?"

"Wait," she repeated. RT—Roy Talbot. She closed her eyes and imagined Fred Barnes reading the Spong book. "Look. Someone must have called Barnes while he was reading. Someone in a hurry. They gave him information about how to find this person—I think that's what those numbers are—and he wrote it down on the only paper he had. He squeezed it into a tiny blank corner on a page. Then Barnes wrote the letter I just mentioned."

"I'm not asking—I want you to notice. But that theory fits nicely," said Tom. "Because what I was going to tell you next is that the numbers—without the letters—works as a phone number. Three-one-two is the area code for Chicago."

Where Dan Talbot goes on business, she thought.

"Does that connect?" asked Tom.

"I have no idea," she said. "Did you call it?"

"No. I thought I'd let you do the honors."

"What's the rest? Give me the rest."

"After three-one-two? Nine-four-one-four-two-six-seven-S-A-F-E."

"Thanks," said Lily.

"Are you going to call now?" he asked.

"Probably not," she said. "It's really late. I'll just wait until tomorrow."

"And then you have a bridge to sell me, right?"

"What do you mean?"

"Just let me know if I can help," he said. "I'll be here another half hour or so."

Lily hung up and dialed the number. The phone rang for a long time, maybe ten rings, but finally she heard the voice of someone young and wide-awake.

"Safe Haven," the person on the phone said. "How can I help?"

"Hi," said Lily. "This is a little awkward, because I'm not sure where I'm calling . . . I mean, I have this number but I'm not certain why it's written down here. Can you tell me what kind of place Safe Haven is?"

"Sure. We're a drop-in center and shelter for teens."

"Homeless teens? Runaways?"

"That's mostly who needs a shelter," came the reply. Lily tried to decide whether she was talking to a young woman or a young man.

"So you probably couldn't give me any information about who's been there over the past few months, who's stayed there with you, say, a month ago."

"Yep."

"Yep, you could?" asked Lily.

"Yep, I probably couldn't."

"Look, I'm a priest, and I'm trying to help a kid in my parish, a teenager. If I leave his name, and my name, with my number, address, whatever's needed, could you post it somewhere, so if there is anyone with information, anyone willing to talk with me, they would at least know where to find me?"

"Yep."

Lily gave Roy's name, her name, both her numbers and her address, then thought of one more thing.

"If I wanted to get in touch with someone I think might be there, is there an address I could write to, someplace I could send a letter or a package?" asked Lily.

"Letter, yes, package, no. It's a PO box, and we don't get packages, just mail. Can you hold on a sec?"

"Sure," said Lily.

There was a thud while the phone was laid down and then the sound of background noises—young voices, male and female, some calling from far off, some talking together, quietly, right by the receiver, almost as if they were speaking to Lily. She thought of Roy, holding out his hands for inspection. Had he been at this place? Had he been all right then?

"Sorry. I'm on my own here. You want the address?"

Lily jumped slightly, then said, "Sure. Yes, please." She wrote down the box number, then they said good-bye and hung up.

She stared out through the window, past the thick branches of the fir tree, to the dark sidewalk. She thought he must be out there somewhere now, in the freezing weather. What was the journey he had taken from Mt. Vernon Street to Safe Haven, to the unnamed streets of Boston?

When the phone rang, Lily grabbed it, with the irrational hope it was the boy calling her from nowhere.

"So, what did you find out?" Tom asked.

"Aren't you ever home?" asked Lily, with the slightest edge of irritation in her voice.

"Not much," said Tom. His voice sounded sad. "I'm kind of a stranger in my own house these days."

Great, she thought, this charming Catholic man ignores his wife and children. Excellent choice.

Lily sat on the cushion in the corner of her bedroom. Her breathing slowed and steadied, she counted in-breath and out-breath. For weeks she had not been able to meditate; her mind never stopped. It was like sitting inside a blender. In-breath. Out-breath. But she still tried. In. Out. If what she had told Mrs. Hanlon was true, the story began to make sense. In. Out. Stanley and Roy had a secret. Fred Barnes had somehow discovered that secret. Roy had run away. And now Stanley was paying Roy not to tell. She stopped pretending to attend to her breathing. She needed to concentrate on the next step.

# chapter ❈ 15

The next morning, Lily called Dan Talbot's office. "Mrs. Hennessey? Hi, this is Lily Connor, Mr. Talbot's rector at St. Mary's. Is he in today?"

Mr. Talbot was not in. Mr. Talbot had traveled to Chicago on business. Yes, he traveled a good bit these days. Yes, he would be back by Monday. Mrs. Hennessey would tell Mr. Talbot she had called.

So Dan Talbot was in Chicago. If Dan had been traveling back and forth to Chicago, did he know Roy had been there, too? Had they been in touch throughout? And did he know his son was in Boston now, and in bad shape?

If Dan was gone, then Sally was home alone. There was no telling in what state Lily would find her. But the meeting last night had convinced Lily that Roy Talbot needed help, and soon. He did say he would call his mother; maybe he had. And Lily couldn't think of anywhere else to go.

She went upstairs and retrieved the Spong book, which still held Barnes's letter, from its spot on the floor by the nightstand. Back downstairs, she first laid the book face-up on the desk, then changed her mind and slipped it into the middle of a short stack of books on the typing table. Then she got her parka and went for a walk. She told herself that if she happened to be near the Talbots' later on, she would stop in.

The curtains in the front French windows of the Talbots' house were drawn, giving the place a shrouded look, as if it sheltered a family in mourning. Although she had walked for almost an hour, Lily felt anxious as she approached the stoop. Her stomach knotted, her breath grew shallow.

Lily rang the bell and listened for the sound of footsteps. She heard nothing, and, after a couple of minutes, she pressed the bell again. Immediately a picture of Sally mouthing "RA-DI-O" and pointing toward the kitchen door came to mind.

When Florence arrived, she looked mildly surprised to see Lily, but only for an instant.

"Hi," said Lily. "I wonder if I could talk to Mrs. Talbot?"

"She is home, but she is in bed," said Florence.

"Could you just let her know I'm here?" Lily persisted. "I could go to her room if she's not feeling well. It's actually sort of important, and it needs to be done right away—church business," she added lamely.

"She can't see you,.I don't think," said Florence.

"Could I write her a note and ask you to take that up? Then she can make her own decision, and at least we could plan to meet soon, another time, maybe at church. Would that be okay?"

"Yes," said Florence. "I will get you a pencil and paper."

Florence allowed her into the tiny vestibule, then turned into the hallway. Oddly, she pushed the second door partway closed behind her, never inviting Lily into the house. Standing in the small space, Lily leaned forward, her ear next to the crack, and heard Florence walk up the stairs and knock. The sounds were faint but clear: the knock, voices, the door opening and closing, opening again, footsteps on the stairs, in the hallway. And Florence returned, pen and paper in hand.

"If you write her a note, I will give it to her later," she said.

"Did you tell her I was here?" asked Lily.

"She is resting," she answered.

"On second thought," Lily said, "just ask her to call me. It's too complicated to write down. I'll be at the church or the rectory for the rest of the day."

Florence nodded.

"Thank you," said Lily.

As she walked down the steep hill toward Charles Street, she thought of the Spong book and Barnes's letter, Roy's letter now. Something had told her to put it somewhere safe—*Safe,* like Roy at Safe Haven, she thought, like Roy would be with me. And safety had suddenly become even more important; it had to do with having heard Dan Talbot's voice upstairs in his house a few minutes earlier, when he was supposed to be in Chicago.

Sally never phoned. Lily knew she wouldn't. On and off through the evening, Lily thought of calling Tom Casey and taking him up on his offer of help. She didn't know what she wanted him to do; she only knew she was too alone. She had told Mrs. Hanlon part of what she feared, but she needed someone who could help, especially someone who could help Roy.

Sally Talbot seemed out of the question—evidently her medication hadn't been adjusted successfully if she was in bed in the middle of the day. Somehow Lily didn't think Dan had meant "meds" the way a professional might mean it—as in Thorazine, anti-psychotics. But she didn't know what he did mean.

As of today, there was a lot she didn't know about Dan Talbot, a lot that made her uneasy. First, there were all the questions about the trips to Chicago. And now there was something else she couldn't shake—the quiet, tight anger she'd heard in his voice that afternoon. It was the voice of a man keeping himself in control, but just barely.

None of the other members of St. Mary's could be trusted. If only she could pray, the solitude might be relieved; she might even know what to do next. But she couldn't.

The next morning Lily called the hospital and was told Roger had been moved. She got directions to the detox center in Jamaica Plain, pulled out her MTA map, and traced the route from Charles Street. The whole journey took almost an hour and the day had turned dark gray, arctic. But Lily had not given up on Roger, either as a pastoral responsibility or as a source of information. She wouldn't mind the cold and the inconvenience if only she could learn something.

The detox waiting room was green and stuffy; a film of grease seemed to coat the floors, walls, windows, and plastic chairs. Insanely bright, chipper posters hung at random intervals: ONE DAY AT A TIME! FIRST THINGS FIRST! EASY DOES IT! She wondered if the room would seem less grim in better weather—doubtful.

When Roger came in, Lily almost didn't recognize him. Already he looked younger, more relaxed, as if his body had actually pumped out all the poison of the last few years, though Lily knew that process took a good deal longer. When he greeted her, he was formal, almost shy. They shook hands and sat down facing one another on two chairs by the window.

"How are you?" she began. "You look great."

"Do I?" asked Roger. "I feel like hell."

Lily laughed. Whatever had happened to him over the past week, he had certainly gotten more approachable.

"You're a lot more sociable than the last time I saw you," said Lily.

Roger blanched. "What was I doing?" he asked her.

"Singing," said Lily. "I think we have the same taste in music."

"What's that?" he asked, still confused.

"Country," she said and was then immediately sorry she had brought it up. He looked embarrassed, uncomfortable. "What else do you listen to?"

He sized her up for a minute before he answered. "Bach,

you know, church music," he said. "I guess they're lucky back at the hospital," he added, deadpan.

"I lost you," said Lily.

"At least I wasn't singing cantatas," he said and smiled, faintly, for the first time. "That could have been really ugly."

Lily laughed out loud again and wondered to herself at Roger's transformation.

"Look," she began hesitantly, "I'm not sure you're ready to talk about this yet, or that you even remember—"

"You're going to ask me what happened, right?" he said. "But the thing is, I don't know."

"Did they ask you about the Antabuse?"

"Yeah, they asked me. But I've never taken that stuff. I've seen people on it, seen them drink, you know."

"Did you . . . were you . . . had *you* had a lot to drink?"

This time Roger laughed, a small, inward chuckle. "By whose standards? You know, that's the question," he said. "Had I had a lot to drink by your standards? Yeah, probably. But by my standards? No, not especially."

"How much is that?" she asked.

"Let's see . . . It was a Tuesday, right, so I wouldn't have had a drink until noon. I never drank before noon, see, not during the week. I had a lot of rules. I've done all this before, you know? Detox, rehab, halfway house, so I know all about how alcoholics act. So I thought, well, if I don't *act* like an alcoholic, then I won't *be* one."

Lily listened patiently. How could she never have noticed his Southwestern accent, his style? He reminded her of the men who worked for her father, telling detailed stories of their last trip to Houston or of a run-in with one of the dog packs in the hills behind town.

"So I had a few beers with lunch," he continued. "Maybe four or five—and then—this is the part I don't remember so well—I came back to the church, to finish something, to work on something—I bet it was the downstairs bathroom, that shelf they want to make into a changing table. Did they ask you about that?"

Lily shook her head, anxious that he not lose the story.

"Anyway," Roger continued, "right after I got back, I started to feel weird, bad, dizzy, short of breath—I thought it was an attack, you know, nerves. So I got out the pint I keep in the basement—or *one* of the pints I keep in the basement, actually. I didn't have more than a few swallows, 'cause what I remember is walking down the stairs, into the workroom, with the pint in my hand, and then—you know what happened after that better than I do. I guess you found me."

"I did, but how did you know that?" asked Lily.

"Mr. Neville told me," he said.

"Has he been here already?" asked Lily.

"Not here. He came up to the hospital a couple of times, once just before I got sent over here. He said you saved my life."

Something about the phrase, or his reverent tone, struck Lily as odd in the extreme. Maybe it was the heroic dimensions the language lent such a small, tawdry scene—her bending over Roger, trying to wake him up and avoid stepping in the vomit.

"I'm pretty sure that's an exaggeration," she said.

"I'm not so sure," said Roger, vaguely, his eyes studying the wall behind her now. "I think that's what he meant."

"Why? What did he say, exactly?" asked Lily, distracted by Roger's subtle drift away from her.

"I don't know," he said, and his eyes shifted back into focus, his voice cleared. "He just said if it weren't for you, I'd be dead. He said I owed you."

"Well, you don't," said Lily, brusquely, surprising herself.

"Okay," he said.

"But Roger, listen," she began again, still determined to get some information, anything, from him. "Did you stop anywhere on the way back to the church, or take something, before you began to feel bad? Are you sure you didn't . . ." Her voice trailed off as she watched his face. Clearly, he had remembered some detail, and now he was struggling with the memory. "What?" she finally asked him.

"My sinuses were killing me, so I took a sinus pill, these

high-power capsules I get—prescription, you know. But there's no reason . . ."

"Have they ever affected you that way before?"

"No, they can make me a little groggy, but nothing like that, nothing like what happened then."

"Do you still have the bottle?" asked Lily.

"No. They took everything when I checked into the hospital."

"Did you get your belongings back when you came here?"

"Some of it. Mr. Neville took my stuff, my dirty clothes and all. The bottle might have been in my pants pocket. It's probably still there. He brought me some clean clothes on his last visit, but I don't think those pants were in the bag. They wouldn't let me have them here anyway—the sinus pills, I mean."

"Could you find out, about the bottle?" asked Lily.

He was quiet for a moment, staring down at the floor. Then he asked, "What do you think's going on?"

"I don't know," said Lily. "But they found Antabuse in your system, so it got there somehow."

He started to stand, then sat back down abruptly.

"Roger, are you all right?"

He raised his right hand to the back of his neck and rubbed it, gently, then lowered his hand and looked at her. "Yeah," he said, "I'm all right."

A blond woman—slender, middle-aged, in a dark, fitted pantsuit and long trench coat—walked into the room, glanced at them, then walked out into the hall. A minute later, she walked in again and sat on one of the lime-green plastic chairs at the far end of the room. Lily glanced at the woman and saw her lean her head against the wall, close her eyes, and sigh.

Lily moved closer to Roger. "Do you want to say anything else, about what you think might be going on here?" she asked.

"No," said Roger, staring out the window.

A handsome, burned-out-looking, dark-haired man in jeans and a T-shirt came into the room. When he saw the blond woman he paused, then walked over to her. He leaned down and said something quietly, then reached out and patted her knee. From across the room, Lily could hear her quiet crying and could hear the man murmuring, "I'm okay. Everything's going to be fine." Over their heads, neon bright letters on a field of blue sky urged them all to LIVE AND LET LIVE!

As soon as Lily walked into the rectory, she felt defeated. From where she stood in the hall of a dead man's house, her whole life looked dismal and forbidding, like the empty rooms around her. She took off her parka and walked into the kitchen to make tea. After she put the kettle on, Lily wandered into her study and began to glance over the handwritten draft of her sermon for tomorrow. She scanned the words but couldn't bring herself to read them, because she knew they would sound hollow. She had given up on preaching from Isaiah and had decided to stick with the Gospel. In her sermon she had posed the question, "What does it mean to be baptized with the Holy Spirit?" But now she realized she had no business asking that question because she had no idea of the answer.

But Isaiah had a message of its own—the consolation of Israel: "Comfort, comfort my people, says your God," she whispered to herself. "Speak tenderly to Jerusalem, and cry to her that her warfare is ended." In Isaiah, God is sending comfort to the exiled people of Israel. In Mark, God has sent John. John doesn't seem like an especially comforting figure, but isn't he announcing the end of our exile—isn't he, too, God speaking tenderly to us while we wait, here, in the wilderness, isn't he God telling us our long service is ended?

The kettle began a slow, rising whistle that tore her from her thoughts. After making tea, she returned, cup in hand, and tried to begin a new sermon. But the concept of comfort eluded her.

# chapter ❈ 16

An hour later, Lily was staring at a page of botched be-
ginnings when the phone rang. Dan Talbot was on the line,
and, according to him, he and Sally needed to talk to someone. They needed to talk to her, and right away if possible.

She walked out into the hall and put on her parka, hat,
gloves, and scarf before she left the rectory. But no amount
of bundling could protect her from the weather. The cold
cast a wretched pall over the world, so that the tasteful
evergreen swags draped along Charles Street, on light posts
and storefronts, looked drab and pointless.

The Talbots' wreath hung on their front door—thick pine
branches with a few sprigs of holly and a single golden
ribbon. It had been put there sometime in the last twenty-
four hours, since her failed attempt to see Sally. She had
a feeling that her visit was what had prompted Dan's call;
maybe it hadn't been a wasted effort.

Sally appeared lucid when she answered the door. She
showed Lily in, took her parka, asked her if she wanted
tea or coffee, then, after Lily declined both, invited her to

sit in the small armchair by the fire. Sally sat in the matching chair across from Lily and picked up an elaborate piece of needlepoint, a baroque-looking floral tapestry in golds and blues and greens. Dressed in gray flannel slacks and a gray cashmere turtleneck, she looked like a picture in *Town & Country*—a wealthy woman very much at home. She even chatted about the Christmas social season for a while, leaving Lily feeling bewildered.

"Dan will be here in a minute, I'm sure" she finally said, having apparently run out of banter.

"I thought he called me from here," said Lily.

"No," said Sally, "from the office. He got another call right after you spoke, so he's been delayed. But it won't be long."

"That's fine," said Lily. "That gives us a chance to talk. I wanted to explain to you why I came by yesterday. I know it probably seemed intrusive but I—"

"Not at all," said Sally. Her voice was calm, but toneless.

"I need to talk with you about Roy."

"Why don't we wait," said Sally. "Let's wait until Dan gets here." She began to work on the needlepoint piece, carefully pulling the long gold thread in and out of the scrim.

"Why?" asked Lily.

"Because Dan asked me to wait until he arrived."

"But I want you to know I've seen Roy," said Lily.

Sally looked up. "Where?" she asked.

"At the church, two nights ago," said Lily. Then she added, "He needs help."

Sally remained perfectly still. After a moment she asked, "Where is he now?"

"I don't know," said Lily. "I was hoping you might tell me."

"I can't. I don't know either. But if you find him, please tell him to stay where he is. It would not be a good idea— it would be a bad idea for him to come back now, to come here."

Lily tried to detect an emotion in the other woman's

voice, but she couldn't. She couldn't make any sense of Sally's responses.

"I don't understand," said Lily.

"I can imagine," said Sally. "But I hope you'll believe me anyway. Please don't tell Dan you've seen Roy." Sally looked up from her needlework. Lily was again struck by her storybook beauty—the Snow White coloring and delicate features—and by how much she looked like Roy, or he looked like her. "This has been very hard on us," Sally continued. "And on our marriage. I just think, right now, it would be better for Roy to work things out on his own. I'm not sure how much help we could be."

Sally turned her head and stared into the fireplace. Lily gazed, too, at the charred log, smoldering on top of a few pieces of kindling. Lily could sense a second persona, someone just beneath the surface of the practical woman who refused to be bothered by her son. Sally was asking for more than a break from a pesky adolescent, she was pleading for help. But Lily wasn't sure what help she wanted. And where was Dan? It seemed to Lily she'd been there a long time.

At that moment she heard a key turn in the lock of the outside door. Sally called out, almost cheerily, "Hello there. Ms. Connor is here with me."

"Good, good," said Dan. "Sorry I'm late." Lily could hear him opening the closet door, hanging up his coat. She studied the photographs on the piano. There in the corner was the picture of Roy and Dan, silhouetted against the sky.

Dan sat in the chair nearest his wife, across from Lily. "I'm sorry we asked you to do this on such short notice," he said. "But I'm glad you could come."

"Me, too," said Lily.

"When you stopped by yesterday, I was upstairs with Sally. I was supposed to have gone to Chicago, but there was too much happening here, so I didn't go."

Dan had talked with Mrs. Hennessey, Lily thought. She told him that I called, and that she said he was in Chicago.

"We've been thinking for a while that it might be a good

idea to talk with someone," he went on. "You seemed a good choice. Maybe your visit yesterday was the kick we needed to get started. But first I should ask if you had something to talk with us about?"

"It wasn't important," said Lily. "I was just checking in to see how things were going."

"Not too well," he said.

She nodded, encouraging him to go on.

"Anyway," he said, "we have a lot to tell you, a lot of hard things to talk about, but there's one problem—a big problem."

"A problem with telling me, you mean?" she asked.

"With telling anyone," he said, "anyone at all. The story involves our son, Roy. And it involves other people, people we don't want to hurt, or really one person whose memory we don't want to harm in any way."

Lily nodded again, careful to register as little as possible on her face. But the phrase *a person whose memory* told her everything; she was about to hear the story she had been dreading.

"You may have guessed some of this already, I don't know," he said, then looked at her questioningly.

Lily shrugged once, as if to imply she had guessed nothing. Throughout this exchange Sally kept her head bent over her needlepoint.

"In any case, because of this person," Dan continued, "nothing we tell you today can leave this room. You can't repeat it."

Lily felt panic begin in her stomach; her heart sped up. With almost physical effort, she forced herself to concentrate on what Dan had just said, not on what he was bound to say soon. He had set her a challenge she needed to answer, but she also needed to be very careful.

Was she here as their priest, their confessor? If so, what they said was essentially sealed, no matter the consequences, no matter who could be saved or damned by the information. But they hadn't come to her, originally, she had come to them. Besides, there might be a boy's life in the balance, and that would give her, she told herself, a small space for maneuvering.

"It depends," said Lily.

"It can't depend," said Dan. "Yes or no." His face was hard in the room's dim light. She could see the small muscles in his jaw tighten and relax. She found herself entranced by the long, white curtains across the room, through which the pale winter light shone and beyond which was the world.

"If someone's safety is involved," she finally said, "I mean, if I think someone could be hurt by my silence, I would have to reconsider any agreement we make here. Also, there are laws—I'm required to report certain things."

She looked at him; he shook his head, smiling a sad, ironic smile. "In any case," Lily continued, "I would come to you first, before speaking to anyone else."

"No one will be hurt by your silence," he said. "Only by your speech."

"Then, yes," she said, "but on those terms."

Dan, evidently satisfied, took a deep breath and began his story. "We've spoken, you and I, a little about Roy. I remember you offered to help, weeks ago. I don't know what you have heard since then."

"Very little," said Lily. "And I'd rather hear the whole thing from you, whatever you think is useful for me to know."

"Let me say something about him first. He's very talented," said Dan. "And complicated, for a kid his age."

"What do you mean?" she asked, surprised by this opening.

"Music, mostly, but he also paints," he said. He glanced at Sally, smiled, and added, "He's his mother's son."

The top log shifted and fell heavily off the grate, sending charred ash and soot onto the hearth. Talbot stood up, moved the log back into place, and swept the hearth with the brass-handled broom resting in the stand by the fireplace.

When he sat back down, he took out a handkerchief, wiped his hands, then continued. "At any rate," he said, folding the handkerchief, square upon square, "whatever he was once, or whatever we thought he was, he changed." He put the handkerchief back in his pants pocket.

"How?" Lily asked.

"We didn't know for a while, of course," said Dan. "We thought it was adolescence. People kept saying—"

Sally's voice surprised Lily. "He started locking his door, the door to his room. He had friends—they'd call. But he never brought anyone home. It was like—I had a sense that his life went on somewhere else, outside the house. He had no life here. One time he left the door to his room open to go downstairs, and I went in. There was nothing there, just the bed, the dresser, things too heavy to move. The walls were blank. There was nothing on the shelves, on the desk."

"Did you say anything to him?" asked Lily.

"No," said Sally. "When he saw me he just said, 'We have too many things. We don't need all the things we have.' Or something like that." For the first time, maybe ever, Lily heard the emotions in this woman's voice. Sally's heart was broken, that was clear now, but it was hard to know exactly what had broken it.

"Anyway," said Dan, "we eventually became sure he was doing drugs. He was still very active in the church— still over there a lot of the time. Stanley was his organ teacher, of course. We were just glad he was involved in something other than those invisible friends."

Sally stared into her lap at the needlework, but her hands were motionless.

"Last year, last spring, his behavior, his grades, all became so bad we sent him to a therapist. It took him a while, but finally Roy told me what was going on. He wouldn't talk to the therapist, and I think he couldn't stand to tell his mother. He knew it would break her heart."

So Dan had the same diagnosis for Sally, thought Lily.

He leaned forward before he spoke. "And it's this information you must keep confidential," he said.

Lily didn't respond. She knew what was coming, and

she had set the terms. There was to be no renegotiating now.

"It was Fred Barnes," he said.

"What was Fred Barnes?" Lily asked.

"Fred Barnes had made Roy have sex with him." Dan Talbot's voice broke on the last few words.

"Once?" asked Lily, idiotically.

Talbot looked blank.

"I'm sorry," she said. "That was—I'm sorry. I don't know what to say. I'm just so sorry you've had to go through all this alone. Have you talked with anyone else, anyone in the church?"

"No. We didn't know what to do. I knew I should go to the bishop, but Fred and I—our whole family—had been so close. I had to talk to him first."

"Did you?" asked Lily.

"Yes," said Dan. "I did. He denied it. I didn't know who to believe. I thought for a while Roy was making it up. I told Roy I didn't believe him, or that I didn't know whether to believe him—then he ran off." The silence that followed was a plea, she could feel that: Dan Talbot needed forgiveness. But Lily was too confused to find any forgiveness. She looked away.

"Did Barnes ever admit to having sex with Roy?" she asked.

"Yes," said Dan. "At the end of the summer, he called me and asked me to come over. He said he'd been given a gift, the gift of sight. He said he had been blind to what he had done—that he hadn't seen the sin." He stopped for a moment, then said, "He was dead a week later."

Information was coming too fast. Lily felt as if she was running alongside a train, and if the train could just slow down, she could catch up, she could get on. "Do you mean he killed himself?" she heard herself asking.

Dan shook his head. "I don't know," he said. "I hope not."

"Have you been in touch with him, with Roy, at all?" Lily asked.

But before Dan could answer, Sally spoke. "No, we

haven't," she said. "We thought he was on the West Coast for a while, but we don't know where he is now."

Lily could read nothing in the woman's face.

"He contacts Stanley sometimes, and Stanley lets us know he's all right," said Dan. "But Roy won't say where he is. He doesn't want us to look for him, and he doesn't want to come home. He's made that clear. We're still looking for him anyway, of course. And if you should ever hear anything . . ."

Lily waited, but he never finished the sentence. "If you knew . . ." she began.

"But we don't, you see?" interrupted Sally. "It's how he wants it. At least he gets in touch through Stanley. At least we know he's alive."

This time Lily saw the mother behind the mask—she was pleading for her son's safety. The emotion was fear. And Lily saw something else—Roy's safety depended on his father's not knowing where he was.

Lily left soon after. She told them what she would tell any couple in those circumstances: She urged them to find help, to tell someone else in the church, to get counseling for themselves. But they weren't interested. None of it felt real to her anyway; her suggestions were like lines from a play. And there were so many possible versions of the script, she couldn't keep track.

On her walk back, she barely felt the cold. At one point, she stopped in front of the window of the liquor store on Charles and studied an elaborate red and gold gift box of cognac with two tiny snifters. Then she saw her own reflection and noticed her parka was unzipped, so she zipped it up and put on her mittens. When she did that, she noticed that her hands were shaking slightly.

This was the story Lily had not wanted confirmed. In fact, she had already talked herself out of this set of suspicions. She had to admit that over the past few weeks she had grown fond of Fred Barnes, through Mrs. Talbot, through Brother Samuel, through the letter to Roy. And she couldn't bear to hurt those people, either, the ones who had loved him when he was alive, the ones who loved him still.

But she couldn't ignore the Talbots' version: Fred Barnes had forced Roy Talbot to have sex. Then, having been forced, himself, to face the truth, the man couldn't live with it. He had given himself an overdose of insulin and ended his own life.

On River Street she stopped in front of the antique store and searched for the triptych. It was gone, probably to some wealthy Beacon Hill matron who wouldn't know what she had, who would balance it on a gilt-trimmed side table and forget the thing existed. As her resentment toward this phantasm grew, to encompass the parish, the neighborhood, and rich people in general, Lily stopped her thoughts and forced herself to acknowledge what was happening.

She didn't believe Dan Talbot. Hearing him tell the story she feared—the story she had already imagined and dismissed—had convinced her it wasn't true. She had already asked herself why Barnes would be looking for a safe place—a sanctuary, Brother Samuel had said—for the boy, if Barnes himself were the abuser? But now she had to ask herself why—if Barnes had been the threat—Sally would *still* be looking for a safe place for Roy, somewhere away from his own father. If Lily were right, if that's what Sally had been looking for.

She crossed the street to the church, noticing how ghostly the neighborhood seemed with the streets emptied because of the cold. She was alone in the world. She didn't know what was true anymore. And she didn't trust her own judgment.

She sat at her desk in the rectory, her head resting on her right hand, the phone in her left. It took a long time, almost twelve rings, for someone to answer at police headquarters. When a woman's voice finally said "Headquarters—Bentley," she almost hung up. Having been given too much time to reflect on what she was doing, she now regretted having made the call and saw the act for the overtired, underfed thing it really was.

"HEL-l-o-o," the voice sang out on the phone. "Anybody there?"

"Yes," said Lily. "Sorry. I wondered, is Tom Casey working tonight?"

"Casey? Lemme see." She put Lily on hold, and after a minute, Lily heard the phone ringing again.

"ID," said a woman's voice, deeper this time.

"Is Tom Casey there?" asked Lily.

"Casey, I don't think . . . Lemme see. Who's calling?"

"Lily, Lily Connor."

Lily heard a muffled version of what sounded like "Is Casey here? There's a woman on the phone that wants to speak to him—Lily, Lily Connor," and then a catcall in the distance. She heard the phone being laid down and more distant noise of the search for Tom Casey.

She began to straighten the papers on her desk, grouping the pages of the first version of her sermon, separating them from the failed attempts at a second version. As she tapped the pages into place, she wondered how they had gotten mixed together. She could have sworn they were in two separate piles when she left.

"Casey," he said.

"Tom, hi, this is Lily. I have a feeling this was not such a good idea, to call you there. I just, I found something out, and I can't tell anyone in the church, well, actually, I can't tell anyone at all, but I thought . . ." What? she wondered. What had she thought? She couldn't say anything about what she'd been told, but she didn't know how to keep her confusions about it to herself. "Oh God," she said, finally, "I don't know what I thought."

"I'm afraid I don't have that information at this time," said Tom in a formal voice.

Lily laughed, a high nervous laugh. "Lots of privacy there? Listen, never mind anyway. I just wanted to see if you were working tonight, if you were free later, but now it looks like I couldn't talk to you even if you were, since I don't seem to have anything to say."

"I'm kind of tied up anyway," said Tom, still in his business voice. "I'm working the weekend here. But I can try to get back to you later on that, Monday, maybe?"

"Fine," said Lily. "Next time I have nothing to say, I'll know who not to call."

"Great," said Tom. "So, I'll check with you Monday on that."

"Yeah, great," said Lily. "Good-bye." She hung up, flushed red with shame. "Oh no," she said, shaking her head, then knocking it gently, once, twice, on the top of the desk. "No, no, no."

At eleven o'clock that night, Lily turned off the desk lamp in her study and sat staring out into the darkness of the courtyard. In her wrestling with the Isaiah text, she had gotten to one of the essential paradoxes of Advent: that while we wait for God, we are with God all along, that while we need to be reassured of God's arrival, of the arrival of our homecoming, we are already at home. While we wait, we have to trust, to have faith, but it is God's grace that gives us that faith. As with all spiritual knowledge, two things are true, and equally true, at once. The mind can't grasp paradox; it's the knowledge of the soul. And since her soul didn't seem to be in working order, she hadn't come up with a sermon. But she was closer. She might have something by Sunday.

Concentrating on the sermon had given her a respite from the Talbots, but the neat pair of unanswerable questions came back when she turned out the light: What had happened? And what was she supposed to do? It was late, and she realized she had forgotten to eat. Soup, tea, and bed, she said to herself a few times, like instructions. I'll think better tomorrow. But she didn't move. Instead, she stared out through the black-limbed pine tree to the right of the porch onto the frozen, moonlit lawn.

Maybe the contact with scripture had cleared her mind. But at that moment, she suddenly knew that regardless of what she wished or guessed or intuited (she had been wrong often enough before), her duty was to the Talbot family now. Of course, she had not wanted to believe that Barnes was guilty. He had been an ordained priest. If they were telling the truth, the Talbots had suffered a kind of hell at the hands of the church, and the church had to save them now. Since she was the only one who knew, she had to save them now.

Lily still hadn't moved. She sat at her desk and felt the cold like a separate presence, through the glass of the window, even, she imagined, through the plaster walls. So she was surprised when she heard footsteps. Why would anyone be out tonight—especially someone walking slowly, someone slowing down, someone stopping on Lee Street, just by the rectory.

Lily tried to judge where he was (a man's footsteps, but a small man) and whether or not he hadn't simply passed by already. She sensed he had stopped at the courtyard gate, but she couldn't see that spot because it was blocked by the looming pine; maybe the steps had continued without her hearing them. She realized, now, that the house looked dark and empty since she had turned off her lamp.

She resisted the impulse to turn on the light, signaling her presence. Instead, she walked cautiously to the front door, then stood with her head against the glass for a moment. She opened the first door of the tiny vestibule and stepped to the outer door, then peered through the glass across the courtyard lawn. Was anyone there? Not in the glow of the streetlight, not in clear sight on the sidewalk. She was starting to feel the first stirrings of relief when she caught a slight movement in the shadow at the corner of the church building, just where the fence began. Anyone standing there would be blocked from the streetlight, and the moonlight, and the sight of any passersby. Impulsively, she reached over and switched on the porch lamp, which meant she could no longer see beyond the railing. But now she was sure she heard footsteps, starting quickly, walking quickly into the dark.

She struggled to steady her breathing, leaning against the door. Late at night, so deeply immersed in this parish and all its secrets, she felt she had lost any sense of the line between coincidence and intention, between chance happening and omen. She saw herself racing down the street, six weeks ago, chasing Roy Talbot into the darkness, and for an instant she wanted to rush down the steps after this second shadowy figure.

But she didn't. She returned through the inside door and locked it behind her, leaving the porch lamp burning. Then she walked to the study and switched on the desk lamp, then to the living room and hit the switch for the overhead light, and did the same in the dining room and the kitchen. "I'm awake," she yelled to no one. "I'm awake. I see you." Her voice came back to her, shrill and pinched in the sudden brightness.

# chapter ❋ 17

At four o'clock on Sunday afternoon, the temperature outside in the teens, the Evensong service at the monastery was sparsely attended by outsiders. Most of the guests had chosen to sit in the wooden chairs beyond the metal railing. Lily sat in a pew inside the railing, facing the nave and the two lit candles of the Advent wreath.

"He hath filled the hungry with good things," chanted the monks. "And the rich he hath sent empty away." Why does it have to be one or the other? she wondered. Why can't God fill the rich *and* the hungry with good things, just different good things? Why does anyone have to be sent away empty? It surprised her when these lines, which had given her pleasure for years and had stood as evidence that the church did have a social conscience after all, now made her uneasy and irritated.

The frail light behind the stained-glass windows high up on the chancel walls faded. She listened to the brothers' voices, and eventually gained a sense of detached appreciation, cocooned in the music and incense, safe from the tumult that had brought her there. "Keep watch, dear Lord,

with those who work, or watch, or weep this night . . ."
prayed the brothers at the end, and she felt an unexpected
chill of fear.

In the muted shufflings after the service, Lily remained
seated, her eyes closed. Soon she heard someone approach,
felt someone enter the pew and sit beside her.

"I want to make a confession," she said softly.

But instead of Charlie's reassuring voice, there was silence. She opened her eyes. Brother Samuel sat next to her,
owl-like, dazed, not what she had expected.

"Sorry," she said.

"No, no," he began, "I'm sorry. I thought you might
have come with some news about—our friend."

Lily studied him blankly.

"The person Fred was helping, the one he wanted me
to help. But I see I shouldn't have presumed. I suspect you
want Charles. I'm awfully sorry. I feel . . . I shouldn't have
presumed."

He wasn't helping him, he was screwing him, she
thought. Did she believe that? She had no idea.

Lily saw Charlie just across the nave, his body silhouetted in the pale light of the chapel like one of the stained-
glass figures, an ascetic saint.

"I was waiting for Charlie, but you couldn't have known
that," she said. Then she added, "I think I may have found
him, the boy, but I'm not sure where he is now. If I find
out anything, anything helpful, I'll let you know, or I'll let
Charlie know."

Brother Samuel cleared his throat. "I certainly hope he's
not out in this weather," he said.

"Yes, so do I," Lily said and managed a limp smile.
Now when she looked for Charlie, he had vanished. "Oh
hell," she said out loud. "Where did he go?"

Brother Samuel proved more alert than Lily would have
guessed. "I'll get him," he said, standing up. "He can't
have gone far." But before Samuel got to the door, Charlie reappeared. The two brothers nodded as they passed
each other, then Charlie came and sat next to Lily.

"I'm skipping dinner. What's up?"

"How do you know anything's up?" she asked.

He looked at her for a minute, then said, "I guess you can't see yourself, can you?"

"I have no idea what you mean. I need to talk to you."

"About what?"

"I've been given some information, you could call it, about someone in the church. But I've promised not to tell anyone else without first letting the person, the informant, know."

Charlie raised his eyebrows and stared at her. "Yes . . . ?" he intoned, his voice implying mystification and impatience.

Before Lily could continue, one of the younger brothers came in with a candle snuffer, bowed to the altar, and began to extinguish, one by one, first the altar candles then the thick candles of the Advent wreath. When he was done, he bowed to the altar again and left silently through the side chapel.

"I need to talk about it, to sort it out," Lily continued, "because I'm not even sure I believe the person who told me, even though what he said makes perfect sense—I mean, perfect sense in that it answers most of the questions."

"So this is about Barnes," said Charlie. Then he added, "You don't have to answer that. Let me just speculate for a minute." He leaned back in the pew.

In the silence, Lily glanced up at the peaked ceiling, where smoke from the extinguished candles still drifted in a pale cloud.

"Roger Frye told you something he knows about Barnes's death," Charlie said.

"No," said Lily, but it occurred to her that she was waiting for that to happen any day. "It has nothing to do with his death. Actually, not nothing, exactly, but that's not what it's mostly—"

"Lily," said Charlie in his most patronizing voice, "just tell me. You don't have to use names. We'll think of it as spiritual direction, and you'll have full client confidentiality."

"What this person, these people, told me," said Lily, "is

that Fred Barnes had sex with one of his parishioners—a boy."

Charlie took a deep breath. He bent his head and put his face in his hands. For a long time, perhaps a full minute, he stayed like that, motionless, then he took his hands away and leaned back again.

Lily said, "Charlie?" quietly, as if asking his permission to speak. He shook his head.

Together they sat in the dim chapel, side by side. "Charlie?" she asked again.

He cleared his throat. "Look," he said. "Either this is true, or it's not. And either way, it's just not bearable. Either Fred Barnes did have sex with a boy in his parish, a boy in his care, or . . ."

Lily waited, again, before asking, "Or what?"

"I don't know, never mind. I don't know what to think," he said.

"Me neither," said Lily.

"Would this happen to be the boy you and Samuel are hunting?" he asked.

"Yes, but I'm not sure I like the verb."

"And how old is he?"

Lily paused, taken aback by her ignorance. "Sixteen, I think," she said.

"And how long is it supposed to have been going on?"

"I don't know."

"Have you found him?" Charlie asked.

"Not exactly."

"But you've talked with his family."

"Yes."

"And they're the ones who told you this happened?"

"Yes."

"We need to think about this," said Charlie. "Think about who this man was—Fred Barnes—not that he was a priest, and a man alone, a man who never married, because then, automatically, we think nasty thoughts about his being in the closet and abusing children in a dark recess of the chancel . . ."

Lily blushed, remembering her dreams at the monastery.

"He was Samuel's oldest friend," Charlie continued. "He was a close friend of Mrs. Hanlon. Now I know you don't much like Samuel, because you don't know him. But think about Mrs. Hanlon. Is this a woman who misjudges character, who misjudges character so badly that she honors a man who would molest a child, someone he was responsible for?"

"I don't know," said Lily thoughtfully. "She's Catholic. You know how we Catholics tend to be about the clergy, see no evil, hear no evil."

"Still, though," said Charlie. "I just don't buy it."

"Look, I don't either," said Lily. "Or I don't want to. I feel as if I was just getting to know Barnes, to find out how much—how much we had in common, in some ways. And now this. The problem is, it answers too many questions. Why does everyone seem so glad to be rid of him? Why so much secrecy? The vestry has been trying to keep it quiet, because they couldn't stand a scandal. That's more important to them than the truth, than helping anyone in the aftermath. It's painfully, achingly typical. Also . . ."

"Also what?"

"I found a letter, a draft of a letter, really," she began and then described the note from Barnes to Roy.

When she was done, Charlie leaned forward and looked at the altar for a while. "All right, fine," he said. "If you think this really happened, you have to go back to the people who told you. You have to tell them that you have a responsibility to the church, to other people in the parish, not to mention the legal requirement for disclosure. You have to let the diocese know—start with Spencer. He'll be rational, at least. Let him handle the reporting. Because there may be others, and if there are, they deserve help. They deserve our help. Silence isn't going to work on this one."

As he spoke, his voice had grown harsh, until by the end he sounded almost angry.

"Charlie," she said, "what were you going to say first, when you said either Barnes had abused this boy or—or what?"

"Or he didn't," said Charlie, his voice still cold.

"But if he didn't, then what's going on?"

"I don't know, Lily," he said. "I guess someone is making it up."

"But why?"

"If I had to guess, I'd say somebody wanted to disgrace him, to smear his name," he said.

This time she waited for him to go on.

"And what's the best way to defame a man in the church, or anywhere, for that matter?" he asked. "The best way to ruin someone's good name is to say he's gay—to say he's one of us."

"He didn't say he was gay, though," said Lily. "He said he seduced a boy, he said he betrayed his parish, that he—"

"You know as well as I do that's what most people mean by 'gay,' it's what they think we are, what most people think we're up to, lurking in corners, waiting for the altar boy."

She didn't try again. She sat with him in the chapel, until they began to hear the sounds of the other monks returning from dinner. Finally, Charlie spoke.

"I think the committee work has stirred a lot of this up for me. If you could see the distaste on these people's faces—some of them, not all of them—whenever we talk about gay people. Anyway, that's not what you came to talk about, is it?"

"Oh, Charlie, please, it's me."

"Still, though, let's finish. I'm actually fine."

"It's up to you," she said, watching him.

"Go on. I'm going to get tired of reassuring you."

Lily thought about the walk back to Harvard Square in the bleak night, about the neon-lit T-station, the bundled figures scattered along the concrete platform. "Charlie?" she asked, finally.

"What?"

"Can we talk more about this tomorrow?"

"What's to talk about?" he asked. "You're going to have

to tell someone, and before you do that, you're going to have to tell the person who told you."

"Okay, okay," she said. "I can see that you're right, but I can't do anything about it now. Maybe . . ."

"Maybe what?" he asked.

"Maybe—nothing."

"I think this is yours, Lily. I think you're on your own with this one."

Lily had almost grown used to the church buildings being inhabited by others, presences she suspected but couldn't confirm—dim shapes in the alcove, weird noises from the basement. So when she rounded the corner onto Lee Street and heard the organ music in the church she felt more relieved than surprised. Things were moving along.

And, since the front door of the church was unlocked, it probably wasn't Stanley, even though she recognized the piece as the simple melody Stanley had been playing last week. She opened the door quietly and stepped into the entryway, grateful to be out of the frigid night air. Inside it was dark, but she could see the faint glow of light from the direction of the chancel. After she paused to catch her breath and take off her mittens and hat, she stepped into the narthex and saw that the organ lamp was shining on Roy Talbot's bent head.

Lily walked halfway up the center aisle and sat in a pew. She leaned against the tall wooden back of the bench, hoping the music wouldn't end, hoping the boy would go on playing.

When he finished, after the moment of silence in which the music rested and disappeared, Lily saw that he was watching her over the music arch. She was afraid to say anything, because she felt sure the wrong thing would drive him away and that he, too, would disappear. So they stared across the darkened church until he stood and walked down the steps toward her.

He seemed different from the last time she had seen him, calm and almost mannerly. He wore the same parka and baseball cap, but his hands were quiet at his sides.

When he sat in the pew and turned toward her, she caught her breath. He suddenly looked so much like his father—he had his mother's coloring, but his father's businesslike manner, and a blend of their features.

"I need a place to stay," he said. "I'm trying to get out of—I'm trying to get clean, and I can't stay where I'm living now. Anyway, there's no heat."

"You've been living with no heat?" she asked him.

"We had a gas stove, you know, so we just kept it on all the time, but it's not working now. I think the gas has been turned off—mainly, though, I can't get clean if I stay there."

"Yeah, especially if you freeze to death first," said Lily, then regretted her tone. Maybe this wasn't the place for ironic detachment.

But he smiled and nodded. "I thought of that," he said.

"You seem pretty calm for someone who's coming off of—what are you coming off of?"

"Don't worry about it. I've got it under control."

"Look," said Lily, "when you're talking about drugs, that line falls in the category of famous last words."

"Fuck you," he said. "What do you know about it?"

"I know some," said Lily, carefully choosing her words. "But not as much as you, so if you say you're okay, I believe you."

"I didn't say I was 'okay,'" he said, warier than before. "I said I had it under control. I'm working on it. I have what I need to make the transition, you know."

"Good," said Lily. "And now you have a place to stay." She had noticed his dilated pupils and had a better understanding of the newfound tranquility. But she couldn't refuse him a bed, and, besides, she couldn't bear to let him disappear again. She watched him decide whether or not to forgive her and realized, as he decided in her favor, how little he had. After all, she was a stranger, and a priest. He wouldn't bother with her if he had anywhere else to turn. "Let's go then," she said. "It's cold in here."

"Wait," he said. "This is the deal. It has to be a secret. You can't tell anyone—no one."

"Tell them what?" she asked, thinking how familiar this felt. Thinking how odd it was, really, the traits we inherit.

"Where I am. I don't want anyone to know where I am."

"You mean anyone in your family?"

"Anyone. Period."

"Okay," she said.

He shrugged his shoulders, turned away, and walked up the stairs to the altar. There he picked up a bedroll and a nylon duffel bag that had been tucked into a corner of the choir stall, then leaned over and, with deft, practiced motions, switched off the organ and the green lamp that shone on the console.

Early Monday morning, Lily sat at the kitchen table drinking tea. Roy still slept upstairs. She felt as if she had a baby in the house, or some fragile, rare creature given over to her protection. All night she had been in and out of the guest room, checking on him. He slept soundly. Between times, she had dreamed of his being hit by a careening car, then of herself standing in the foyer of his father's office in the pitch dark with a cold wind blowing through the halls. She had woken trying feverishly to remember what came after "We believe in the Holy Spirit . . ."

When the phone rang, she stayed at the table. It stopped after nine rings and began again a few minutes later. She worried it might wake the boy, but she didn't think it would, since there was no phone upstairs.

The third time it started, she made herself go answer.

"Was I too hard on you last night?" asked Charlie. "I realized after you left that I didn't really—"

"No, no," she said, interrupting. "You're right. This is my job here, and I need to do just what we talked about. It's up to me."

"Look, before you go on, I want to tell you I talked to Samuel last night, after you left. I didn't tell him what you'd said, but I did tell him that it was very, very important that if he knew anything at all about what went on between Barnes and the young man you were trying to find that he tell me, or you, that he let us know."

"And?"

"It took a while—"

"I'm stunned."

"All right. So, anyway, he said I could tell you that the young man had told Fred Barnes a secret, something he knew about someone else in the parish, and that Barnes was worried about the boy's safety."

"But what if the secret was about Barnes?"

"I asked him that. I asked him that specifically. At first he just looked confused, but then he understood perfectly, he got it, and he said he could assure me, without hesitation, that was not the case. Those were his exact words: 'I can assure you, without hesitation, that was not the case.'"

"Did he seem angry?" Lily asked.

"No. He just seemed sad."

Lily felt the word "sad" like a tiny pin stuck in her heart.

"I'm sorry," she said. "But I—"

"It's not your fault, Lily. And it still has to be investigated. It may be he told his parents that, or it may be . . . who knows. You still need to tell Spencer everything, but at least you can tell him with a different perspective in mind. This is way over our heads now."

"I know," she said, after a pause. "I'm going to talk to Spencer today—and the person who told me." As she said it, she realized she would indeed do that. She would speak to them both, but she would not mention the child asleep upstairs in the rectory.

"Good. Just—be careful."

"What do you mean?" she asked.

"I can't help but think that if there *is* some kind of secret, something, I don't know, something Barnes knew, something the other guy, Roger Frye, knew . . ."

"Oh," said Lily, frightened by Charlie's wholehearted conversion to the story she and Mrs. Hanlon had been assembling over the weeks. When Charlie had been skeptical, there remained some slim chance that the truth might turn out to be a bizarre series of misunderstandings, accidents, coincidences. But now, she thought, that possibility was gone.

"Maybe somebody else was abusing the boy," said Charlie, "and Barnes found out."

"Yes," said Lily. "Maybe so."

"The point is," he said, "you've got to go on with this and get it cleared up, as soon as possible. I just hope we're not getting all caught up in some inflated drama that doesn't have anything to do with reality."

"Actually," said Lily, "that wouldn't be the worst end to this story."

# chapter ✳ 18

Lily called both Talbot and Spencer as soon as Charlie hung up. She was afraid if she didn't do it then, she wouldn't do it at all. What she wanted to do was stay in the rectory with the door locked, keeping watch.

She called the cathedral, claimed it was an emergency, and got an appointment with the bishop for two o'clock that afternoon. She phoned Talbot's office next, and Mrs. Hennessey said if Lily came right away Talbot might be able to see her before his next appointment. She left Roy a note on the floor outside his room: Lily would bring lunch back for both of them—she would not be gone long. She refrained from writing *Don't move and don't let anyone in and don't get hurt and . . .*

She cut across the Common toward Talbot's building on Tremont. Gray clouds had moved in, and wide, airy snowflakes drifted past tree limbs strung with loops of Christmas lights. The temperature was in the high twenties. After the frigid days of the past week, this weather struck Lily as almost whimsical. She lingered another minute on the sidewalk, trying to prepare herself for the scene with Dan Talbot.

Then she entered the downstairs lobby and told the young, uniformed Japanese man behind the counter why she was there. He didn't much seem to care. He nodded toward the elevator and went back to his newspaper, with its vertical headlines of Japanese characters. She pushed the call button and stepped into the elevator, all the while thinking, "Breathe, breathe, breathe."

When the doors opened onto the tenth floor, Lily saw Mrs. Hennessey and her desk framed by swirls of white flakes in the picture window.

Mrs. Hennessey smiled brightly. "Oh good, you're in time," she said. "I think he's just—oops." The phone buzzed, she answered it, her face becoming serious. While she listened, she cast Lily a subverted glance. "Fine," she said more than once, "Fine," and then hung up, less cheerful, more brusque. "Mr. Talbot is ready to see you now," she began. "But," she continued, in a rush, "he wants to be sure you understand he's on his way out, so . . ." She paused, evidently hoping Lily would fill in the blank.

But she didn't.

"So . . ." Mrs. Hennessey began again, "anyway." She stood and led Lily through the secretary's office, empty today, and to Talbot's brass-handled double door, where she knocked and inclined her head to listen for an answer.

Once she heard his voice, Mrs. Hennessey opened the door wide and disappeared, leaving Lily to walk in alone. Talbot stood facing her at one end of the room behind the desk, a dark wood and chrome structure that seemed to stretch the width of the office. He wore a charcoal wool suit, a pin-striped shirt, a red tie, but something was different. He looked as if he'd dressed in a rush. The tie was slightly crooked, there was no handkerchief, and Lily saw a small spot on his lapel. His choirboy face looked flushed and swollen. He gathered papers, stacking, assembling, and tamping them into piles, which he then placed in a briefcase on the desk in front of him.

"Did Mrs. Hennessey tell you I'm on my way out?" he asked

"Yes, she did," said Lily.

"What can I do for you?" His tone was distant, formal.

"I understand you're in a hurry," began Lily, "but the thing is, I need to talk with you now, and I—"

"Will it take long?"

"That's hard to say," she answered.

"I hope you're not going back on our agreement," he said.

"No," she said. "I'm actually here to fulfill the terms."

"I see you are—going back on it, that is." He snapped the briefcase shut, then grasped the handle. Lily saw that his hands shook.

"Not at all," she protested. "We said—"

"We said," he interrupted, "that you would not repeat a word of what I told you." He was keeping his voice calm, but just barely.

"—unless someone could be hurt by my silence. And then there's the legal question—"

"Which is?" he interrupted again.

"There's a law that requires me to report any child abuse, no matter how I learn about it."

"The man's dead," said Talbot.

"I know," she said. "I'm not sure how it would apply here, but I have to find out. In any case, I think someone, maybe a few people, will be hurt by my silence."

"For instance?"

"Your son, and possibly other members of the parish. I can't say for sure until I know more about it."

"*It?*" he asked.

"About Barnes, about Roy. Look, if Fred Barnes sexually abused one parishioner, he may have abused others, maybe even other young people. It's not fair—"

"He didn't," said Talbot. "That's as far as it went."

"How do you know?" asked Lily, incredulous.

"He told me."

"Who?"

"Barnes."

"No offense," she began, "but just because—"

"I'm leaving now," he said, his voice suddenly loud. Lily noticed that his jaw was clenched, the muscles working. "I can understand—" he began, then gave a quick shake of his head. "I am sure you think you're doing the right thing. I can only say to you that you are not, and I have to ask you to wait until I'm back and we can discuss this further . . ."

"I'm really sorry, but I can't," she said. "I haven't come here to get your permission. I've come to tell you what I'm doing. I'm going to Bishop Spencer today. It will be up to him and the diocese after that."

Lily looked at his hands on the briefcase. His knuckles were white.

"I refuse to let you ruin our lives," he said. "We trusted you."

"I'm sorry."

Years ago, when Lily had done field work as a hospital chaplain, she had sat with a man who had run over his two-year-old son. The father had been rushing, and he hadn't checked behind the car where the child was bent over, playing with something in the driveway. She remembered a look on the man's face, the last stage of refusal, just before defeat—the look of a prisoner gauging the strength of the bars.

Dan Talbot picked up his coat from the chair and walked past Lily, only inches away, without glancing at her or speaking. She caught a whiff of whiskey and sweat. And she thought of that man at the hospital. Dan Talbot had the same look on his face as he swung open the door and left the office.

Lily arrived back at the rectory with two bags of sandwiches, chips, and drinks. It was still early for lunch, but she had said in her note she would bring food, and it seemed important just now to do exactly what she said she'd do, for things to go, as much as possible, according to plan.

Roy sat hunched at the kitchen table, his elbows propped on either side of a cup of coffee, his head in his hands, his eyes closed. When he heard her come in the room, he glanced up and almost smiled.

"Thanks for letting me do this," he said.

"What?" asked Lily.

"You know. Stay here."

"You're welcome," she said. "I got some food. Are you hungry?"

Roy seemed to think about the question for a few seconds before answering. "Yeah," he said, almost surprised. "I am."

"Great. Let's eat," she said. Her voice sounded singsong cheerful—the voice of a nurse in a locked ward. I can't treat him like a crazy person, she thought, or a baby. She couldn't remember the last time she had been alone with a teenager—a teenager on tranquilizers.

He looked up and gave her the same almost-smile. "Are you nervous?" he asked. "I mean, in general?"

"Yes," said Lily, without thinking. "I didn't used to be, or I didn't used to know I was, but I am now. This parish has made me a wreck." She laughed, a brief, surprised chuckle, at the truth of the statement.

"I believe that," said Roy, watching her closely.

"Also," she said, "I've had a hard year." She turned to the counter, her back to him, and began to unpack the food. "Do you want roast beef, chicken salad, or tuna?"

"I don't know," he said. "You choose."

"I'll put them all out. We'll graze."

"Whatever."

There was a stretch of silence while Lily got down three plates, put the sandwiches on one, and put it in the middle of the table. Then she set a plate down in front of Roy and put one at her own place, next to him. Finally, she put the bags of chips and cans of soda on the table by the sandwiches and sat down heavily in her chair.

"Thank God," she said. "That just about did me in."

"I bet you hear this a lot," said Roy, "but you don't actually look like a priest."

"I know," said Lily. "I don't hear it all that much, but I can see in peoples' faces that they're thinking it."

"No shit. So, are you gay?"

Lily had decided on the chicken salad and was just leaning forward to take a bite out of the thick, messy sandwich when Roy spoke. She stopped, the sandwich midair, her mouth half open. "No," she said. "What makes you think so?"

"You're tall," he began, as if thinking out loud. "You're old, well, middle-aged, you're single, and you wear cowboy boots. I just thought . . ." He shrugged.

"I see," said Lily. She took a bite of the sandwich and put it down on the plate.

"Did I offend you?" he asked her, more guarded.

"Not at all. I see that question in people's faces, too."

"But you can't be gay and be in the church, right?" he asked.

"Who told you that?"

"I don't know. A lot of people. It's in the Bible, right?"

Lily reached for a can of seltzer, popped the top, and took a sip.

"Look, never mind," he said. "I don't usually talk this much, anyway. It's the pills."

"Just wait a minute," she said, holding up her hand to silence him. "I want to answer your question—questions. Then will you answer some of mine?"

"I doubt it," he said.

"Okay. I'm going to answer yours anyway." She took another drink and set down the can, then got up and started to leave. At the door, she turned and said, "Don't go anywhere. I'll be right back."

He gave her a look of disdain.

A couple of minutes later she returned with the NRSV translation of the Bible and John Spong's book, the book that harbored Fred Barnes's letter. Lily wasn't sure what to do next, but she didn't want to lose the moment, to lose him. She was afraid, suddenly, that she would fail this boy.

She began talking as soon as she sat back down at the kitchen table. "I brought these because I want you, sometime, not necessarily right now, to read this guy and see what you think. He takes on the arguments against homosexuals based on what's said in the Bible. And it's good, he's good at it."

"But?"

"But for me that's only part of the answer."

He stared at her, waiting.

"For me," she went on, "these kinds of questions—"

He was eating chips, hundreds of them, it looked like to Lily. He'd finished the first two bags and was working on the third. I've got to talk fast, she thought, before the chips run out.

"In Christianity, at least in the Episcopal Church, these questions—about who's in and who's out, who gets included and who doesn't—are only partly about what the Bible says. The other part is about our—well, we call it 'reason,' but that includes more than just what we *think*. It includes insight, a wisdom of the spirit. On Pentecost—you know Pentecost?"

He didn't deign to speak, just nodded.

"On Pentecost, we pray for the Spirit to send us 'a right judgment in all things,' and that means a way of seeing and measuring and acting that's inspired by Scripture, by God, by Jesus, by the Holy Spirit—" Lily stopped. He sat slumped in his chair, staring at the half-eaten sandwich in front of him. He was gone; she had started preaching, he didn't want to hear it, and she wasn't sure how to get him back. "Do you think you've ever experienced the Holy Spirit?" she asked.

"I doubt it," he said.

"I have," said Lily. "And what's been most amazing to me is that sometimes it really feels like a wind—" He wasn't listening. "Anyway, the point is," she said, having no idea what she was going to say next. He stirred. "The point is that reason—my reason—tells me that the church is wrong about this."

"Yeah, but so what?" he asked. "The Holy Spirit seems to be telling a lot of people just the opposite. If nobody agrees with you, what difference does it make?"

"But other people do agree with me. Fred Barnes agreed with me—or he would have, if we'd ever met."

"You think so?" he asked her, with a sad smile.

"Listen," said Lily. "I need to talk with you about this. I need to ask you some questions now. You don't have to answer them, but I need to know—I need to know anything you're willing to tell me."

He avoided her eyes. But he didn't object.

"Can I ask you something about Fred Barnes?"

He didn't respond.

"I'm going to ask the question anyway, and you can answer or not." She watched him for a few seconds—still no response. "Did you ever get a letter from him, while you were away?"

He shook his head.

"This book belongs to him," she said, pointing to the Spong. "He read it carefully. One night I was looking through it and I found a copy of a letter he was writing to you. I read it, because I didn't know what it was at first. I think it means he had changed his mind about whatever went on here, about something that happened between the two of you or something he knew . . ." She trailed off, hoping he'd tell her more, tell her what had happened.

"Do you have it?" he asked, his eyes still on the plate.

"Yes. It's right here. Do you want it?"

He nodded.

She opened the book at the back and thumbed through the final pages, expecting them to fall open at the letter, but they didn't.

"Shit," she said. "I can't believe this." She held the book by the spine and shook it over the table.

"What?"

"It's not here. I know it was here. This is where I put it."

"Lemme see," he said, taking the book from her hand. He shook it upside down again, then went through the pages, section by section.

"Maybe I just put it somewhere," she said and started toward the door. But she stopped when she remembered the evening she'd come home to find her papers in unfamiliar piles—as if someone else had straightened her desk.

The book had been there, too, on the typing desk, with the letter in it.

"Forget it," he said. Then after a moment, he asked, "What did it say?"

She turned to face him and saw that there was still hope; he wanted the blessing of the letter.

"It said . . . it said he was sorry. That he had made a terrible mistake. It said that he'd been given the gift of sight and could see how wrong he had been. He wrote that God loves all of us equally and that with God's help the past could be amended, by becoming a more loving person in the present. He also—"

"What?"

"He also mentioned your father, that he could be helped. Do you know what that means?"

"Yeah. I know."

She waited, hoping he might say something else.

"Can you tell me Fred Barnes's part in all this?" she blurted out.

No response.

"Did he have anything to do—was he part of the reason you left home?" she asked.

He looked up at her now and said, "I left home—if you want to call it that—because my parents threw me out."

"Why?" Lily asked him, trying to sound calm.

"Because I told them I'm gay," he said. He stood and stretched. "I need a nap." He turned toward the door. As he walked past her, she almost reached out to touch him, to take his arm, to take him in her arms, but she knew better. He walked by her without a word and climbed the stairs slowly, the book still in his hand.

# chapter ✳ 19

It had been hard to get on with her day, hard to go very far away with Roy asleep upstairs, so she had compromised and gone only as far as the church office. Through the window, the courtyard lay quiet before her, a snow-covered square with indentations of the walks and borders and a set of footprints clearly marking her path from the rectory to the church. She had planned to return phone calls, but her mind was too busy with what she'd just learned.

She had no idea what to make of Roy's matter-of-fact revelation. At sixteen, he could think he was gay because an older man had seduced him. Or he could know he was gay because he was. But Roy had also said his parents threw him out. Dan Talbot had told her the boy ran away. Lily wasn't sure if they were two different versions of the same story or two different stories altogether.

When the gate clicked, clear as a hammer-strike in the still air, she sat up and looked out into the courtyard. All the emotional chaos of Saturday night—her despair after talking with the Talbots, her call to Tom Casey at work—

came flooding back to her. Casey stood just inside the fence, looking at the rectory, then at the church. He seemed a threat to the safe and secret world she'd created around Roy. Lily's only thought was how to get rid of him as fast as possible. She walked over to the door and opened it before he had reached the steps.

He smiled his wide, genuine smile; it threw her off guard. "I didn't expect to see you," she said.

"Ever again?" he asked.

"I just felt like such a fool. I still do."

She stood in the doorway; Tom had stopped with his right foot on the bottom step. A light snow had begun again, but a breeze had started with it this time, and the temperature was dropping toward its standard single-digit freeze.

"You mean Saturday night?" he asked. "That wasn't your fault. It's just a tough situation, because I'm the only single guy. There's a lot of joking around, and not much privacy. But that wasn't your fault."

"That's generous, but not entirely true. Anyway, I'm sorry I called you at work, and I'm truly sorry I was so confused, that I wasted your time. I was—confused."

"And how are you now?" he asked.

"More confused," she said. "But I'm about to meet someone over in the rectory so . . . So you're the only single guy, huh?"

"More or less," he said. Blood rushed to his face, coloring his cheeks.

"More or less *only,* more or less *single,* more or less *guy . . . ?*"

"Single—more or less single," he said. "It's a long story, and I'm not sure this is the best time, but if you want to hear it . . ."

"I do want to hear it, but not right now," she said.

"How long will it take—this meeting?" he asked. When she didn't answer, he said, "A long time. So I'll talk to you soon." He took his foot off the step and stood with one hand on the railing, squinting in the diffused light of the sky, the reflected light of the snow. His face was drawn, as if he had not slept much. He watched her, waiting for her to say something.

When she didn't, he said, "I'm working tomorrow. Maybe I'll stop by then."

"Great," said Lily. "I'll be in the office most of the day. That would be great."

"So you said."

She squinted now, too, and forced a smile at him. "I'm actually going to run back in to check my messages, then I've got to get over to the rectory, so I'll see you tomorrow. Thanks for coming by."

"Sure," he said. He nodded to her, walked slowly to the courtyard gate, waved, and left.

Lily returned to the office. Back at her desk, she thought of the ways in which her life and vocation had always been so clear to her, the terrain mapped miles into the future—mountains and plains, good guys and bad guys, right and wrong, faith, friendship. Now she groped down a dim corridor, feeling her way inch by inch, barely able to tell where she stood at that instant, much less where anyone else stood, much less where she was headed.

She pressed the answering machine replay button. She heard a woman's voice, familiar but too soft to be immediately recognizable. Lily missed a couple of words, then caught, ". . . tonight at our house. I don't know why it's so secret, but I thought you should at least know about it. He said 'vestry,' but it's not the whole vestry, just a select few. In any case, I thought you should know." And then the click and the dial tone.

Next, Mrs. Hanlon had called to check on her. "Today is Monday. I'm not waiting until Thursday to know what's going on over there. Call me just as soon as you get this. If I'm not home, someone can tell you where I am. For Heaven's sake, take care of yourself." Mrs. Hanlon had known about Lily's original plan to ambush Roy when he came to collect the money in the chapel, but that was all she knew, and all she could know for now. Mrs. Hanlon would have to wait for the rest.

The third message sounded as if it was from a pay

phone. "Ummmm," he began—a young man with a light Southern accent, slow and heavy-voweled. "So I read the notice, about Roy, and I knew him, know him, and if there's money in it, I could tell you what I know. Or if it would help. Or both. Both would be good. So you can't call me, but I'll try you again, maybe tonight, but soon. Or you could tell the guy here at the desk when I should call. Okay." And he was gone.

The last three messages were all from parishioners, one with a question about the Christmas Eve service, two with requests for appointments. She only half listened. Did she need information about Roy when she had the real article here with her? Besides, the guy hadn't left his name. When the messages stopped, she replayed them and jotted down the numbers of the parishioners. Now that she had no time for and even less interest in pastoral work, the people of St. Mary's seemed to need a pastor—another of God's punch lines.

She liked her vantage point from the office window: Since both the front and back doors of the rectory were visible to her, she could keep an eye on Roy without his knowing it. She had an appointment with Spencer at 2:00. She would keep watch here for a while and then check in at the rectory before she left.

An hour later, she opened the outer door to the rectory vestibule and then, quietly, the inner door, not wanting to wake Roy up. But he was awake already. She could hear cabinets being opened and closed in the kitchen, a chair dragged across the floor. Lily stood for a moment, taking in the urgency of the sounds, then crossed the front hallway to the kitchen door.

He was standing on a chair, rummaging through the cabinet above the stove, his head completely inside.

"Can I help you find something?" she asked.

"No," he said, not turning around.

"What are you looking for?"

Finally he turned and looked down at her. "What happened to all the sherry he used to keep in here?"

"I threw it out."

"Yeah? Great. Why?"

"I don't drink."

"How come?"

"I used to, but I drank too much, so I stopped," said Lily, then added, "And my mother's a drunk."

"So's mine. That never stopped me."

"Why do you want a drink?"

"Why do I want a drink?" He was still standing on the chair, peering down on her at an odd angle. "Because I'm losing my mind here. The pills aren't enough."

"Can I see the bottle?"

"What bottle?"

"The bottle the pills came in. Can I just see what they are?"

"I didn't get these at a pharmacy. There's no label."

"Fine. Do you know what they are?"

"Xanax."

"How do you know?"

"Because the guy I bought it from told me. Besides . . ." His voice trailed off as he climbed down and pushed the chair under the table.

"Besides what?" Lily asked.

"I know what they look like. I used to get them from my mother." He paused and smiled at her, mocking them both, she thought. "And it says so on the pill."

"Let me see them," said Lily calmly.

He reached into his back pocket and retrieved a small, plastic bag with the green seal strip—quality stuff. After he tossed the package across the room to her, he pulled out the chair and slumped down into it. Lily opened the bag and poured five or six of the tablets into her hand— pale blue ovals with XANAX/1.0 inscribed on them.

"Looks like Xanax to me," she said. Then she poured the pills back in the bag and set them on the table. "How many are you taking?"

"Not many. They didn't come with instructions."

"Yes, but how many?"

"One every four hours—sort of. I'm just trying to make

them last as long as possible," he said, cockiness gone. He looked at the large, kitchen clock on the wall across from him. "So I get another one in fifteen minutes."

"Listen, I want to call someone," said Lily. "She'll know about detox; she'll know about Xanax. But I need to know what you've been doing."

"Are you going to make me go somewhere else?" he asked.

"No way," said Lily.

He believed her. "Mostly drinking," he said. "Then I got into speed for a while. That's what fucked me up. The drinking's not the problem."

"So the Xanax makes it easier to quit taking the speed?" Lily asked.

"Supposedly."

"I'm going to make that call," she said. "Then we'll decide what to do next."

He nodded and with both hands began to play the counter like a bongo drum.

Maybe miracles still happen, thought Lily. Lena was working today. Lily sat at the desk in the study, waiting while the hospital operator paged her. She could hear noises from the kitchen across the hall—a complicated tattoo being worked out on the kitchen counter, then silence, then Roy opening the refrigerator, more silence, and the refrigerator door being slammed shut. Finally, she heard Lena's voice on the phone.

"You probably don't remember me," said Lily. "I'm the priest who was a friend of Roger Frye, the guy who was detoxing on your floor two weeks ago, the guy—"

"The country singer," Lena said, flat-voiced. "And you're the tall dark-headed one with the weird accent and the cowboy boots. Yeah, I remember."

"Oh, good," said Lily.

"Is he out already?"

"No, no. I'm actually calling about something—someone else."

"Yeah?"

"There's a young man here—a teenager—who's trying to detox on his own. He's got Xanax from the street."

"Detox from what?"

"Alcohol and speed."

"So he's using Xanax to detox?"

"Yes. I know it's not the greatest idea—"

"What's the dosage?" asked Lena, cutting her off mid-sentence.

"One milligram."

"Are they blue?"

"Yes."

"Sort of pale, oval, like an Easter egg?"

"Yes."

"Sounds like Xanax. What's your question?"

"Now he wants a drink."

"No kidding. That's why he's detoxing, right? What's your question?"

"My question is, what should I do?"

"You should get him into a rehab. He can't do it on his own. I mean, people have. I know a guy that decided to kick heroin on his own. He locked himself in a room with water, a toilet, a mattress, for a week. He got clean. He had half a tongue, but he was clean. And that's the rare exception. This kid needs help, and you can't give him enough."

"I know, but he doesn't trust anyone, and I think—he could hurt himself if he's left on his own. So I just want to help him get started until I can talk him into it, slowly, when he feels a little better."

There was a brief silence on the other end of the line. Then Lena said, "I thought you knew something about this stuff."

"I do, some, anyway."

"Then you know as well as I do that you're playing with fire. You know better, right?"

"Yes. Look, I know what you're saying is right, and I'm going to get him in there as soon as I can, but I don't want to scare him away now. I don't want to send him back out to the street."

Lena sighed, then said, "I can't tell you what to do, but you're not doing him any good if you don't get him help. At least get him to a meeting, something. Don't try to do this on your own. Do you want me to come over there? You don't sound too great yourself."

"I'm fine," said Lily. "But thanks. I'll call you if I need some backup."

After another short silence, Lena said, "Sometimes people like us—people in service professions—sort of lose sight of what we're doing. We start playing God. But the work's not about you and me, it's about the people we're working with."

"Right," said Lily. She wondered why it was so quiet in the kitchen. "I know. Thanks for the reminder. I'm definitely going to get him to go somewhere."

"Now."

"I know. I appreciate it."

"Right."


"You told me you weren't going to send me somewhere else."

Lily sat across from him at the kitchen table. She had told him a little of what Lena had said, but she'd softened it, using *sometime soon* and *when you're ready*.

"I'm not," she said. "Not now. But eventually you're going to need more help than I can give you."

"I'm not going to the monastery."

Lily looked at him, surprised. "Where did that idea come from?" she asked.

Roy hesitated. He picked up the plastic bag and toyed with it, slapping it on the metal edge of the table. Finally, he looked at the clock on the wall across from him, opened the bag, took out a pill, put it in his mouth, and swallowed. Lily said nothing. He sealed the bag, put it down in front of him, and began to tap, with his fingers now, against the metal edge. The sounds drove Lily crazy.

"Will you tell me?" she asked softly. "Did you talk to Barnes about going to the monastery?"

"Yeah," he said.

"And what did he say?"

"You know—sort of what he said in the letter. He wanted me to come home. And then he said if I needed a safe place to stay, I could stay there, he'd set it up."

"Why not here?" she asked him.

"I don't know," he said, his voice edgy. "It wasn't a safe place."

"Why not?"

He put the bag in his pocket and stretched his legs under the table. When he raised his head, he looked fed up. "You want me to get you killed, too?" he asked her.

She put her elbows on the Formica surface of the table and leaned forward. "I understand that you don't want to tell me what happened between you and Fred Barnes, or you and your family. So I can't help you very much. But whatever happened, I don't believe you got anyone killed."

He laughed to himself, a muffled, not-amused laugh. "But you don't know, do you?"

"No," she said. "It might seem to you now that something you did, or said, or told someone, brought on Fred Barnes's death. But I'm willing to bet you that it's more complicated than that."

He put his right hand behind his neck and twisted his head to the right, to the left, releasing tension. Then he sighed and said, "Yeah. It usually is."

"The more you tell me," she began, "the more—"

"—you can help me. I know." Suddenly all energy drained from him. Lily could feel it happen, like a plug pulled on his soul. "I'm just not too good at this." His face softened; he sounded younger and vulnerable.

"What? Do you mean talking?"

"No. The whole thing—living. Making decisions. Making money. Other people. I don't get it. I don't think—" he stopped.

Lily didn't know whether or not to touch him, to reach out and put her hand on his arm, so she didn't. She waited for any signs that might tell her what to do next. Finally she asked, "Do you have any faith at all?"

"No," he said.

"Is there someone you care about? Anyone you're close to?"

"There was. She came down here with me. She was, like, my best friend. But she's living with an older guy, a dealer. He doesn't like me, so I left."

He pushed back the chair and stood, then went to lean against the kitchen counter, facing away from her, drumming his fingers on the yellow Formica.

"Roy?" she asked, wanting to make him turn to her. But he was gone; she had lost him. "Look—" she began.

"Don't worry about it," he said. "I took another pill. I'm gonna feel okay in a minute."

*Okay,* but for how long? she wondered. She'd talk to him about the Xanax later tonight. This wasn't the time.

"I've got to go out again," she said. "But I'll be home by dinner. Then there's something this evening—" She felt uneasy even alluding to the vestry meeting at his father's house, so she let it drop.

"Will you be back before dark?" he asked.

"Yes," she said, "I'll be here." It was almost two now; she would be late for her meeting with Spencer, even if she left immediately. But she would be back by dark.

Though she needed to rush, she couldn't move. Finally, she turned toward the hall, then turned back. "Look," she began, "what we're talking about here, this is a long talk. We've only started. There's a lot more—"

He raised his hand, palm out, to cut her off. His eyes were closed, but he opened them and smiled at her. "I'm okay," he said. "You can go."

For the second time that day, she hurried across the Common toward Tremont. She arrived at the Cathedral breathless but only ten minutes late. Lily didn't like to be late. As with so many things, it was, at bottom, a moral issue for her: Good people were on time. And, now especially, lateness contributed to her sense that life was spinning out of control—too much, too fast, and too much of it unmanageable.

But Spencer was running late, too. She suspected it

was not a moral issue for him. She had time to sit in the pale-green reception area with this month's *Episcopal Times* in her lap and have a moment of peace—time to collect her thoughts, to think through what she had to tell the bishop and what she wasn't going to tell, what she knew and what she guessed. That would have been the ideal plan, but that's not what happened.

Instead, she pictured Roy in the rectory alone. He would take another nap. He would wake up in an empty house. She almost got up and went back, but Bishop Spencer appeared beside her chair.

"I was about to call you, you know," he said, ushering her toward the elevator.

"I saved you the trouble," she said. "Are we going up to your office? I like the basement better."

"Me, too, but it's just been painted and the stench is awful. Besides, I've got to put in my show time, you know, let people see me walking around, having meetings, doing my bishop thing . . ." He pushed the button for the fourth floor and leaned against the elevator wall. They rode together in silence, and after the doors opened they walked silently across the green carpet to his office. He closed the door behind her, showed her to a leather armchair, walked around behind the sturdy walnut desk, and sat down.

He remained silent until Lily asked, "What?"

"What, indeed?" he responded. "As in, what in the world is going on over there?"

"Why?"

"Why? For starters, I've got the big bishop breathing fire, you know, furious that a grieving parish is now having to appeal to the diocese for a new interim rector—"

"I don't know what you're talking about," said Lily, trying to sound calmer than she felt, "but I want to tell my part of this before I hear any more."

"That seems fair," said Spencer. "Tell."

"This is hard," she said. "Frankly, I'm not sure what I can even include—"

"Yes, that seems to be part of the problem," said Spencer.

"What do you mean?" she asked.

"Something about 'betraying confidences' was mentioned as one of the issues. What would that be?"

"Do you want me to betray them further by answering that question?" she asked him.

"Good point," he said. "But I think you should, don't you?"

"Yes," said Lily. She had to tell him everything, what she suspected, what she had been told—or almost everything.

"From the start . . ."

"Wait," he said. "Do you want anything, coffee, Coke . . . ?"

She shook her head and continued. ". . . there have been suspicions, about Barnes's death and then about other parish members—"

"What do you mean," he interrupted, " 'there have been'? Been where? And held by whom?"

"Do you know Mrs. Hanlon?"

"I don't think so. A parishioner?"

"No. She cleans the church and the rectory. She became close with Fred Barnes over the years, and to her his death seemed, let's see, improbable. Suspicious."

With his coaching and clarifying, Lily told him all she had learned from Mrs. Hanlon, then included the search through Barnes's belongings.

"So that's why you were feeling guilty when we had lunch," he said with a smile. "I wondered. It seemed out of character."

"It's not out of character," said Lily. "At least not anymore."

She continued with Roger Frye's collapse, her discovery of Barnes's letter, her meeting with Brother Samuel, and her slow understanding that the Talbots' son seemed to stand at the center of the picture. "Then I ran into Stanley Leonard lurking in the side chapel. The next day, Mrs.

Hanlon found a wad of money and a note. I guessed that Stanley had left it for Roy. Cynthia had said—"

"Cynthia?"

"Cynthia Babcock. Vestry. You know, short, squat, solid—"

"Oh, yes," said Spencer. "I like her, I think."

"Me, too, I think. Anyway, she had said that Stanley and Roy had been very close. So for a while I thought Stanley was at the heart of all of this, that maybe he'd done something wrong, something involving the boy, and Barnes had found out. But then Dan Talbot called."

"Why?" asked Spencer, his voice sharp.

"I had stopped by their house to talk with Sally about her son, the note, the money, and to try to find out what she knew. But she was in bed and couldn't see me. After that, Dan called me. He said that the two of them had decided they needed to talk to someone and could I come over right away."

He nodded. "Go on," he said.

Lily told him, word for word, what Dan Talbot had said that evening in his living room.

He stood and walked over to the window. Then he came back and sat down again. "What do *you* think?" he asked her.

"I don't know what to think. I don't want to believe him, but why would he lie?"

Spencer smiled. "With most people, that would be a reasonable question, but with Talbot you never know. He's been known to stretch the truth before."

"What do you mean?" asked Lily. "How do you know?"

"Mr. Talbot and I, or I should say Mr. Neville, Mr. Talbot, and I—they work as a team—have gone a few rounds together over the years. They raised quite a rumor campaign to keep me from being elected bishop. Our relationship has deteriorated from there."

"But why didn't you tell me all this at the beginning?" asked Lily.

"I didn't think it would be helpful. I was afraid it would affect your view of them."

At that moment, she understood the answer to one of the questions that had nagged her from the beginning. "So that's why you were so eager for me to take this job. You're the bishop, they're the knights, and I'm the pawn, the sacrificial front line. I see," said Lily, letting anger into her voice. "You were using me as a kind of spy."

"I hadn't thought of it that way," said Spencer. He seemed genuinely surprised at first, but when he spoke next, his voice sounded resigned. "But, yes, I can see how it would look that way to you."

"Did you know all along something was wrong over there?"

"I didn't *know* anything. But I had my suspicions. It made it all the more important to have someone of your insight—"

"Please," said Lily. "Let's keep the flattery to a minimum. You weren't interested in my pastoral skills. You wanted me there in some weird undercover job. It wasn't about how well *they* were being served. They didn't matter to you. It was about how well *you* were being served."

"I'm struck by your sudden concern for these parishioners. A few weeks ago you were in here telling me they weren't worth your time," he said. "I think you even called the place a 'spiritual wasteland.' Besides, the simple truth is I wanted both. I wanted them cared for, and I wanted to know what was going on."

Lily felt too lost, too angry, to challenge him. She needed something, an apology, something more than what she had gotten from him already. She wanted him to admit he had been wrong. But she also had to admit that some of what he said was right.

Spencer seemed to sense the shift. "Do you know there's an emergency meeting between your vestry and the bishop tomorrow morning, concerning you?" he asked.

"I'm not surprised. There's a secret vestry meeting tonight, at Talbot's house—I bet that one is about me, too."

"How do you know, if it's so secret?"

"His wife left a message on my machine."

"Sally? Good. Do you think she'd be willing to talk with us, or you, without Dan? You might get something closer to the truth, that is, if what we have isn't the truth."

"I think so, maybe."

"And what about the boy? Do you know where he is?"

"No."

# chapter 20

Lily was outside again by four, but it felt much later, the sky dark, the wind strong. Sleet blew diagonally, stinging her eyes and face, so that for a moment the world looked blurred. She stood across from the cathedral, surrounded by Christmas rush-hour traffic, the T-stop, and Dan Talbot's discount store, his building rising above it, floor after floor, up to the top floor, where a light shone in what Lily knew to be his office.

Then she turned and set off through the Common, hunching her shoulders against the wind. She pulled the hood of her parka up and walked in a kind of muffled, panic state, aching to be back at the rectory, to see that Roy was all right. Too much was going wrong at once. She should never have left him alone. And now she had broken her promise to be home by dark.

Lily knew when she entered the hall that the rectory was empty, but she took the stairs two at a time and pushed open the door to the extra room where Roy had slept. His blue duffel bag lay on the floor by the bed, open, most of its pathetic contents visible—two Ivory soap samples, still in their wrappers, a gray T-shirt, a paperback missing its cover, and a bright, turquoise blue hairbrush, a child's brush. She would search the bag if she had to, thought Lily, but not yet.

She walked into her own room and scanned it—bed neatly made, meditation corner untouched for days. When she saw the Spong book, her heart stopped for an instant. It lay on the night table, a small wedge of white paper stuck out of the top. For an instant, she thought that it must be Barnes's letter returned from the void, but she immediately knew better.

The note had been written with a blunt pencil on a file card found, she suspected, in the desk of the extra room where Lily had stashed some research materials. "Thanks for loaning me this but I'm having trouble reading right now. Maybe we can talk tonight." *Maybe we can talk tonight.* That meant he planned to return.

She walked downstairs, entered the study, and sat at her desk. Searching the bag upstairs was pointless; Roy wouldn't have a leather-bound book with alphabetized names, addresses, appointments. He had moved himself into another world, because this one hadn't worked for him. She could think of no one to call. She was in this alone, and for now she could only wait, wait and hope he'd come back.

She heated a can of soup and made a grilled cheese sandwich, ate a few bites, cleaned up the kitchen, walked upstairs to check his room, her room, the bathroom, for something more, a sign that he was all right, a hint as to where he might be. Around eight o'clock, she walked into her study, sat in her chair, put her head in her hands, and stopped. There was nowhere else to go and nothing left to do. She got on her knees and put her elbows on the desk chair, determined to stay there until she could pray.

She asked that Roy be kept safe in God's hands. But that was not an image that worked for her; she always thought of old life insurance ads. She waited. Her mind was filled with the sound of his voice asking if she'd be back by dark, with a picture of a gray, unlighted room without heat.

Finally, she reached across the desk and picked up the prayer book. She had stopped saying the daily offices over the past few weeks. The book felt almost foreign in her hands. But she was desperate.

She turned to the Penitential Order and began to read out loud to herself. *Bless the Lord who forgiveth all our sins,* she read. *God's mercy endureth forever.* At the bottom of the page she reached the passage in Matthew from which she had preached her first sermon at St. Mary's: *And the second is like unto it: Thou shalt love thy neighbor as thyself. On these two commandments hang all the Law and the Prophets.* How little I knew then, she thought, and how proud I was of that knowledge.

She remembered standing in the narthex, shaking the hands of parishioners, gauging their responses to see how well the sermon had gone over, to see if she had gotten some of them on her side. She had been like a politician taking a poll. Now she realized she couldn't recall one name or one face from that scene in the church door, only that she had tricked them into liking her. From the beginning, these people had not seemed real, and they had certainly not seemed like her equals. They had simply been part of a problem she needed to fix. Bishop Spencer had been right about that.

As she began the prayer of confession, Lily felt a shift within, like a sheet of ice floating into warmer waters. *We have not loved thee with our whole heart; we have not loved our neighbors as ourselves,* she prayed.

The silence afterward was not the empty silence she had felt before. She stayed on her knees, eyes closed, and after some time she turned to the prayers for a sick child. *Lord Jesus Christ, Good Shepherd of the sheep, you gather the lambs in your arms and carry them in your bosom: We commend to your loving care this child Roy. Relieve his pain, guard him from all danger, restore to him your gifts of gladness and strength, and raise him up to a life of service to you.*

When she had finished praying, Lily folded her arms on the chair and lay her head down on them. Tears ran sideways across her face, over the bridge of her nose and onto the cushion. She did not sleep, but she rested for the first time in many days. And when she finally raised her head, she thought she knew where to turn.

After four rings, Lily heard Jo Leonard's taped voice telling her Stanley and Jo weren't home right now, to please leave a name and number. So Lily left a short, unrevealing message for Stanley and refrained from using the word "urgent," but barely. Then she dialed the Talbots' number and waited through five rings, six, then seven. Just as she was about to hang up, a man answered.

"Is this Dan?" she asked.

"Yes. Who's speaking?"

"This is Lily Connor. Look, I'm sorry to bother you, but I need to talk to Stanley."

"What makes you think he'd be here?"

Lily sighed, quietly, then said. "Call it a hunch."

"I may see him later tonight. We're having friends—"

"Dan, I know about the meeting. Right now I don't care about the meeting. I just need to ask Stanley one question. If it weren't extremely important, if it weren't urgent, I wouldn't be calling you."

"If you want to talk to Stanley, you'll have to call him at home."

"Please, I know we haven't—"

"If I see Stanley, I'll tell him you're looking for him, but I suggest you leave a message at his home." His voice had the odd, high pitch it got when he was angry and, she now suspected, frightened. She had also come to suspect he was frightened a lot.

It didn't take long for someone to answer the door at the Talbots'. When she peered out onto the stoop and saw Lily, Sally looked relieved. She opened the outside door wider and let Lily into the tiny vestibule between the two doors, then whispered, "They just started. Stanley was late, and Dan waited for him. What are you going to say?"

"I'm not going to say anything, to the group anyway. I just need to talk to Stanley."

"Why?" asked Sally. Lily saw now that Sally's delicate face was unusually pale (no lipstick), her fine, dark hair uncombed. She wore jeans and an oversize black sweater and looked like a different woman from the one who had opened the door to her only last week; now she seemed both older and younger, more human and more vulnerable. She wasn't a pretty doll anymore.

"It's about Roy," said Lily. "I need some help."

Sally's face went blank for a moment, then she focused on Lily again. "What should I do?" she asked.

"Just see if you can get Stanley's attention, quietly. Don't say my name, just say you need to ask him something."

"But what?" asked Sally.

"It doesn't matter," said Lily, struggling to keep from raising her voice. "It doesn't matter, because you're not going to talk to him. I am. Just go in and say you need to ask him something, privately, out here."

"No one will believe me," said Sally, matter-of-factly, and Lily knew she was right, that there was no precedent for Sally Talbot's interrupting a meeting run by her husband.

"All right," said Lily. "I'll go in. But you've got to do something for me. You need to keep Dan busy for just a few minutes so I can have my time with Stanley. If it weren't important, I wouldn't ask."

"I just don't—" began Sally, then she touched Lily's arm and said, "Wait a minute. Follow me."

She led Lily into the darkened dining room on the right of the foyer. A moment later Dan called out to his wife, and Sally crossed the hall, opened the sliding doors to the living room, and explained the doorbell—a liquor delivery. Not their usual guy. She had sent him around back.

At least she's a good liar, thought Lily. But then, of course, she would have to be.

Sally walked past her into the kitchen. After a pause,

Lily heard, through a crack left by Sally between the doors, the sound of voices in the living room. At first they were only sounds, unintelligible, and then she recognized Dan Talbot's voice and could make out the words.

". . . the seriousness of this information being out, into the general public."

Then Lily heard Cynthia's voice but couldn't tell what she said.

John Neville spoke next, cutting Cynthia off. He must have been near the door; Lily could hear him perfectly. "Excuse me," he called out, "but I think we all know how quickly this kind of thing leaks and what it looks like once it's out. We must agree, as a group, to keep this quiet."

The kitchen door swung open and Sally came out, pen and paper in hand, followed by Florence, holding a silver tray with two cut glass bowls, one filled with peanuts, one with black olives, and a plate of crackers. Sally looked at the tray and shrugged. "It was the best we could do on short notice," she said and handed Lily the pen and paper. "Write Stanley a note. Florence can deliver it."

"Is that okay?" Lily asked Florence, who nodded. Lily wrote five words, then folded it and passed it on.

Florence took the note and tucked it in the palm of her right hand, where it rested, invisible, between her hand and the tray. Then she turned and walked toward the living room. Sally followed.

In a moment, Lily heard Sally's voice rise above Dan's objections. "I know," said Sally, "but there's no reason to have all these people here working and not offer them something. Go on, anyway, with the meeting. I'm sure everyone here is smart enough to be able to chew and think at the same time. Let's just leave the tray, shall we, Florence, and then everyone can help themselves."

In the silence that followed, Lily imagined Dan's round, angry face and knew what an effort it had been for Sally to do what she had just done.

Florence reappeared from the foyer. As she passed Lily, she paused and said, "He got it and read it."

"Thanks," said Lily. "I really appreciate it."

"I have been hoping Mrs. Talbot would get some help. I hope you can help her—and the boy."

"I'll do my best," said Lily.

Sally came back into the dining room. She waited until the kitchen door swung shut behind Florence, then asked Lily, "Is Roy all right?"

"Yes. I think he is. But I want to find him now, as soon as possible. Can you stay here and make an excuse for Stanley?"

"If it will help," said Sally.

"I think it will," said Lily.

"You won't bring him here, though, will you?" Sally wasn't pretending anymore. It seemed clear Roy was in danger, and at least part of that danger came from his father.

"No," said Lily. "I won't."

When Lily glanced up, Stanley Leonard stood in the dining room doorway, the note in his hand. As always he was impeccably neat, his hair slicked down, his black turtleneck tucked neatly into flannel trousers, but his face betrayed him: It was tight, lined, a picture of worry.

"I waited so it wouldn't look glaringly suspicious," he said.

"I have to talk to you," said Lily.

"I'll be in the hall," said Sally, "that way, if anyone comes out . . ."

"Great," Lily said and turned to Stanley, who stood beside her, staring down impatiently. She thought how rarely she had to raise her eyes to other people and then thought, I bet that accounts for something.

In whispers, she told him a quick story of the last two days and of her fears for Roy Talbot now. "He's scared and confused. He thinks he's responsible for—too much," she said, leaving Barnes's death out of it for now. "He's got a bag full of sedatives, and he's completely alone. The point is," she said, "do you know where he might have gone, where he was staying before? He mentioned an apartment he was sharing, where the heat had been turned off—"

"Wait one moment," said Stanley. "I haven't actually signed onto this enterprise yet. As you may have noticed,

I'm otherwise occupied." He inclined his head toward the living room. "It's unclear to me—"

Lily interrupted in turn, her voice hushed, insistent. "Stanley, listen to me. I don't care what you're doing in there, and you don't have to come with me if you don't want, but you're his teacher, and, I think, his friend. He's in trouble, maybe in danger. He knew something, knows something, that involves Fred Barnes's death and Roger Frye's accident—" She stopped, partly because the look on Stanley's face was such an arresting mix of sadness and dawning comprehension, and partly because she remembered she had no idea where Stanley stood in any of this. But the answer to her prayers had been the thought of Stanley as a person who loved Roy, and she had trusted that answer.

"I know one place," he said. "But it's where he was last spring, when he first left. He wouldn't be there now."

"Do you have your car here?" she asked him.

He glanced toward the hall, out the window, and back at Lily. Then he said, "I'm not going to tell them I'm leaving. Let's just go."

They walked together into the foyer. While Stanley got his coat from the closet, Lily went over to Sally, standing sentry outside the living room door. Lily put her hand on the woman's arm. Sally looked directly at her, pleading, as if she had placed her soul in Lily's hands.

On the Charles River dam, in front of the brightly lit Museum of Science, Lily asked, "Where are we going?"

They had been silent up until then, except for a few stilted niceties: "Here's the car," "The heater doesn't actually work. It's more or less a conceptual source of warmth." Maybe Stanley was taking in what she had told him at the Talbots'. Whatever the reason, she was grateful for the quiet. She had said all she knew already; she was certainly not in the mood for parish chat.

"East Cambridge," he said. "There was a place, a sort of hut, I found him there once, last spring. I seriously doubt—" Stanley interrupted himself, shaking his head.

"It's a start," said Lily. "Maybe somebody there will know more, know where he moved to—the heat was off in this last place. That's why he left, or one of the reasons."

"Good Lord," said Stanley.

"Yeah," she said. "That's what I thought."

The silence returned while Stanley maneuvered the Monsignor O'Brien Highway and ended up on Cambridge Street, just behind the Middlesex County Courthouse. He slowed down and leaned forward, squinting, struggling to locate street signs. Each time they passed beneath a pink halogen streetlight, Lily could see Stanley's breath, a pale circle of fog.

"I have no earthly idea where I'm going," he said and pulled over to the curb. He closed his eyes, then opened them and turned to her. "That meeting, at Dan's—"

Lily raised her hand and cut him off. "I know this sounds a little feeble, but I can only do one thing at a time these days. And the one thing I'm doing right now is looking for Roy."

"That's fine," he said. "But you should know he's out to get you, as they say. Like in the Westerns. As in, he's out for blood."

"I figured," said Lily.

"What did you do, besides take the sensible act of revealing our little parish secret? Or was that—"

"Stanley—" she began, exasperated.

He raised his hand. "Yes, yes. Fine, fine. I have a morbid fascination with this process—you and Talbot squaring off. It's hypnotic, like watching a python digest an elephant. But you're right, as I suppose you usually are," he said. "I just have to think for a moment." He leaned his head against the headrest. Then, almost to himself, he said, "I'm going to take the next left. At a bar and grill on a corner, I'm going to turn again—right, I think. Then halfway up the street on the left is this tiny, flat house, a hovel, with the address spray-painted on the door. And that's it."

He sat up and pulled away from the curb, then turned left at the corner.

"Can I ask what parish secret you meant?" Lily asked him.

He hesitated before answering, then said, "Didn't Dan tell you about Fred—about his—" He seemed uncertain now about how much he should or could say.

"About Fred Barnes and Roy?" she asked. "Yes. Do you believe it's true?"

He turned left onto a narrow one-way street with empty lots lining the right side. At the corner, he glanced up at the street sign and sighed. "Now *I'm* on overload," he said. "I don't think I can have this conversation while I'm wandering these particular streets."

"Fine," she said. "Sorry."

They drove for another five minutes in silence, but there was no bar in sight.

"This isn't working," he said. He continued to drive, to turn right, then left. All the streets were one-way, making their progress seem hopeless and illogical. They passed through a canyon of tall, empty buildings; on their left a bright blue NYNEX sign lighted a glass entrance. Across the street loomed a polished, modern genetics engineering site, then the AT&T offices. At the end of the street, in the distance, an elevated garage stood, its skeletal beams and levels silhouetted against a starless sky. The streets were deserted, the cold forcing everyone inside; it was a moonscape. Lily wanted to stop, to go home, but she had no real home, and there was no stopping now.

After two more turns, they saw a pink and green neon sign above a shingled, one-story building; one of the letters blinked erratically. Stanley slowed down and turned right at the next corner. "I believe this is the block," he said, sounding awestruck. He pulled the car over in front of a skinny three-decker, deserted, a Board of Health certificate stuck in a front window. Across the street was the house he had described. A streetlight shone on the single window by the door—its incongruous venetian blinds closed. The number 29 had been scrawled across the door in black spray paint, and, beneath that, the word SCORPION. They sat together in silence for a moment, watching the house. "Is that tar paper?" Lily finally asked. One corner of the front wall appeared to be missing and was covered with a rough, dark patch.

"I think so," said Stanley.

"Let's go," she said, and opened the car door.

# chapter 21

Lily heard Stanley open and shut the car door. When she reached the other sidewalk, she paused and glanced behind her. Stanley stood halfway across, in the middle of the street, staring at the downstairs window.

"It doesn't seem like anyone's there," he said.

Lily walked to the ravaged door and knocked. They waited, Stanley still midway into the street, until Lily knocked again, louder, three times. Finally, she walked to the window and rapped on the glass. Though the blinds were shut, Lily thought there was a dim light around the edges from inside. She tried to see through a narrow space between the blinds and the window frame. The street was silent, Stanley and everything in the frozen world motionless.

The blinds were pushed suddenly to the side, and Lily saw an eye staring back at her through the gap. Lily gasped. She could hear Stanley give a sharp yelp of fright behind her, but she didn't dare to turn around. A girl stood in the narrow space, only a sliver of her visible, half her face, a quarter of her tiny, skeletal body—Lily could see her cheekbones, jawbone, the arched bone socket above her eyes. She wore a dark wool jacket, open at the neck, and a black wool watch cap. She looked like a haunt from a mariner's tale, a child lost at sea.

As soon as she got her breath, Lily leaned toward the girl and said, "I'm looking for Roy. Is he here?"

The girl disappeared, and Lily could hear her speaking quietly to someone in the house. A man's voice, not a boy's, replied in low tones. The girl reappeared and shook her head, slowly, as if dazed.

"Do you know him? Do you know where he is?" asked Lily.

The man's voice again, louder now, nearby but indistinct.

The girl blinked twice, then said in a clear, high-pitched voice thick with a British accent, "Do you have any money?"

She spoke through the glass but the sound traveled in the still air. Stanley snickered behind her; Lily put her face closer to the glass. "Yes," she said. "Do you know where he is."

The girl nodded once, then twice.

"If I give you what I have, will you tell me?"

The girl nodded once.

Lily pulled her wallet out of the hip pocket of her jeans and opened it. She had two dollar bills. Without moving her head, keeping her eye on the girl, she asked, "Stanley, how much money do you have?"

"I don't know," he began, sounding incredulous, wounded. "I'm not going to give them anything, if that's what—"

Lily turned to faced him. "You need it for something, do you, right this minute?" she asked.

"Oh, Christ," said Stanley, reaching into his pants pocket. He pulled out a money clip, peeled off two bills, walked over, and handed them to Lily, then returned to the middle of the street.

Lily held the two ten-dollar bills up for the girl to see. "Where do you want me to put this?" she asked.

The man spoke again. The girl unlocked the window and raised it half an inch. Lily slid the bills inside, thinking there were no storm windows—No, she said to herself, and probably no central air in summer either.

After handing the money to the man behind her, the girl reappeared. "He's at Serena's," she said, her high, clear voice carrying out into the night. "Over that way," she added, pointing to her right, down the block, toward the bar and the ghostly high-rise garage. "On Paul Street. The one with the garden. It's the only one with a garden. You'll see. And a fence."

Without warning, the blind slid back into place. The girl was gone. Lily reached out her right hand to tap on the glass, to call her back, then stopped herself. What would she say?

Back in the car, heading in the direction the girl had pointed, Lily felt relieved. If Roy was staying with someone who had a garden and a fence, the only one on the street, surely he would be fine. Stanley drove on, and both of them craned forward to make out the street signs.

"Paul Street," Lily almost shouted.

Stanley slammed on the brakes and stopped in the middle of the intersection, then backed up and turned right. It was a short, one-block street directly behind the looming AT&T offices. Lily saw no houses, only squat, single-floor concrete buildings—garages, a foundry, a loading dock.

Halfway down the block, they came to a six-foot-tall chain-link fence with a single strand of barbed wire strung along the top. A street lamp in front of the gate lit the yard, the skeletal stalks and weeds of a winter garden, the remains of a scarecrow on a frame of crossed poles—a T-shirt, a stuffed head, and a one-legged pair of overalls—and to the right of the garden plot, a small house set sideways on the lot, facing the scarecrow. Lily could make out a front porch and light coming through a pair of curtained windows. Her hope, though dampened, was not extinguished.

"That's it," she said. "Wait here."

"Don't you want me to come with?" asked Stanley.

"No thanks," she said, half joking. "If I need more money, I'll let you know."

The gate was latched but not locked, which surprised her given the KEEP OUT quality of the fence. She followed a narrow path between two halves of the garden, then walked up the steps of the porch to the storm door. A warning sticker was plastered to the center of the top glass pane: BEWARE OF DOG! with a red circle around the silhouette of a Doberman.

Lily could hear music from inside; it sounded like Sarah Vaughan singing "Isn't It a Pity?" and another off-key woman's voice singing along. She rang the buzzer once, loud and long, and waited for the aggressive barking of a guard dog. Instead, there was a volley of yaps, querulous and high-pitched.

The music was turned down and a woman called out, "Who is it?" from somewhere near the door. Lily tried to answer but the dogs never stopped, so she found herself yelling, "I'm a priest. I'm looking for a kid, Roy Talbot. Someone told me—"

The inside door opened. A massive woman in a flowered muumuu, her long, curly blond hair tied back with a brightly patterned scarf, stood framed in the storm door. Two of the tiny dogs—terriers? Lhasa apsos?—began to throw themselves against the bottom pane of glass, and the volume of the barking grew unbearable.

"Sorry," said the woman. "But I can't be too careful."

Somehow, Lily could hear her. "That's okay," she shouted over the din. "I'm sorry to bother you but I'm looking for a young man in my parish, Roy Talbot. Someone told me he might be here. Are you Serena?"

"Who's that?" asked the woman, looking over Lily's shoulder.

Lily wheeled around and saw Stanley standing at the bottom of the porch stairs.

"I heard the yelling," he said and shrugged his shoulders.

"Thanks," said Lily. She smiled at him and turned back to the door. "He's in the parish, too. He was Roy's teacher."

The woman studied him skeptically. "He looks like that guy that used to play Dracula," she said.

"He's helping me look for Roy. We're worried about him—"

"Honey," said the woman, "I don't blame you. As cold as it's been lately. But I haven't seen him for, oh, a week at least. He and the girl were renting the unit out back—" she said, tilting her head toward the rear of the lot. "But they couldn't pay utilities, nothing. So I had to run them off. I hated to do it, but I can't afford my own, hardly, much less paying for them. The girl said they had someplace to go, but then I saw her and she said he'd split. They do, you know. They don't most of them last too long. That's why I try to give them a decent place to live. But I can't support them. I don't have enough. I wish I did."

She took a breath then and picked up one of the dogs. Another one took his place at the bottom of the door. There must have been at least six of them. Either the barking had died down, or Lily had gotten used to it. Anyway, she could hear.

"Do you mind if we just look out there?" Lily asked, not sure why, but sure she needed to do it. This was the end of the trail for now. If he wasn't here, they had nowhere else to go. She couldn't leave yet.

"I don't mind, but he's not there. There's nothing but a couple of mattresses. Nobody's out there now. It's all been shut off, shut down, there's no lights, no nothing. I even took the stove out. You have a flashlight?" she asked.

"I do," said Stanley from his post at the bottom of the porch stairs. "In the car. I'll get it."

"Thanks," said Lily to him, again, and smiled a genuine smile of gratitude. She had been sure he'd want to drag her home. "And thank you, too," she said to the woman.

"I sure hope you find him," she answered. "Serena'd be heartsick if she thought anything happened to one of those kids."

Lily stopped for a moment, just before she turned away.

Was the woman talking about someone else who lived there or about herself in the third person? Lily couldn't tell. The door closed, and she stood alone on the dark porch.

Without waiting for Stanley, she started down the stairs and across the backyard to a tiny blockhouse in the far corner, against another stretch of chain-link fence, this time without the barbed wire. There was no window, and it wasn't until she got around to the side that she saw the door, no more than five and a half feet high, the lintel just at her nose. She could hear Stanley walking up behind her, and suddenly she felt the cold, sharp as glass, making it impossible to breathe or move.

"I found it," said Stanley, flicking the light on for a minute, then off. "Can't you get it open?" he asked, after a moment's silence.

Lily forced herself to put a hand on the metal latch and push. The door swung open into darkness. Stanley turned on the flashlight and shone it over her shoulder onto the opposite wall. She stepped aside and he moved past her, into the single room, more like a storage crate, like a cage. He passed the light over the cinder-block walls and down to the floor, first the right-hand corner, lighting up a part of an empty mattress, a black milk crate with a paperback book lying on top, coverless, next to a Mickey Mouse alarm clock, silent. Then he shone it into the left-hand corner, onto the second mattress, onto the curled figure of a boy, his knees jammed up inside his blue parka, eyes closed, right arm trapped beneath him so that the hand, white, delicate, lay crazily twisted palm-up on the concrete floor.

Stanley dropped to his knees beside the mattress, taking hold of Roy's wrist.

"He's got a pulse," he said. "Call nine-one-one. And give me your coat."

Lily pulled off her parka, tossed it to him and raced back down the path to the front porch. She pounded on the door, rang the buzzer, calling above the dogs' shrill barks, "Hello, hello. We've got to use your phone. He's out there. We've—"

The door swung open. The blond woman stood open-mouthed behind the storm door, the dogs swarming at her feet.

"Roy's out back. We've got to get an ambulance. Can I use your phone? Or do you want to call? Just call nine-one-one—"

She broke off when she saw the woman's face, slack, empty.

"Where's your coat?" the woman asked.

Lily repeated what she had just said and added, "May I please come in and use your phone?"

"Oh, honey," she said. "I don't have a phone."

"Where's the closest one?"

"Let me think," she said, slowly, so slowly Lily began to doubt she could come up with an answer. "The bar around the corner. I don't have neighbors, you know. And nobody around here would let you in to use the phone. Not at night, anyway. Not—"

Lily ran down the steps and out the gate, focusing on her memory of where they had seen the bar and grill, which direction she needed to turn. Then she reached the corner; down the street, at least four blocks, shone a green-and-pink neon sign, one letter stuttering erratically in the night.

She ran without thought, but thinking all the time, Did she have a quarter? Would they make the call for her? Where the hell was she supposed to tell them to go? Paul Street. Halfway down the street. The chain-link fence, the hut in the back.

Twenty minutes later, she stood at the gate wondering how she could be watching a pair of EMTs wheel a body on a stretcher down a narrow path and into an ambulance. Hadn't she just done this? Hadn't she just done it twice before, once at home with her father, once at St. Mary's with Roger Frye? How could this be happening?

Not until Stanley wrapped her parka around her shoulders did she know that she was shaking, her teeth chattering uncontrollably.

"Take my car and meet us there," he said, handing her the keys. "I'm going to go in the ambulance. I'll call Dan and Sally from the hospital, unless you think you should be the one—" He broke off in mid-sentence. "Perhaps not," he ended.

"Where are they taking him?" she asked, putting on the parka, zipping it, grabbing mittens from the pockets.

"Cambridge Hospital," he said. "Do you know how to get there?"

"I don't know where I am," she said, staring out at the street. "Don't worry. I'll get there. Just go."

"Fine," said Stanley, then hesitated an instant and gave her an awkward pat on the shoulder.

Lily watched him climb into the back of the ambulance. She gave a half wave with her right hand, as if she were sending someone off on a sad voyage.

Lily decided to retrace the simplest version of their path to Serena's house, ending up, she hoped, back on Cambridge Street. She passed the bar and grill on the corner and recalled the young girl's hollow face at the window, her small, clear voice. There was no time for that now, she thought. But the one-way streets disagreed. A couple of minutes later, she found herself at the other end of the short block. She could see the tiny house halfway down on the right.

She passed the corner, then put on the brakes, backed up, turned and drove wrong way down the narrow street, parking directly in front of the house. For a few seconds, she stared at the window, trying to make out if the light was still on, trying to know what to do. Finally, she reached in Stanley's glove compartment and rummaged for a scrap of paper.

In the end she found a handwritten list of hymns, numbers and titles, pulled out a pen from her inside coat pocket, and wrote on the back, "We found Roy and took him to Cambridge Hospital. If you want to see him, or if I can be of any help, please call." She wrote her numbers at the rectory and the church office, put the pen away, then leaving the engine running, she got out of the car and walked first to the window, where she tapped twice on the glass.

In a few seconds she tapped again, but no one moved the blinds this time. There were no signs of life. She walked to the front door where she discovered a vestige of the house's former life as a home: a mail slot. She folded the paper once and slid it through the opening.

Back in the car, she waited, watching—she wasn't sure why or for what. She closed her eyes and said a prayer for Roy. She said a prayer for the young girl in the house, whose name she did not know. She prayed for herself, for Dan and Sally, for Stanley, for the doctors at the hospital who were caring for Roy, for her father's soul, and for all the sick and suffering. "Keep watch, dear Lord, with all who work, or watch, or weep this night," she prayed, "and give your angels charge over those who sleep. Tend the sick, give rest to the weary, bless the dying, soothe the suffering, pity the afflicted, shield the joyous; and all for your love's sake." Then she pulled away from the curb, drove down the block to the corner, turned left, drove toward the lights, and found herself on Cambridge Street.

# chapter 22

The guard in the booth of the emergency entrance parking lot at Cambridge Hospital waved her through. She parked Stanley's car and rushed into the waiting area, but she found no one she knew. At the information desk, she was told that Roy had arrived, Stanley was with him; they couldn't comment on Roy's condition at that time. Lily wanted to go in to see the boy, but the receptionist asked her to wait until the family arrived.

So Lily got a cup of coffee from a vending machine by the elevators. She stood at the front windows and watched the traffic on Cambridge Street, half listening to an argument between a woman and a teenage girl who wore a short-sleeve T-shirt and ripped jeans. They sat behind Lily on a red banquette against the wall. The fight had something to do with the girl's clothing and the weather outside. Lily thought the girl was about Roy's age. She had long, curved fingernails, painted black, and Lily found herself wondering how the girl could play the piano, or do her homework, or make a sandwich with nails that long.

When Lily returned to the waiting area next to the emer-

gency room, she found Sally sitting very erect on a plastic chair directly below the television. She still wore jeans
but now had on an immaculate off-white parka with a fringe
of thick, pale fur around the hood. Her hair was recently
brushed, her small, fine-boned face freshly made-up.

Lily couldn't think of what to say. She had the cup of
coffee, untouched, so she offered it to Sally. The other
woman nodded and smiled appreciatively, but when Lily
handed her the Styrofoam cup, she said, "I don't drink coffee."

"Me neither," said Lily, and noticed that Sally's pupils
looked large and round, her face oddly tranquil. Lily walked
over, threw the cup away in a trash can by the water foun-
tain, then came back and sat next to Sally. Above their
heads, *Dr. Quinn, Medicine Woman,* played with the volume low.

"Have you seen him?" Lily asked.

Sally shook her head. "Dan went in. But we can't be
with him now. They're working on him. They couldn't tell
us much, just that he's got a lot of alcohol in him, and
probably tranquilizers. What does that mean—they're working on him?"

"I don't know," said Lily. "I think it means he's getting
the help he needs," she added. She had remembered at the
last minute that she was supposed to provide some pastoral comfort.

"But how is he?" asked Sally. "What happened?"

"Stanley and I found him in his—where he used to live.
The heat was off, so it was cold."

"He's all right, though—he's going to be all right?" Just
beneath the tranquil surface lurked panic, the beast below
the waters.

"I think so," said Lily. "But he didn't wake up when
we found him, or when they put him in the ambulance."

Sally nodded, as if to signal she understood, but Lily
couldn't tell if she did or not.

"Where's Dan?" Lily asked.

"He's in Admitting. He wants to get Roy moved."

"Why?" asked Lily. "I mean why does he want to get Roy moved?"

Sally looked around at the small, dingy waiting area and said, "This place is not up to his standards."

"But—" Lily started to object and thought better of it.

"He was my pharmacist, you know."

"Who?" asked Lily.

"Dan. He went to pharmacy school here, in Boston. I met him at the drugstore across from the T-stop."

"Where is he from, originally?"

"Illinois," said Sally. "Somewhere outside Chicago. He grew up in foster homes, but no one knows that. He didn't even tell me for a long time. He made up a family for himself, when we met." She stopped talking and twisted around to look up at the television.

"Are he and Roy close?"

"No," said Sally. "They never were." She sat back and stared at the wall across from them. A sign in six different languages instructed patients and their families to register at the front desk. "What's that language at the bottom?"

"Tagalog, I think. It's a language of the Philippines," said Lily.

"I think maybe he's afraid of Roy," said Sally. "Afraid that Roy's bad, from his own family, from Dan's family, the ones he never knew—that there was, I don't know, bad blood."

Her eyes began to fill, and her mouth trembled. When she spoke next, her voice sounded connected to her body for the first time that night. "They said—the doctor said that he lay there for a long time, and he did something to his hand, somehow, he had it kind of—" Sally twisted her right arm across her chest, and then raised her hand to her face. Lily leaned forward and put her arm around the woman's shoulders. Her body was so tiny, so narrow, that it was like holding a young girl. Lily thought of the girl's face in the window in East Cambridge. Finally, Sally took her hand down and studied it, wet from tears, smeared with black makeup; the cuff of her parka was stained as well.

"Oh God," she said. "I don't even have anything to wipe my nose with."

"Stay right here," said Lily. "I'll get you something."

Lily walked back down the hall to the front desk. The receptionist was on the phone, but Lily mouthed the word "Kleenex?" and the woman gave her a small handful from a box under the counter. As she turned to go, Stanley and Dan emerged from a hallway on the left. Dan stared straight ahead, intent on some goal in the distance. When he spotted her, his face changed. Lily could see the hatred.

He said nothing. He walked past and stopped a few feet down the hall, his left hand in his pocket, his right hand smoothing back his hair. Then he continued toward the waiting area.

Lily stood beside Stanley until Dan was out of sight, then asked, "What have you heard? Have you talked to a doctor?"

"Briefly," said Stanley. "His body temperature was low, extremely low, and the alcohol level was high. It appears they don't know how much he had in his system, as far as I can tell. I wish they'd taken him somewhere else."

"But how bad is it?" she asked.

"They said he was lying on his arm in some strange way, and twisted it so that the blood was cut off. And there may be frostbite. His breathing's depressed; he's still on a respirator. But no one seems to have any prognosis—at least not one that they'll tell us." He paused, then said, "The point remains that he might not have survived if you hadn't acted as effectively as you did." He patted her back awkwardly.

"I'd like to stay—" Lily began but stopped when she saw Stanley's face.

"I'm not sure that's a good idea," he said. "Dan's being quite unreasonable."

"But someone from the church should be here, don't you think? I could at least wait until they know more . . ."

"I wouldn't, not right now. Dan's desperate for someone to blame, and I'm afraid—"

"I'm who he came up with." Lily handed the Kleenex to Stanley. "Here," she said, "give these to Sally."

"What do you plan to do?" he asked.

"Go home. Please call me if . . ." she began, then found herself unsure about how to finish the sentence. "Just let me know how he is." She fished Stanley's car keys out of the rear pocket of her jeans and held them out to him.

"How will you get home?" he asked.

"The T," she said. "Don't worry. I do it all the time."

Stanley pulled out the now-familiar money clip and handed her two more ten-dollar bills. "Call a cab. We've had sufficient drama for one night."

"Thanks," she said and noticed, with a distanced surprise, that she never considered refusing. She took the money and walked toward the pay phone at the end of the corridor, to the right of the emergency entrance. She found a quarter in her back pocket and called the cab company, whose number was displayed on a bright yellow sticker on the Plexiglas shield surrounding the phone. Beneath the number, on the bottom of the sticker, someone had written what looked like "Blow jobs while u ride" and a second, smaller local number.

A stretcher was being wheeled through the glass entryway—a young girl, her face covered by an oxygen mask, her body wrapped in a blood-soaked blanket. An older woman walked behind, carrying an infant bundled against the cold in red bunting.

The cab was stifling—hot, dry, and filled with the sweet scent of cheap aftershave, whether from the driver or the last passenger, Lily couldn't tell. She leaned forward and gave the driver directions to St. Mary's, then unzipped her parka and stared out the window. When she glanced toward the front, she caught a glimpse of him studying her clerical collar in the rearview mirror.

"Everything all right?" he asked, loud enough for her to hear him. He was Eastern European, judging from his name on the licensing tag and his heavy accent. From the back he looked like a set of attached squares—square head, square neck, large, square hands.

"No," said Lily. "Or I guess it's all right for someone out there tonight."

"But not for you?" he asked.

"Not for me," she said. She dreaded returning to the empty rectory. She was scared, cold, tired; she could think of nothing that would comfort her. Then she thought of having a drink. In the dark backseat, she knew exactly what a shot of brandy would feel like—bitter in her mouth, hot in her throat, warm. She leaned forward and asked, "How much is this going to cost, I mean, approximately?"

He looked at the meter, then at her in the mirror. He shook his head, reached over, and shut the meter off. "Please don't worry about it," he said. "The world is round."

"The world is round?" she asked.

"Yes. You do good for people. I do good for you. Someone does good for me. It's a circle."

Lily looked back out the window. "I got a friend you should meet," she said.

"You don't agree?" he asked her, surprised.

"Yes," she said, "I think I do. But I keep waiting for the evidence to support that thinking."

He was silent for a minute, decoding her answer. "So here it is at long last," he said. "A free ride." He raised his right hand in a gesture of offering.

Lily didn't answer him. The whole conversation was being carried on at high volume over the rattle of the cab and the low hum of "Yesterday" on the easy-listening station.

"Is it a family member who is ill?" he asked.

"No," said Lily. "Someone in my parish."

"You are Catholic?" he asked her, raising his eyebrows.

"No. Yes. I was but not anymore. I'm an Episcopal priest," she said. "Anglican."

"Ahhhhh," he said, nodding. "Here you never know." They were almost to the Longfellow Bridge. Lily could see the orderly reflection of lights on the film of ice coating the river. "Is he very sick, your friend?"

"Yes," said Lily. The lights of the bridge blurred and faded. Through her tears she said, "He's a young man—a boy."

She wiped her nose on the back of her hand and thought of Sally, of the immaculate cuff of her off-white parka, stained with mascara. "I—" she began, and then stopped, cut off by the tears, heavy now, and by the impossibility of yelling intimate doubts at him through the open half of the grimy Plexiglas partition.

He pulled out a handful of Kleenex and passed them back to her. She took them, blew her nose, and began to laugh. He glanced in the mirror at her. "Maybe it is round," she said. Again his eyes looked back at her in the mirror, confused. "I just got Kleenex for someone, and now you have some for me."

He nodded.

Lily wiped her nose and continued to cry, bitter fits and starts that hurt her throat, constricted her neck, made her miserable. Catching his eye in the mirror once more, she said quietly, "I don't do good for people."

He nodded again, but whether in agreement or sympathy, she couldn't tell.

The Christmas lights on Charles Street clicked off.

"What was that?" she asked him.

"They are requesting everyone to turn off unneeded electricity. Because of the cold, and all the heaters, and all the lights—too much at once." He pointed outside to the store windows.

As the cab reached the corner of Charles and Mt. Vernon, Lily noticed the still-bright window of the liquor store, open late, across from her favorite deli. If the taxi turned out to be free, she would have Stanley's twenty dollars in her pocket.

"You can just pull over here," she said.

He stopped in front of the deli. "You want out here?" he asked. "Or should I wait for you and drive the rest of the way?"

"This is fine," she said. "Thanks."

He turned around to face her. "It's very hard when they're young," he said. "The young ones are the hardest."

"Yes," she nodded, "yes," wiping her nose, fumbling to stuff the dirty tissues into her pocket. As she did, she found the two bills, took one out and handed it to him over the seat. "Are you sure I can't pay you?" she asked.

The driver shook his head.

"Okay," she said.

He shook his head again. "I won't get credit for my good deed," he said, smiling at her. Then he added, "I will wait here if you want."

"No thanks," said Lily.

Lily rounded the corner onto Lee Street and thought she had never felt so cold. In a brown bag under her left arm she carried the gift box containing a small bottle of Remy Martin and two miniature snifters. She would have one shot and give the rest to Charlie—a Christmas present.

A car sat parked just in front of her at the rectory gate. The headlights were on, and the engine was idling. A man sat alone in the front seat.

She walked toward the small gray sedan; she could hear loud music from inside, the rhythm but not the tune. As she approached, the driver leaned forward, saw her, shut off the engine, and got out. Then Tom Casey walked around the front of the car toward her.

They sat at the kitchen table, Lily with a box of Kleenex in front of her, Tom leaning back in his chair, hands in his pockets. When she first came in, she had tucked the gift box into a small space on the closet shelf. (Maybe she'd just give the whole thing to Charlie, unopened. It made a nicer present.) Then she had invited him into the kitchen, put water on to boil, and told him the bare bones of the story: that she had been looking for and found this boy—someone from her parish; that he had stayed with her for a while; that she had just come from the hospital, where he lay in a coma, or, at least, not awake yet; that she was waiting to hear if he would be all right.

"But what happened?" Tom asked now. "Did someone do something—I mean, did he OD by himself, or did he have some help?"

"I don't know, but I don't think so," she said. "Not exactly."

The kettle whistled behind her, so she got up and made tea for them both. When she put the mug in front of him, Tom said, "Maybe you could use something stronger. Have you got brandy—anything?"

"No," said Lily, sitting down at the table across from him. "What if you tell me the story you promised me this afternoon?"

"That's fine," he said. "That's one reason I came by. But then I'd like to know what's going on here with you and what happened tonight."

Lily noticed that she was having trouble meeting his gaze. Part of her was grateful for his company; part of her wished he'd leave so she could have a drink. She nodded her head a couple of times and said, "Okay. It's a deal."

The story began with his best friend. "You know," he said. "First communion together, altar boys together, navy, Police Academy." While they were in the academy, his friend, Scott, married someone they'd grown up with.

"Had you dated her, too?" asked Lily.

"No," he said. "But that's a miracle."

In their rookie year, Scott and his partner, an older cop, arrived just as a young white man was backing out of the corner store three blocks from where their families still lived. The man had a red bandana tied around the lower half of his face and a long-barreled shotgun held up against his shoulder.

"Scott said he looked like a bandit in an old Western. He couldn't take it seriously. And then he recognized the guy. So he called out his name. Of course, the kid was wired, so when he heard his name, it scared the shit out of him. He turned to Scott and shot him—in the face."

Tom stopped talking and took a sip of tea. "The bullet took off the right side of his jaw," he continued, "from his chin to his ear. So, they're building him a new one, but it takes a really long time, and meanwhile, you know, he can't really talk, he can't really eat—well, he can, but it's messy. He doesn't want anyone to see him, especially his kids. He's afraid they'll be scared of him. He says he looks like a Halloween mask." Tom took his right hand off the mug and drummed once with his fingers on the metal edge of the table. "He does."

"Look like a mask?" asked Lily.

"Yeah. I wouldn't let anyone see me either," he said. "He basically lives at his parents' house now, and the VA center."

"What about his wife and his family?"

"He asked me to help out, be around, make sure they were all right. We told the kids that he was really sick, but getting better, that he'd be home soon."

"So you took his place at home?"

"That wasn't the idea originally."

"But that's what happened?"

"Yeah, that's what happened. It was like we all knew and didn't know at the same time. And then, one day, I was the daddy in the house—and then I was the husband." He took another sip of tea before he went on. "Our lives—Scott's and mine—weren't that separate to begin with. We'd done everything the same, even become cops."

"But you weren't a cop. Not exactly."

"I was," he said. "Then I went into ID."

Lily wadded up a piece of Kleenex and tossed it into the sink. "Oh," she said.

"Yeah, I know."

"And where does this all stand now?" she asked him after a pause.

"I'm moving out," he said.

Lily felt surprised at the strength of her response: immediate relief.

"Everyone's feeling shitty about all of it," he continued. "I thought I was helping them, you know—helping her out, helping him out, helping the kids—but I've made it worse. Anyway, moving's the right thing to do. I'm already looking for a place."

Lily walked to the sink, retrieved the wad she had just tossed, and put it in the trash can.

When she sat back down, Tom asked, "So do you want me to leave?"

"Why?"

"Because—I thought you probably wouldn't approve of my living arrangements."

"I'm not in a position to be disapproving of anyone at the moment."

"What do you mean?" he asked.

"The boy's father blames me for what's happened. I'm beginning to think he's right," she said.

"How is it your fault?" he asked.

"He came to me and asked me if he could stay here, so he could get clean—"

"When was this?"

"Last night—was it only last night? I can't believe it. Anyway," she continued, "I—"

"Wait a minute. So he was here today, earlier, when I stopped by your office?"

"Yeah, he was," she said.

"Okay," he said. "Go on."

"He's been treated badly by a lot of other adults—by his parents, for sure, and maybe by someone here in the parish. I think—he may have been molested. I don't know for sure, and I don't know who was involved. Anyway, there wasn't anyone else he could trust—at least that's what I told myself."

She filled in some more details of the story, then added, "I should have gotten him some help—gotten him in somewhere, helped him to get clean. I wasn't thinking clearly. I wanted to be the hero. Now he's lying in Cambridge Hospital—or he was when I left—he hadn't woken up yet. He's done something to his right hand."

"But do they think he'll be all right?" Tom asked.

"He was a—is a musician, an organist, pianist," she said.

"I'm really sorry," he said.

"Thanks," she said.

"I'm not sure what you could have done differently, though. The kid came to you. He asked for help."

"Just the way your friends came to you," she said.

He looked down at his empty mug.

"It's not necessarily the same," said Lily. "I shouldn't have even said that."

"Let's say that's all true, I still think you should—and I should, too—get some credit for doing our best, helping at all. A lot of people—"

"A lot of people would have done nothing, some would have done worse, some would have done better."

"Yeah, but let me finish. The thing is, first you take full responsibility for getting it all right, then you take full responsibility for getting it all wrong. Everything's either your product or your fault. What's the difference? There's a lot going on here, with the family, with this church, whatever, and it started a long time ago, way before you came on the scene."

"I think you're in the wrong line of business," she said.

"Just one more thing—it's not over yet. You need to be around for all this. So the guilt's no good, it's no help to anyone. You can feel it on your own time."

"This is my own time."

"Yeah," he said, glancing at his watch, "you can sit here and feel shitty for about six or seven more hours. Or you can go to sleep. Speaking of which, I don't suppose you have a couch available—" He watched her face. "No couch," he said.

"No, no. There is one, and there's a guest room upstairs, but . . ." Roy's bag was still lying open on the floor. The room still smelled like him. It was still, to her, his room.

"I'd rather have the couch, but I could drive out to my parents'. Oh, which reminds me, Mrs. Hanlon said to tell you that she has some information from Mrs. Hennessey that might be of interest."

"Mrs. Hennessey?" asked Lily, bewildered. She searched around for the face to fit the name and suddenly saw the plate glass window in Dan Talbot's office, framing an impressive desk and an older woman in cashmere and pearls. "From Talbot's office?"

Tom shrugged. "I think so."

"How in the world do they know each other?"

"The Hennesseys live one street over from my folks. They're the Hanlons' neighbors. I think maybe Mrs. Hanlon got her that job. Anyway, Mrs. Hanlon wants to come by tomorrow afternoon, teatime."

"Yes," said Lily, quietly, "I could use some of Mrs. Hanlon's tea."

"Me, too," he said.

They sat for a moment, then he took her hand and held it, briefly, before standing up.

With Tom ensconced on the living-room couch, Lily could hardly carry a brown paper bag upstairs—or so she thought. She felt better now, too. She didn't need a drink.

She fell asleep easily enough, but she hadn't planned on the dreams. There was a crowd, nicely dressed and very angry. They included the antiques dealer from across the street, the young receptionist from the diocesan offices, Mrs. Hennessey, a couple of members of her mother's family whom she had never met but recognized, wondering how they had gotten here so fast.

They wanted to bury someone in the courtyard, but the box, the casket, was flimsy plywood streaked with black paint and the way they were handling it, trying to shove it over the fence, the box was going to splinter into pieces. The child in the box wasn't dead, but only Lily knew that, and no one would listen. When she tried to tell the man next to her, he turned to show only half a face, the other half blown off, exposed, like a bombed building.

At two A.M. she woke up, chilled with sweat. She tiptoed down the stairs. From the top of the first flight, she could see Tom's head tucked at an odd angle against the arm of the couch. She thought of how bad his neck was going to feel in the morning. After a moment, she crept to the study and phoned Cambridge Hospital, only to find the Talbots had refused to allow them to release any information about Roy. She sat in the dark; she wasn't sure how much time had passed. Then she stole to the closet, opened the door, took down the bag, and crept back up to her room.

The sheet and blankets lay neatly folded at the foot of the couch. It was almost eight in the morning, but the gray sky barely lit the windows. Lily stood at the bottom of the stairs again looking into the living room, then walked in and sat on the edge of the couch. She ran her hand over the cushion next to her. Then she stood and walked into the kitchen where she found a note on the table—large, legible script in pencil on a yellow, lined pad: "Thanks. I've got to be at work by 8. See you around 5—Take it easy today, Tom."

She stared at the note for at least a minute, trying to focus on what it meant. He had gone to work, but he planned to come back this afternoon because Mrs. Hanlon was going to be here. Would Charlie come, too? She didn't know. And she didn't know why anyone was coming anyway.

She did know that she could no longer do what was expected of her—call the hospital, visit Roy and the Talbots, track down Stanley—and she had told Roger Frye she'd be back to see him today, or was it yesterday? Anyway, she owed him a visit.

She didn't feel sick to her stomach but she ached all over, her eyes ached especially, and she couldn't focus on any single thought. She couldn't remember opening the bottle and pouring the first drink into the ridiculous snifter that came with the box. But she had a clear memory of holding the bottle vertical, straight up above the glass, and catching the last drops. It was not a very big bottle, but it was cognac, and she felt as if she had drunk a great deal of something very cheap. She felt the way she always felt with a hangover—sick, and sick with fear.

Her hands shook as she filled the kettle. Her mind kept drifting to an image of Roy's bag in the room upstairs. She should take it to him in the hospital, even though there wasn't much in there. Even though there might be drugs in there that he shouldn't have, maybe tranquilizers.

She climbed the stairs and paused at the door of the guest room. She could at least check the bag before she took it back to him, to be sure. She walked in and sat on the edge of his bed. She picked up the bag and held it on her lap, then opened it and stared at the bleak contents: the child's brush, the soap samples, the T-shirt and a dirty pair of jockey shorts. There were no drugs, none for him and none for her. She lay down, with her head at the foot of the bed, her feet curled up by the pillow, the blue duffel bag clutched to her stomach like a baby's comfort toy. She closed her aching eyes and listened as the kettle began to whistle in the kitchen below.

She tried to focus on anything in the moment—her cold feet, the handle of the blue bag scratching her chin—but instead she found herself searching for the melody Roy had been playing on the church organ, that first, cold night. The notes eluded her. But she had a clear picture of his right palm lying on the cement floor of the shed. She saw Roger Frye's bared ankle on the basement steps, white and thin. And she saw her father's wrists on the white sheets, his wrist bones like shining knobs, no longer human, unfamiliar.

Over time she began to notice another sound, a kind of percussion accompaniment, behind the constant whistle of the kettle. Short, staccato blasts—she realized it was the phone. It rang at least ten or twelve times, then stopped, then started again, another ten or twelve rings. She imagined a Disney animation of domestic cacophony downstairs—phones and kettles rushing around in search of a maestro. After a long pause, the phone started again, and then stopped altogether.

She found herself looking down, somehow, at her own body curled around the bag and wanting, more than anything, to help this woman in so much pain. The phrase "in so much pain" lingered. If she was going to help the woman, curled there on the bed, she needed to help gently.

It was the silence that roused her, the silence and the

odor of scorched copper. She would have to boil the water in something else, she thought. She would make herself tea and have something to eat. And maybe the person who called would try again, and Lily would answer the phone.

# chapter ✤ 23

when the phone rang again almost half an hour later, it was Stanley, still at the hospital.

"His hand's better than they thought," he said. "They're worried he might lose a finger—that's all."

"But?" asked Lily. She could hear in his voice that news was being withheld.

"He's not awake yet. They're worried about that."

"Isn't this a long time? The doctors think he's going to wake up, don't they?"

"Yes, of course," said Stanley. "You know how it is—they're guarded."

"Did you talk to the doctors yourself?"

"No. Dan won't let anyone near them."

"How is Sally?"

"It's hard to tell, as usual, but I have the sense she's glad to have him there—Roy there—with her, someplace safe."

"That makes sense," said Lily. "I'd like to see him, just to make a visit. Do you think . . ."

Stanley hesitated, then said, "No. I'm afraid I don't. But I do promise to keep you posted."

"Did someone from the church show up? Should I call the bishop?"

"I'm quite certain they know," said Stanley. "John Neville just left. So you can be sure the bishop's already been phoned."

Lily searched around for some duty she could perform, some way to make herself feel useful. "At least tell Sally they're in my prayers, and if I can do anything—she can always call me on her own."

"I'll tell her. And I'll talk with you again later in the day. Will you be there this afternoon?"

"I told Roger I'd visit him at the detox center, so I'll be over there for a while."

"Give him my best, would you? I've always liked Roger. I was sorry to hear about his troubles."

"I didn't know anyone liked Roger," she said.

"I think they do, we do, some of us. He's always had a good relationship with John and Dan. He'll be sad about Roy. Are you going to tell him?"

"I don't know," she said. "I hadn't thought about it. Do you think I should?"

"Goodness. I'm not sure. I'll leave that up to you. You seem to be quite good at your job."

For an awful moment Lily thought he was mocking her, and then she realized he meant it. "Thanks," she said, "for everything. I hope . . ."

"Yes," he said. "So do I."

Lily drank as much tea as she could, ate three pieces of toast, and started out on the journey to visit Roger. She thought the cold might shock the hangover out of her, but it didn't seem to help, at least not at first. She began shivering on her walk to the Charles Street station, so that by the time she got to the platform her teeth were actually chattering. She leaned against the wall and breathed into her hands, trying to steady herself. Eventually the shaking stopped. The trip seemed endless, but somewhere in her tedious journey to the VA center she noticed she felt better. Her eyes didn't hurt so much, and she could focus her thoughts.

She had left a message at the switchboard that she would be there by one o'clock and was already a few minutes late. Roger hadn't yet appeared in the reception area. There was a large family in one corner, filling at least a quarter of the room. At first, they seemed to be there for a pleasure outing, the children using the plastic chairs as houses and tents, ladders and horses, but eventually Lily saw that the adults were all gathered around a young man in his late twenties. He had a small child in his lap and a younger woman kept her arm draped across his shoulders, while an older woman, who had the young man's light brown coloring and thin features, sat across from him, patting his knee from time to time. As she watched, Lily became aware that they were celebrating; the event had a prodigal-son feeling to it.

At 1:20 she began to glance at the wall clock every few minutes—had she been unclear, had he come and gone exactly at one, had she messed up again? At 1:25 the family started to say good-bye to the young man. As they left, in groups and pairs, Lily's hope left with them, so that by the time Roger appeared in the empty room at close to 1:45 she had given up.

"I'm really sorry," he said. Roger's transformation had continued. His eyes were clear, his face had lost its strained, angry expression, and he seemed almost happy, if exasperated at the moment. Lily felt self-conscious. Would he be able to read her state of mind as clearly as she read his? "I got into this—well, here's the thinking at this place," he said. "There's one area where you can smoke here, in the smoking lounge. Makes sense, right? Not too hard to remember. Anyway, my roommate smokes in the room, all the time, morning, midnight, whenever. So I go to the hall counselor and say, you know, 'He's smoking in the room.' So instead of the counselor just going to him and saying, 'Cut out the smoking in here,' we have a meeting, all three of us, that lasts for . . ." He looked over his shoulder at the large black-and-white wall clock. "It lasts for over an hour."

He shrugged and raised his hands, palm up, a "what-are-you-going-to-do-about-it" gesture. She shrugged in return.

"Are you okay?" asked Roger.

"It's been a hard few days," she said. "But let me say this first—if you're here, I think it's best just to do what they ask for now. That way, you don't get confused between your job, which is getting sober, and the details. You know, 'I can't get sober because they make me talk about everything.' You must be getting something useful. Focus on that. And stay clean." She was instantly struck by the horror of her giving someone else that advice in her present condition.

"Good idea," he said. "So what's going on?"

"It's a long story," she said, "and it's about the parish, people in the parish. I wasn't sure if I should talk to you about it or not."

"I'm getting really good at talking about shit," he said, straight-faced.

"So I heard," said Lily. "You know Roy, Dan and Sally Talbot's son?"

"Yeah."

"He hasn't been living at home for the last few months."

"Longer than that," said Roger. "Since last spring, right?"

"Yes," said Lily. "Right. Two days ago, he came to the church and asked me for a place to stay. He was trying—" She paused, unsure about how much she should say. "He was trying to get off the street."

"Go on."

"He stayed overnight, but the next night—last night—he ended up back in this sort of garage where he had been living, with no heat, no power—"

"Jesus," said Roger.

"Yes. And he was out, passed out for a few hours in this place—"

"Is he okay?"

"I think he's going to be okay, only, you see, he's not awake yet, and they're worried about his hand . . ."

"Frostbite?" asked Roger.

"Something like that. How did you know?"

"It's not that unusual among this particular population," said Roger, nodding toward the dorm. "If that's all that happens, he's lucky."

"We're hoping."

"How's the family doing?"

"Not so good. You know this is the third event like this in a short time."

"What do you mean?"

"Fred Barnes's death, your fall down the stairs—"

"I wouldn't call that an event. That was just carelessness. That was just an old drunk being careless."

Lily studied his face. Roger glanced at the wall clock, at the poster across from them, the one suggesting that everyone LIVE AND LET LIVE.

"I had the impression the last time we spoke that you thought something else had happened."

"I know. But since then I've been noticing how I always want to blame other people for my situation, you know? How I never want to be responsible. And so now I'm not sure." He unclasped his hands and rested them on his knees.

"How about this?" she asked. "How about you tell me what you were thinking, last time, and we work out together whether it makes sense or not, whether or not it's just an excuse, a way out of responsibility? Would that work?"

"I don't know," he said. "I'm afraid I'm going to tell you something, something that might not be right, that will start some ball rolling and then I won't be able to stop it."

"Okay," said Lily. "How about this: If after we've talked you still feel unsure about your suspicions—is that too strong a word?"

He shook his head.

"Then I won't do anything. I won't share them with anyone, and I won't act on them, okay?"

"Okay," he said.

"So," Lily said, trying to sound matter-of-fact, even cheerful. "Just tell me what you thought, or suspected, and we'll look at it together."

"Fine," he said, nodding in agreement. "What I was thinking last time was that maybe—I talked to you about taking the allergy pills, right?"

"Oh, yeah," said Lily, "I remember that." She tried to seem casual but attentive; she didn't want her eagerness to scare him.

"What was strange was that Mr. Neville and I—we'd just had a kind of argument because I'd been seeing him around too much."

"What do you mean?" asked Lily.

"After Father Barnes died, he was in the office a few times, sometimes at night, cleaning out drawers, going through stuff. I didn't think much of it then, but later, when you were already working at the parish, I saw him again."

"In the church office?" she asked.

"Yeah. It was at night that time, too. No one else was there. I surprised him, and he didn't like it. He made up some story, and I'd had enough to drink that I just told him what I thought was going on."

"What was that? What did you think?" she asked.

"That wasn't the only place I'd seen him. I'd seen him over at the rectory, too."

"When? After I'd moved in?" asked Lily, feeling goose bumps rise on her arms.

"Yeah. Once. And once before that. I saw him leaving the rectory just after dark—the night Father died."

By the time Lily finished listening and talked Roger through his doubts, walked back to the bus, transferred to the subway, and arrived at Charles Street, she felt well enough to visit two parishioners at Mass General—an older woman with a broken hip and a friend of Cynthia's at Eye and Ear for surgery on a detached retina. She was back out on Charles Street around four o'clock, in plenty of time for tea with Mrs. Hanlon and Tom. Despite the garlands of fir and red ribbon that decked the street, there was an air of siege mentality in the city now; the cold was a constant presence, and there were requests to save on electricity by turning off space heaters and lights whenever possible. Lily walked hurriedly past store windows stocked with presents—gold enameled pens, a huge bottle of Chanel N° 5, a pair of porcelain rabbits holding a brass umbrella stand.

At the bakery on the corner of Mt. Vernon, she stopped and bought a sandwich. She wanted a beer; she could remember how good a beer felt around this time of day, when she was just getting rid of a hangover. But if she didn't stop drinking now, she wouldn't stop at all. And she needed to be around for whatever was going to happen next. She owed Roy that much. She forced herself to ignore the liquor store across the street and headed for the rectory.

Yesterday's snow coated the courtyard, lending the church the feel of a country parish in the north of England—safe, cozy, harboring people, not secrets. Lily went to the church building and unlocked the door, pausing in the hallway to listen for any warning sounds of occupancy. She leaned over the banister to be sure the basement was quiet. When she felt satisfied she was alone, she walked into the office and sat in the desk chair.

As she watched out the window, Mrs. Hanlon appeared at the gate, lugging shopping bags in both hands, wearing a new red wool coat and a white knitted hat and scarf. She looked exactly like Mrs. Claus, thought Lily, with a surge of affection. A few minutes later Charlie arrived, brisk and efficient in his black parka and watch cap, not looking much like a monastic, looking more like a teenager.

The image of Roy on the frozen bed last night remained a constant; it merged with the frantic buzz of guilt and a certain sense of worse things to come.

She played back the messages on the answering machine, jotting down the names and numbers, two parishioners and a stranger wanting to know about Advent services. As the last message began to play, Tom Casey's car pulled up just outside the gate. Her heart tricked her, seeming to stop for an instant and then beating so hard that she put her hand to her chest. She watched Tom at the gate and listened to a message left by the boy with the soft Southern voice: he would be at Safe Haven tonight; she could call there and leave a message telling him when to call her back; he'd hang out by the desk, that way he wouldn't miss her message. His name was Reese.

Lily stared down at the machine, as if it could produce the boy or at least answer some questions. But he hung up and the machine's voice informed her only that there were "zero messages remaining." She thought of her response to seeing Tom, of her exaggerated responses to everything right now. She thought of the phrase "wearing her heart on her sleeve." She thought of "a bundle of nerves" and *heart like a wheel, when you bend it, you can't mend it . . .*

She added the words *Safe Haven—Reese* to her list of calls, then stood up from her chair and stared out again into the afternoon. She tried to think through all the things she needed to say to the group in her kitchen, the questions she wanted to ask, the help she meant to request. But it occurred to her she was beyond thought. She was going on faith.

In the warm, steamy kitchen, with Mrs. Hanlon standing by the stove and Charlie and Tom seated at the table across from her, Lily let herself drift for a few minutes away from the world outside the room, away from their reasons for being there. They talked about the cold, about the Christmas lights being turned off, about Advent. Just beneath the talk, Lily was aware of Roy's absence and Tom's presence, a distant worry and a sense of promise, not unlike Christmas without lights.

It was Charlie who broke the unspoken pact of avoidance. "Look, I hate to do this," he began, "but I don't have very long—"

"What are you doing here anyway?" asked Lily.

"Thanks," said Charlie. "Always good to feel indispensable."

"I didn't mean *that*," she said. "I just didn't know you were coming, that's all."

"Mrs. H. called me," he said.

Mrs. Hanlon nodded. "I thought you could use the company." After a moment's silence she said, "The water's boiling at last. What in the world happened to the kettle?" With that she turned and looked at Lily over her shoulder.

"I burned out the bottom," she said.

"How in the world—" Mrs. Hanlon began, then seemed to think better of it. "You'll have to get a new one. It's no good making tea out of a saucepan."

"I know," said Lily, meekly, sensing a narrow escape. "I saw Roger today," she added.

"How is he?" asked Mrs. Hanlon.

"He's better. I think this one might really take."

Mrs. Hanlon poured the water into the pot and put the pot in the center of the table. "I've made a mess, but there's no way to pour it without making a mess," she said, as if to herself.

"He said—" Lily began and then realized she didn't know how to tell them what Roger had said.

"What?" asked Tom. He had been so quiet Lily felt startled when he spoke.

"It's a long story, but it all begins to make sense, finally," Lily said. "I just don't know how to start."

"But do it anyway," said Charlie.

"Do what?"

"Start."

"Have you got a date?"

"What kind of question is that?" asked Mrs. Hanlon, joining the group at the table.

"She says things like that to me all the time," said Charlie. "Isn't it awful?"

"Tell your story," said Mrs. Hanlon. "He may not have a date, but I do. And I have something to say, too."

Lily nodded, poured out a cup of tea, and began. "Roger was working in the basement the day Fred Barnes died. When he got ready to go, in the evening, he saw John Neville leaving the rectory." She wrapped her hands around the warm cup and breathed in the fragrance of bergamot. "He didn't think much about it—but then later, he says, he began to wonder. Roger asked Neville about that night, and Neville lied, said he'd never been there. He said Roger must have seen someone else."

"But why didn't Roger mention this?" asked Charlie.

"He did, but that's—Let me tell it in order or I won't get it right. Afterwards, after Barnes died, Roger found Neville in the office cleaning out the desk. I guess that didn't strike him as so strange, but then later, when I had moved in, he saw him there again, and once coming out of the rectory."

"Was he visiting you?" asked Charlie.

"Who, Neville?" asked Lily with a chuckle. "Mr. Neville and I have a lot of social chats."

"So that's a 'no'?" asked Charlie.

"I thought he was the one doing the packing," said Mrs. Hanlon, out loud but to herself. Then she looked up at Lily and added, "But he didn't get much packed, did he? Just the desks, some books. He was looking for something."

"Yes, and I think I know what it was," said Lily.

"What?" asked Charlie.

"Letters from Barnes to Roy, or from Roy to Barnes. I think Barnes must have told Talbot that he was in touch with the boy, that he'd written him. And Talbot didn't want anyone else seeing what they'd written."

"Why?" asked Charlie.

"I'm not sure," said Lily. "But I've lost my place again."

"You just said that Roger had seen Neville leaving the rectory," said Mrs. Hanlon.

"Thank you," said Lily. "Do you remember that day Roger asked me if he could talk to me, when you and Cynthia and I were in the hall by my office?"

"I do," said Mrs. Hanlon, nodding her head.

"That's what he wanted to talk about, but then you two had words—"

"Good Lord, to think I could have kept my mouth shut for once and saved him some misery."

"I doubt it," said Lily. "The die was pretty much cast

by then. Somehow it got back to Neville that Roger had tried to see me. Roger said Neville found him one evening in the basement and as good as threatened him; he told him to stay out of parish business and, specifically, not to talk with me—to come directly to him with any questions. Roger thought he was kidding at first; he said Neville sounded like someone in an old western. He was drunk, and he told Neville to fuck off. Excuse the language. The next week Roger ended up lying comatose in a pool of vomit at the bottom of the basement stairs."

"But those things aren't necessarily—" began Charlie.

"Hush," said Mrs. Hanlon. "She's not through yet."

"Before Roger blacked out, he took one of his allergy pills. He gets them from SDT pharmacy."

"Which is?" asked Tom.

"Dan Talbot's store," said Lily. "Or one of them—he owns the whole chain. The main one's over on Tremont, by the cathedral. Usually Roger picks his allergy pills up for himself, but this time Dan Talbot brought them over when he came to see Roger at the church."

"Came to see Roger about what?" asked Tom.

"Sorry. I left that out. Roger called Talbot and told him about John Neville, about his being there at night, about the fight. Roger wanted Dan to go to the police, to tell them about Neville's being over at the rectory the night Barnes died."

Mrs. Hanlon's right hand went to her chest. She sat that way for a few seconds then put her hand on her tea cup and shook her head.

"What?" asked Tom.

"Mr. Talbot supplied Father with his insulin, too. I'd never thought of it until this minute. Often Father would phone in an order and Mr. Talbot would drop it off when he came for a visit. As a favor, you know."

"I thought that might be the deal," said Lily. "And was the Xanax you found on the nightstand from there, too?"

"I'm trying to remember," said Mrs. Hanlon. "I think so—I'm not completely sure. Anyway, I've been told something else about Mr. Talbot."

"What?" Tom asked again. He had been mostly sitting back, watching.

"I caught up with Frances Hennessey after church on Sunday. We had quite a long talk on the way home. She says she's been concerned about Mr. Talbot. First I should say she's devoted to the man, so none of this comes easy to her. But I had asked her how everything was, mentioning the boy, and once she started . . ."

"Yes?" asked Charlie, urging her on.

"All right, all right," said Mrs. Hanlon. "She said that he had started traveling a good deal to Chicago last spring. One of the big companies—K-Mart, one of them, I can't recall—wanted to buy SDT. At first, she or Marjorie, Mr. Talbot's personal secretary, made all the flight reservations, hotel reservations, and whatever else he needed. But then, after a month or so, Mr. Talbot started being strange about the traveling. He began making his own arrangements, coming and going at odd times, saying he was gone when he wasn't. Last month he got two calls from the folks in Chicago when he was supposedly *in* Chicago."

Lily thought of how she had phoned him at the hotel after she had found Roger in the basement, of the runaround she'd gotten from the concierge. She remembered hearing his voice upstairs when she tried to talk with Sally, only an hour after Mrs. Hennessey said he was out of town. "I've found him in town, too—sort of—when he was supposed to be gone."

Mrs. Hanlon nodded and continued. "After a sherry or two, Frances told me he was acting more and more secretive. She said it was like he had this other life, alongside his real life."

The room was silent when Mrs. Hanlon stopped. Finally, Charlie said, "Poor guy." Then he added, "So John Neville and Dan Talbot have been working together to—to what?"

"To find something they didn't want anyone else to find," said Mrs. Hanlon. "And to keep people quiet."

"But what are they hiding?" Tom asked.

"I can think of a couple of possibilities," said Lily.

"But—" She certainly wasn't going to introduce the story about Fred Barnes and Roy right now. She didn't believe it anymore, if she ever had. She'd gotten another idea—she had to wonder what was going on in the Talbot household—but she didn't want to drag Roy into this any more than necessary, at least until she was certain she was right.

"But you're not going to tell us either of them," said Charlie.

"I'm sure one of them isn't right. And the other one is speculation. Let's just say there seem to be two possible scenarios. One is that Talbot and Neville knew something about Fred Barnes, something they're trying to hide."

"And the other is that he knew something about them," said Tom.

"Yes," said Lily. "I think that's the more likely one."

"But we can't entirely dismiss the other possibility," said Charlie, avoiding Lily's eyes.

"We certainly can," said Mrs. Hanlon. "The man had no bad side to him. There would be nothing to hide."

"Still," said Charlie.

"Still nothing," said Mrs. Hanlon. She stood up abruptly, pushed back her chair, and walked to the sink with her cup. "I'm running late. I'll just leave this here, if that's all right." She set the cup down in the sink and turned toward the door.

Lily got up and followed; she said the woman's name and reached out her hand. "We'll get this cleared up," she said.

"I'm not going to listen to that," said Mrs. Hanlon. "I won't hear people speak ill of him." She squeezed Lily's hand and left.

Once again, Lily and Tom sat alone together at the table. Charlie had left just behind Mrs. Hanlon. He'd hoped to catch up and apologize, "though I'm not sure what for," he'd added. "But I can't stand to have her mad at me."

"She really *was* mad," said Lily.

"You can't blame her," said Tom. "She loved the guy."

"What do you mean, 'loved'?"

"You know, *love*. She loved him."

"Romantically?"

"Probably not, not to her mind anyway. Do you know anything about her husband?"

"No," said Lily. "I know she's always rushing to get home to him, to give him dinner. I get the impression he likes to have things on time."

"She's rushing to get home before the day nurse leaves. He's paralyzed from the neck down. I think maybe he has some use of one hand."

Lily stared at him, unbelieving. "But she never said—"

"It was some kind of accident on the job. He worked construction."

"But when?" asked Lily, still stunned.

"A long time ago. Since I've been around, I think. Right after they were married."

"I never even asked," said Lily. "I never knew."

"How would you? You don't start off by asking people, 'So what's the tragedy in *your* life?' "

"No. But sometimes I think we should. Just cut to the chase."

"Not everyone's into sharing, you know. Mrs. Hanlon's made her life. I think Fred Barnes was an important part of it. And I certainly don't mean anything kinky. But it was pretty clear when she first came to me that this was a big deal to her."

"Clear to you, at least," said Lily. "I'm so impressed with how much I've missed here," she added.

At the exact moment Tom reached over and took her hand, Lily heard a tiny boom in the distance, like a cannon firing. Were the two connected, she wondered, idiotically. He leaned forward and put his other hand on her cheek.

"What was that?" she asked.

"In this country, we call it making a move," he said.

"I mean that noise."

"A plane breaking the sound barrier?" he asked, shrugging, still very close to her.

She finally looked at his face, now inches away. "Are you going to kiss me?" she asked.

"I was thinking about it," he said.

"Well do it fast, because something else is about to happen," she said and leaned forward the rest of the way herself.

# chapter 24

Lily stood in the kitchen doorway watching him. He sat at the table, facing her empty chair. She had just hung up the phone in the study.

"There's been an explosion," she said, "on Tremont, in front of St. Michael's. Something about a transformer. I've got to get over there. They've set up some kind of first-aid station in the cathedral, and they need help."

He turned to her then. "I'll come, too. We can take my car."

"There's no point in the car," she called out over her shoulder as she headed toward the hall closet. "You won't be able to get near. They said to walk."

But when they opened the gate and stepped onto the sidewalk a blast of cold air caught them broadside. He grabbed her elbow and steered her toward his parked car. "I've got my official police permit," he said. "We can get near enough."

At the corner of Park and Beacon, Tom flashed his badge to one of the policemen and explained their destination. The cop told them to find a place to park near this end of Park Street and walk the rest of the way, but Tom ignored him and drove slowly toward the flashing lights of fire trucks and emergency vehicles, toward the black mass of smoke rising in the night sky. More than halfway down the block, he pulled over into an empty space at the top of the Common. "We walk from here," he said. "Bundle up."

When they reached Tremont, Lily's eyes began to tear from the smoke and fumes. "My God," she said, when she saw the corner of Temple. "It looks like a war zone."

Five fire trucks formed a kind of ring around the intersection, while beyond them waited police cars, EMT vans, and hundreds of onlookers. In the exact middle of the ring, orange flames poured out of a hole in the street, and above that hung the smoke. Through the blur, Lily could see the remains of two vehicles—a small sedan and, a few yards away, a panel van on its side, the rear end blown off. Surrounding the van was a crazy haphazard design of pots, dirt, plants, poinsettias, paper whites. A massed bouquet of bright red tulips lay by itself in the street on the driver's side of the sedan.

Smoke also poured from a corner of the building next to the SDT Discount Services store. Firemen sprayed foam into a hole at the base of the concrete wall. From Temple Street down, all the storefronts were dark, except for pale green emergency lights.

"I've got to go," Lily yelled, pointing across Tremont.

"I'll come with you," he said. "It'll be easier." They walked up Tremont away from the flames. Across from Bromfield, Tom found someone he knew, a plainclothes officer leaning against his car. They spoke briefly; when Tom returned, he nodded to her and they headed across Tremont toward the cathedral.

"What did he say?" she called to him. As they walked back toward the fire, the noise grew louder.

"You were right. A transformer blew, or at least one, maybe two. One of them's just under a manhole in the middle of the street. They think there was a methane leak down there, too. That's what caused the big boom, and all the flames. And that's what happened to the people."

"What people?" she asked, almost yelling.

"There was a family in one car and two young guys in the other—a driver and a delivery boy."

Lily saw the sedan—its front end charred and crushed—and the ripped end of the van.

"Are they okay?" she asked.

"Nobody was killed. The cop said he thinks they'll be okay. No one knows for sure."

"Was it because of all the lights and heaters?"

"More or less. Probably an overloaded transformer—too much coming in too fast. It could be that the first explosion caused a major electrical fire under the building. They can't go down to look yet." Tom glanced toward the cathedral. "I guess a lot of the witnesses are in there, in the church."

Lily, too, glanced up at the doors. "I know," she said. "They want us there to talk with them, and to listen."

"You don't have to do this right now, you know," he said.

She hesitated. "I'll check it out," she answered. "I'll see what they need. I said I'd come."

"What?" he asked, leaning toward her.

"Nothing," she yelled. "I said I'd do it."

They stood under the portico at the top of the cathedral stairs. She could see the van and the sedan farther down the street, the flames, lower now, still pouring from the hole.

"I'll wait around here until you're finished," he said.

"No," said Lily, after a pause. "Go on back to the rectory. I'll call you when I'm done. Or I'll walk."

"What's with this *walk* business?" he asked. "It's sub-Arctic temperatures and the streets are exploding."

She fished in the pocket of her parka for her keys, removed the key to the rectory, and handed it to him. "Here," she said, finally, "take this. I'll get home."

"Just call, would you?" he asked, exasperated.

"No," she said. "Probably not. But I'll be fine. I've done this a long time."

"What?"

"Stayed alive on my own. I think I've got it down."

St. Michael's Cathedral had been turned into a kind of haven for those who had seen the explosion or who knew someone who had been hurt. In the far corner, in front of the side chapel, stood a small makeshift medical station. A woman with an inhaler was lying down on a cot in the center aisle.

The pews near the front of the church were filled with people sitting, kneeling, talking. To Lily's right, in a corner near the door, Bishop Spencer stood listening to a small group, a few of whom seemed to be speaking at once, maybe a family. She thought she recognized the man who ran the deli across from the cathedral bookstore. The young receptionist from the diocesan offices sat on the steps near the altar with a woman holding an infant. The baby screamed, the woman talked, and the receptionist looked baffled. In the far corner, a group was setting up two vast urns of coffee. As she watched, Lily saw Cynthia in her red parka, carrying a thick orange extension cord searching the baseboards for an outlet. Lily started toward her, immediately comforted by the presence of anyone who knew about the other, more private tragedy being played out in their lives.

When Lily reached the corner, Cynthia had her back to the room. As she turned and saw Lily, her face fell; she remained motionless, the cord held out in her right hand like a kind of offering. Finally, she said, "I need to talk to you."

"I need to talk to you, too, but I'm not sure this is the time."

"No," said Cynthia, lowering her hand, "probably not. But it has to be soon. I don't like what's happening."

"What do you mean?" asked Lily.

"Dan told us, last night, about Fred—about what he claims happened between Fred and Roy."

"You hadn't known before?"

"Nothing specific. There were hints about improper behavior. But I thought it was all about getting Fred out of the parish."

"Why, though?" asked Lily.

"Because of the homosexual issues. You know, ordination and the rest. Dan and John can't stand not to have complete control. They couldn't brook Fred's disagreeing with them—about anything."

A tall, thin gray-haired woman at the coffee station called out Cynthia's name impatiently. "Haven't you found the plug yet?" she asked.

"I need to do this," said Cynthia, brandishing the extension cord. The room was filled not so much with specific noises as with a muted commotion of fear and bewilderment. Cynthia glanced over her shoulder at the tall woman behind her, involved in telling someone else what to do, then continued. "But I want to say—I know this is no time for confession—but something's been on my mind for a while now. Can I just mention it to you?"

"Yes," said Lily.

"One day, a while ago, you and I and—what's her name?—Mrs. Hanlon were talking in the hall. Do you remember?"

"Yes."

"It's when John and I were on the outs, and for some reason, to get him to like me again, I told him about what you'd asked me, about Fred's belongings. And he just—I can't remember exactly what he said, but he had this extreme response, much too big. I knew immediately that I shouldn't have told him. I've felt bad about it since."

"Cynthia, do you by any chance remember Roger Frye coming through while we were there? Do you remember his asking to speak with me?"

Cynthia nodded.

"Did you say anything, did you tell John about that, too?"

"Yes," she said, after a moment. "Yes. I did."

Lily stared across the cathedral at Bishop Spencer, sitting with four young children, listening to what appeared to be—from the exploding sounds and gestures they made—their own version of the accident. She thought briefly about how small things sometimes make big differences, and how you so seldom know which small thing you do or say is going to make the difference—and even whether the difference will be good or bad.

"Are you all right?" Cynthia asked her.

"Yeah, yes. I'm okay. I'm just going to see what can be done here."

"Cynthia," screamed the woman at the table. "What in the name of God are you doing?"

Instinctively, Lily leaned down and kissed Cynthia Babcock on the cheek, surprising them both, leaving the older woman red-faced and flustered.

Two hours later, Lily stood again on the top step outside the portico. She had spent most of her time inside talking with a young couple from Framingham who had been out doing Christmas shopping after work, who had seen the explosion and heard the screams. The young man was quiet and attentive; the young woman was six months pregnant. She kept asking if Lily thought she would lose the baby. Or would seeing all that hurt the baby? Would the baby remember it? Would it be an unhappy child?

Lily had also helped Spencer with the children who, as it turned out, had been on an after-school program adventure to see the lights on the Common. Slowly, their parents arrived, terrified, harried, grateful. As she watched the Bishop talk with the mothers and fathers, Lily felt some of her old admiration for him. He remained a man good at his job—not perfect, but good.

The scene on the street outside had changed dramatically. Lily was struck, first, by the emptiness. The van and the sedan had been towed away, the hole covered with sheets of metal. Tremont was cordoned off from Park down to West Street. A single police car lingered on the Common side of Tremont, facing up the hill, motor running; a fire truck sat parked further on. Beyond the stillness she could hear the static and bark of police radios, and car horns honking erratically a few blocks away.

No one seemed to notice her as she walked down the steps and started off along the empty side of the street. Just in case, she kept her parka open, collar visible, so she would be recognizable as part of the cathedral crew. She was drawn to the spot of the explosion; she needed to witness the source of all this damage.

At Temple Place she paused across from Talbot's building. The small side entrance was lit eerily by green emergency lights. As she tipped her head to look toward the top, toward Dan Talbot's office, something small and square came sailing down from above. She let out a muted cry as it smashed in the gutter on Tremont. Lily looked up again, but the front of the building was dark; there were no signs of occupancy.

From where she stood, she could see splintered wooden fragments among pieces of broken glass. As she began to move closer, a second object sailed out into the air and smashed a few yards away. She ducked, covered her head with her hands, and ran back. Suddenly she needed to sit down, but there was no place to sit.

This time she let minutes go by before walking over to the gutter. Scattered in the street were shards of two black enamel boxes, surrounded by small, square notepads with black printing on each one. Lily bent over to look more closely. They were prescription pads, with a doctor's name at the top. She saw at least two different names, which meant there were at least two different sets of pads.

She returned to the corner and stood, hands on her hips, staring at the shattered boxes, the small square pads, the glass shards. Then she walked to the side door of Talbot's building and pulled it open. The back section appeared to have escaped all damage from the explosions. The foyer stood empty. Knowing better than to trust the elevator, she found the stairs and started up the ten flights to the top floor. She didn't rush, but she climbed steadily, knowing it would take a measured amount of energy to get there in time. At the seventh-floor landing she paused, sat on a step,

and put her head down between her knees. She felt breathless and dizzy. As soon as she could stand, she started again
in the dim green light.

At the tenth floor, she stopped with her hand on the
door knob. She noticed her heartbeat—fast and loud—and
felt a moment of pure fear. Whatever waited in there, in
Dan's office, she asked God to be with her. She opened
the door and walked into the reception room. There were
no lights inside. For a second she was struck by the beauty
of the scene before her, Boston and the river at night, a
sky full of frozen stars. Then she felt the wind, a cold blast
through the halls.

When she reached his office, Dan Talbot stood facing
the skyline, his back to her. He wore a white shirt, with a
black handkerchief tied around his right forearm. In front
of him, a narrow panel of glass was gone. Cold air poured
in through the emptiness.

Slowly, deliberately, he turned his head to look at her,
then turned back to the window. "I thought you might show
up," he said. His words were as precise as his movements.
He was taking great pains to appear sober, but even with
the outside air filling the room, Lily could smell whiskey.
Whether it came from Talbot or from a bottle nearby, she
couldn't tell. "I want you to hear my confession."

"I'll hear your confession, but we have to go into the
next room. I'm freezing," said Lily, hoping to get him away,
from the shattered window.

"That's fine, but I'm going to jump anyway, so it won't
much matter," he said.

"Let's do one thing at a time," she said. "Come into the
next room with me, I'll hear your confession, and then
we'll talk about what's next."

"On second thought," he said, "let's stay here."

"Fine," said Lily, sitting in the beige armchair, the same
one she had sat in the first day she visited.

"No, let's kneel," said Dan. "I want you to kneel with
me."

He walked toward her, shoved the matching armchair

next to hers, then knelt in front of it, elbows on the cushion. "You do this, too," he ordered.

Lily hesitated. He reached up, grabbed her forearm and jerked her out of the chair. She half fell, half knelt on the floor. Then he pulled her arm toward him, to turn her so she was facing the chair. But she lost her balance and fell into him momentarily. When he caught her, the force of his grip was painful. He shoved her back against her own chair. The whiskey smell was overpowering.

She hadn't thought again about being afraid until she felt his hand on her arm. He was stronger than she'd imagined. He was drunk. He planned to kill himself. And he hated her. She leaned forward and put her elbows on the chair seat.

"There," he said. "Say your part."

She struggled to recall the opening words of the Rite of Reconciliation, but all she could remember was the Penitential Order that had saved her last night.

"Blessed be God: Father, Son, and Holy Spirit," she began.

"And blessed be his kingdom, now and for ever. Amen," Dan responded.

"Bless the Lord who forgiveth all our sins," she said.

"His mercy endureth forever."

Then she recited the passage from Matthew and began the prayer of confession. "Most merciful God," she said.

"No, the old one," said Dan. "Almighty and most merciful Father," he began, "we have erred and strayed from thy ways like lost sheep . . ."

Lily joined in, ". . . we have followed too much the devices and desires of our own hearts, we have offended against thy holy laws . . ."

Here his voice trailed off, and she found herself praying alone. ". . . we have left undone those things which we ought to have done, and we have done those things which we ought not to have done . . . Dan?" she said, after a moment.

"I'll just tell you. It'll be faster."

"Fine."

There was silence, in which Lily noticed she was no longer so afraid. The words of the prayer had calmed her.

"I have followed too much the devices and desires of my own heart," he repeated.

"Can you be more specific?" she asked.

"Are you making fun of me?"

"No."

Lily waited.

"I lied," he said. There was a long silence. "I can't tell you everything."

"That's fine. Tell me what you can."

"A lot of people called Fred 'Father.' I couldn't do that."

Lily was shivering. But she listened.

"I wish I knew exactly what I'd done," he said. "That would be easier."

"What do you think you did?" she asked.

"I thought I was—warning them, Fred and Roger. I thought if Fred seemed incompetent, like he couldn't take care of himself, they'd have to get rid of him." Dan shifted and put his face in his hands. "I don't think I hurt Roy, though. I don't think that was me. Not this time."

Lily didn't ask what he meant. She had stopped shivering and no longer noticed the cold. She watched him, and waited.

"I miss the part, 'and there is no health in us,' " he said.

Her face was inches from his. She was getting used to the smell.

"Why?" she asked.

"Because it's true," he said.

"No," she said. "I don't think so. I think God is always in us. There's always goodness somewhere in us."

He raised his head. "I want you to forgive me," he said.

"Have you completed your confession?" she asked.

"Look at me," he said. "I don't want God to forgive me. I want you to forgive me."

"I can't," she said.

"Why not?" he asked.

"I'm not—" she began. "A person can't do that for you."

"You can," he said.

"I can't," she repeated. Her voice was loud. She pulled back from the chair.

She stopped when she saw his eyes. She had scorned him; she had scorned the parish. She had judged them all because of who they were. And now she hated him because of what he'd done. But if what she'd just said were true, then God was in her, too. God would work through her, if only she would get out of the way.

Lily leaned toward him and raised her hands. He flinched and lurched backward.

"It's all right," she said.

She laid her palms on the crown of his head. "Lord Jesus Christ," she prayed, "Good Shepherd of the sheep, you gather the lambs in your arms and carry them in your bosom: We commend to your loving care this child Dan. Relieve his pain, guard him from all danger, restore to him your gifts of gladness and strength, and raise him up to a life of service to you. Hear us, we pray, for your dear Name's sake. Amen."

"Amen," he said, never moving.

They stayed like that, her hands on him, for some time. The air around felt warmer. With one part of her mind, she heard a set of noises, not too far away, nearby, coming closer.

The room was light. Someone was outside the room. Someone was calling.

The air and light poured through her. She opened her eyes, took her hands from his head, and returned his gaze.

"Mr. Talbot!" a man's voice called out in the darkness. "Anyone up here?"

For a moment Dan stayed on his knees beside her. Then he stood, holding his arm, and Lily saw the blackness on the handkerchief was blood that had spread down his sleeve.

Lily stood, too, and turned to the young Japanese man she had seen yesterday in the lobby. He remained in the doorway, frozen, staring at the two of them.

"They radioed me," he finally said. "The police thought someone was up here trashing the building, throwing things down."

"I'm afraid Mr. Talbot's cut himself on some glass," said Lily. "We'd better call an ambulance."

But the young man didn't move.

"Mr. San," said Dan, gently. "You had better call an ambulance for me." Then he sat down heavily in the leather chair.

After getting Dan into an ambulance, Lily walked home across the Common for the third time that day. Dan hadn't wanted her to come with him, and she felt relieved. She wasn't tired; in fact she felt calm and filled with energy. But she was glad to be alone.

At the gate to the church courtyard she remembered she had given Tom the rectory key. She could ring the bell, but she didn't want to see anyone right then. So she went to the side door of the church building, unlocked the double doors, and walked into her office.

She sat down in the desk chair, switched on the light, and mindlessly read through a list of calls she needed to return. At the bottom she saw the words "Safe Haven—Reese." She knew the number by heart.

The voice on the other end sounded like the person she had spoken to the first time she called, but she couldn't be sure.

"Someone left me a message to call him there," said Lily. "A young man named Reese. He said to leave the number where he could call me back."

"Hold on," said the voice. It had to be the same person. There were not two people on the planet so noncommittal. "Give me the number," the person said.

"Is he going to call me?"

"Collect."

"Fine," Lily said and told him—she thought it was a him—her number there at the office.

Fifteen minutes later, the phone rang.

"So, we meet at last," she said.

There was silence on the other end. "Not exactly," said the boy in his soft drawl.

"Good point," said Lily. She had no idea how to tell him about his friend.

"How's Roy?" he asked.

"He had a bad accident," said Lily.

"An overdose?"

"In part. He passed out in this cold place—" she began.

"Is he alive?"

"Yes. But he's—we don't know how he's going to be. I'm sorry."

"I didn't really know him that well," he said. "We hung out together some, and we stayed in the same places a couple of times. You don't get to know people that well up here, or I don't."

"Where are you from?"

"Alabama."

"Why don't you go home?"

"I don't want to," he said. "What did you want to know?"

"I wondered how much you knew about Roy, what he was like, what had happened to make him leave home. But I guess you answered my questions already. You didn't really know him."

"Yeah," he said. "We didn't talk that much."

He paused. She felt despair.

"I saw his dad once though," he offered.

"You saw his father, there, in Chicago?" she asked.

"Yeah. Well, I saw a picture of him first," he said. "Then I saw *him.*"

"Oh," said Lily. "Did Roy have a picture of him?"

"Yeah. One day Fowler—he was one of the older guys. He hustled for a while—now he mostly handles the newcomers, the young girls. I think he actually owned the place we crashed. He went into Roy's wallet to take some money. Roy was passed out from the night before. Fowler said he owed him rent."

He paused again. It came to her that he was smoking while they talked. The pauses were drags on his cigarette.

"He found a picture of Roy's parents in there. Fowler thought it was funny. I think we all did. You know, we all left home because—you know. And here's Roy with this picture of his folks." Another pause. "It turned out, after he looked real close at the picture, that Fowler recognized the guy."

"Wait. Fowler knew Dan Talbot? He knew Roy's father personally?"

He laughed. "He didn't know him too personally, but some of the girls definitely did," he said. "He was a john."

"I don't understand," she said.

"A lot of us hustled. I don't do it anymore. I got a job. But Fowler's been out on the street for a long time—longer than most."

"And he recognized Dan Talbot? He knew him from the street?"

"Yeah. Talbot goes with the girls—the real young ones, Fowler's group. There's one in particular I guess. Fowler told me he's run up quite a tab."

"Did Fowler tell Roy?"

"Oh, hell yeah. Everybody thought it was a big joke, you know. I don't think Roy believed him at first, but Clark, this other kid, told me that Fowler showed the picture around later, on the street, without saying who it was. You know, in front of Roy. A few people knew him, at least two of the girls knew him. They said he'd picked them up, that they'd gone with him. Described him, too."

"So Roy believed them then?"

"Yeah. He believed them. They were telling the truth."

"And later you saw Talbot—Roy's father?"

"A couple of weeks after that. Fowler showed him to me one night. This guy drove up in a Ford, a rented car— you can tell by the plates. I left before he picked anybody up—it freaked me out a little, knowing who the guy was."

"Did Roy see him?" she asked.

"I don't know."

Lily thanked him. She took an address so she could send him money. She told him to keep her number there, in case he ever wanted any help. But, she added, he'd have to get clean.

# chapter 25

Mrs. Hanlon had arrived with a new kettle and was now making tea for the four of them. Tom and Charlie had tried to ask Lily questions, but Mrs. Hanlon wouldn't have it—not until the tea was ready and Lily had time to absorb the comfort of their company.

Only forty-eight hours earlier Lily had sat at this table with Tom. They had kissed, and the phone had rung, and all hell had broken loose; she considered how apt that phrase was, with the flames shooting from the hole in the street and the red tulips lying by the burned-out sedan. Yesterday St. Michael's Cathedral had held a healing service for all those affected by the explosion. Lily had gone and recognized many of the people there—the young pregnant woman and her husband, the crowd of children, the owner of the deli, witnesses, and family members. She felt at one with them, as if they had all arrived on the same bleak ship, refugees from an unjust homeland.

Mrs. Hanlon put the teapot on the table and sat in the chair next to Lily. She poured, passed the sandwiches, then turned to Lily and said, "All right. Tell it in your own time, however you want. We'll just listen."

"Okay," said Lily. "I can tell you what I told the police. Tom was there so he's heard most of it. And I can tell you the parts I've filled in on my own—guesswork, mostly. But there are some questions I can't answer, because of how I know, and because it's just too private."

"That's fair," said Charlie.

"All right," Lily said, then found she couldn't start. "Also, nothing I say can go beyond this room." The other three nodded. Finally Lily said, "Why don't you ask me something?"

"What happened to Father Barnes?" asked Mrs. Hanlon.

"We were pretty close to the truth the other night. Dan Talbot and John Neville had been warring with Fred Barnes over issues in the church. Father Barnes had begun to believe the church should ordain homosexual priests, and John and Dan were very strongly opposed—very strongly."

"So they killed him?" asked Mrs. Hanlon, eyes wide, hands clasped tightly together on the table.

"No. That was just the background. The real story has to do with Roy Talbot and his father. When Roy was away, he found out something about his father, something damaging that the boy told Fred Barnes, something Barnes then took back to Talbot. I think—I imagine Barnes did that because he thought he could help Dan, that he could help him face the truth about who he really was, and bring the Talbot family together."

"What had happened there to begin with?" asked Charlie. "Why had the boy left?"

"I'm not sure about all of it," said Lily. "And again, some of this is really private. I know that Roy Talbot is gay. He told his family, and his father couldn't handle it. Then Roy went to Fred Barnes, but I don't think Barnes did a much better job. So, eventually, Roy left. There's more to it than that, a lot I don't know."

"So Fred Barnes tried to use the information about

Dan to bring the Talbots together?" asked Charlie. "I don't get it."

"He knew he'd failed Roy the first time around," said Lily. "He didn't want to do that again. Roy came to him with a second problem—his father's problem. I think Barnes needed to help, to try to make things right. Maybe he believed that having the truth out in the open would heal them all."

"But it didn't," said Mrs. Hanlon.

"I'm not sure it ever got out in the open," said Tom. "Wasn't that the point?"

"Yes," said Lily. "When Dan Talbot knew that Barnes might expose him, that his secret might be told, even just to his own family, he couldn't handle that either. Dan had spent years constructing a life for himself, and almost all of it was a lie. He'd made up a background and an identity. He had to be thought of as an upstanding man, a wealthy, prominent member of the church. It must have felt like the whole thing was crumbling at once."

They were all silent for a moment, then Charlie asked, "So he killed Barnes to protect himself."

"He said he didn't intend to kill him," said Lily.

"What in the world is that supposed to mean?" asked Mrs. Hanlon.

"I'm not sure," said Lily. "That's something he'll work out with his lawyers, I imagine."

"But what did he do? How did he do it?" asked Charlie.

"The day Fred Barnes died, he had spoken with Talbot, told him he was sick, and Talbot offered to get him some antibiotics. Barnes had ordered some insulin as well, and Talbot offered to bring it all at the same time."

"Aren't antibiotics prescription medicine?" asked Tom. "I wondered when I heard you say that yesterday."

"I don't know how he did it, but I think Talbot had developed a system in which he wrote prescriptions under a doctor's name—or a couple of doctors' names. Then he could give people drugs—himself included—because he could fill the orders at night, after the pharmacy closed."

"So Talbot was bringing Barnes antibiotics and insulin," said Tom.

"Yes. Maybe the whole idea came to him when he was packing it all up, but I'm just guessing. Anyway, he packed two vials of triple-strength insulin, and when he got here, he switched the vials of insulin in the kit Fred always kept there in the meat drawer. He gave him three times the dosage of both."

"But what if someone had checked the insulin vials afterward—the ones Talbot put in the drawer?" asked Charlie.

"Dan came back the next day, after you'd found Father Barnes," Lily continued, looking at Mrs. Hanlon. "After he learned he'd died. He says he was in shock. He switched the vials again. He also exchanged the antibiotics for tranquilizers. Do you remember," she asked Mrs. Hanlon, "how you found one bottle the first time, and a different one the second time?"

The other woman nodded.

"What was that all about—the Xanax and the rest?" asked Tom.

"Dan knew Barnes really well. He knew he'd notice details—if the vials looked different, if they weren't exactly the same as when he used them last. He gave him a heavy dose of Xanax instead of Ceclor, the antibiotic Barnes was supposed to take. He assumed the Xanax would make Barnes less aware, and less able to help himself. Dan also made sure they had some sherry together."

"So that's where the glasses came from," said Mrs. Hanlon.

"Yes," said Lily. "He even stuck around to wash up, because Barnes was already feeling dizzy. Then when Dan switched the vials the next day, he also switched the pill bottles, to make it look like Barnes had been taking tranquilizers on his own. That way, if there were any questions and they found any Xanax in Barnes's blood, there'd be an explanation."

"Doesn't really sound like the actions of a man in shock, does it?" asked Charlie. "Did John Neville help?"

"In a way," said Lily. "But it's not clear how much Neville actually knew. He disagreed violently with Barnes on the issue of gay ordination and the blessing of gay marriages. By the end, he just wanted to get rid of him. I don't think he knew Talbot killed Fred Barnes, or I don't think he let himself know."

"But I thought Roger Frye saw Neville leaving the rectory that night, not Talbot," said Charlie.

"I think Neville went on his own, to see Barnes, not even knowing what Dan was planning," said Lily. "Talbot had suddenly backed off from the fight over church politics, and he'd told Neville to do the same. But Talbot wouldn't tell him why. And Neville couldn't let go. He may even have felt guilty later, as if their talk—it was probably more than a talk—had brought on Barnes's heart attack."

"What about Stanley Leonard?" asked Charlie. "Where does he fit in?"

"Stanley really loves Roy," said Lily. "He didn't like the news about his being gay, but he stayed in touch with him throughout, sent him money, tried to get him to come home."

"That's why we found the money there in the side chapel," said Mrs. Hanlon.

"Yes," said Lily. "They had elaborate arrangements— just what you'd expect from Stanley, a kind of liturgy of meetings and notes."

"Is he all right for sure now—the boy?" asked Mrs. Hanlon.

"I think so," said Lily. "He woke up and started breathing on his own Tuesday night, the night of the explosion." She paused, then went on. "He's lost one of his fingers, from frostbite—the little finger on the right hand. But he goes home tomorrow." Lily said a small prayer of thanks, a spiritual knocking-on-wood.

"Isn't he a musician?" asked Charlie.

Lily nodded.

"Maybe he can still play," said Tom, after a short silence.

"Maybe," said Lily.

"I take it Talbot was responsible for Roger Frye's accident, too," said Charlie.

"Yes," said Lily. "You know Frye saw Neville going through the church offices, and in and out of the rectory, even after I arrived."

"You already told us that," said Mrs. Hanlon. "After your visit with Roger. Was Neville after the letters?"

"I'm not sure," said Lily. "My guess is that by this time Talbot had Neville convinced that Barnes—" She stopped and looked at Mrs. Hanlon. "I haven't mentioned this part yet. But Talbot created a story to cover everything—Roy's disappearance, Fred Barnes's defection, Sally's drinking. He told Neville, and later told the others, that Fred Barnes had—" She couldn't say it.

"I know," said Mrs. Hanlon. "Or I guessed. Mr. Talbot said Father had done something horrible to the boy. But I always knew it wasn't so."

"You were right, of course," said Charlie.

"But Neville believed him," said Lily. "So now there was a perfect reason to remove Barnes and also to keep everything very quiet. Talbot told Neville they had to be sure there was no evidence to suggest that this had happened—no notes, no phone numbers, no letters between Roy and Barnes. For Roy's sake. And for the parish. In the end, I don't think Neville found much—but Talbot did."

"What do you mean?" asked Charlie.

"When Talbot asked me over to his house to talk—to tell me his version of what had happened—he wasn't there when I arrived. And it took him a long time to get there. I think he went to the rectory and searched my office himself. He found a letter from Barnes to Roy that I'd stuck in a book by my desk."

"Why did he want the letters so badly?" Charlie asked.

"At that point, he wanted to be sure I didn't know too much, to be sure I'd believe his story."

"Okay," said Charlie. "Where were we? Frye saw Neville coming and going and wanted to know why. Neville told Talbot. Talbot brought Roger Frye his allergy pills, and—?"

"Talbot filled a capsule with Antabuse," said Lily. "He assumed Roger would take it when he was drinking. Because that's when his allergies bothered him, of course."

"I suppose he didn't mean to hurt Roger either," said Mrs. Hanlon.

"It's hard to know what he meant," said Lily. "I don't think he knows."

There was a moment of silence around the table.

"Dan Talbot created his own world," said Charlie. "But the world had problems. So he created a story that would explain all the problems—his son's problems, his wife's problems, his priest's change of heart—he found a way to blame it all on someone else."

"And to persuade John Neville to help him with the cover-up afterwards," said Lily. "And to discredit Fred Barnes just in case he had told anyone Dan's secret. And to keep the vestry quiet."

"Father would never have harmed him," said Mrs. Hanlon, suddenly, through tears. "He would never have told anyone. He wasn't that kind of man."

Lily got Mrs. Hanlon a paper napkin from the red plastic holder to the right of the sink, then stood with her hand on Mrs. Hanlon's shoulder.

Mrs. Hanlon blew her nose and asked, "It was all for nothing, wasn't it? Who's the better for any of it?"

Tom stirred in his chair. He took a breath, as if to speak, then paused.

"What?" asked Lily.

"Maybe we can't really know that yet," he said. "Maybe it's too soon to tell."

Lily glanced down and saw Mrs. Hanlon nod.

"My man," said Charlie and slapped Tom on the back.

The following morning, Lily sat in the same room where she had watched Sally Talbot fall asleep by the fire, where

Dan had told her his lies about Fred Barnes, where the vestry had met. There was no fire in the fireplace, but the room felt warmer and lighter. Of course, the temperature outside had climbed back into the thirties and sunlight streamed through the French windows.

Sally sat across from her. The transformation that had begun the night of the vestry meeting continued. She wore no makeup; her hair was pulled back from her face. She had on jeans and a black turtleneck. She had deep circles under her eyes, but she looked awake and alert.

They had gone back through the story, step by step, with Sally filling in the few details she knew. Roy had told them he was gay. At that point, Dan had been drinking for a long time, and doing some kind of diet pills, she thought, and sleeping pills. At one point he'd threatened to kill Roy. That was what made Roy leave the first time. But then he came back. There'd been more fights. During the last one Sally saw, Dan had grabbed Roy and thrown him against the wall, and Roy had left for good. And Sally had, in her own words, taken a pill and gone to bed.

After she finished the story, Sally sat with her elbows on her knees and her head in her hands. "Of course," she said at last. "Roy could just as easily have died. And it would have been my fault."

"It would have been a lot of people's fault," said Lily. "But he didn't."

"Thanks to you," said Sally. She raised her head and sat back.

"And you and Florence and Stanley and the doctors and Serena—I think that's her name—you know, the woman at the house where we found Roy. And the girl, his friend in East Cambridge."

"Maybe we can find her," said Sally. "Roy wants to find her."

"That would be good," said Lily. "She could use some help. How long is he going to stay in detox?"

"Two more weeks."

"And Dan?"

"He's still in the hospital. They're having trouble stabilizing him, or so they say. He has a lot of friends—doctors, lawyers, bishops. I imagine they'll keep him there as long as he wants to stay."

"When's the trial?"

"I don't know," said Sally. "Dan doesn't want me to testify, so I can't. It's just as well. I wouldn't want to. I don't trust myself right now. I'm afraid I'd try to get some kind of revenge."

"How are you?" asked Lily.

"I'm all right. In fact, I think I'm better than I've been in a long time. I've quit drinking."

"Have you gotten any help?"

"I'm talking to you, aren't I?"

"Yes, but you can't do this on your own. And I—" Lily started and then stopped herself. "Just think about getting more help, for yourself, okay?"

"Okay," said Sally.

She wouldn't do it now, thought Lily; she clearly didn't think she needed help. But maybe later Sally would change her mind—when she saw she had no choice.

After a few more minutes, they walked together to the front door. "Where's Florence?" asked Lily.

"She's gone," said Sally. She took Lily's parka out of the closet and handed it to her. "I couldn't pay her. Actually, she hadn't been paid for a while, but I didn't know that. We're broke. More than broke. Dan's been stealing from the company, and from me."

Lily stopped with one arm in her parka. "God. What will you do?"

"The house is in my name. I'm selling it," said Sally.

Lily finished getting her jacket on and glanced at Sally, who stood staring into the living room.

"I grew up here," said Sally. "But somehow I'd never been alone in this house before, not for any amount of time. The past few days—"

"What?" asked Lily.

"I tried to pray. I couldn't. But then afterward, the thought came to me that this might be better. Not the loss, not the suffering. But it might be better to leave the house, to start again—at least for Roy and me. It was as if my prayer had been answered, even though I couldn't pray. Do you now what I mean?"

"Yes," said Lily. "I do."

# chapter 26

one week later, mid-December, just past the mid-point of Advent, Lily sat with her back against a gray boulder, barnacled and damp. The extreme cold had broken last week.

She hunched down out of the wind, facing the Pamet harbor and the golden marsh. Charlie had suggested coming to the outer Cape, to a beach he knew from childhood, where the Pamet River met the bay. He had borrowed the old Ford station wagon from the monastery and brought Syro, the brothers' one-eyed mutt. The two of them were off down the beach now, walking all the way to the other end of Corn Hill.

Only two boats remained anchored in the harbor this late in the season. As the tide went out, the river flowed toward the bay; gulls wheeled and sounded up from the sandbars on either side of the channel. At midday the sun was high and white in the blue sky. Behind and to her left, the Cape swung out toward the Atlantic. Provincetown gleamed in the clear air. Across the bay lay Boston, a shadow on the water.

Shielded from the wind, Lily had begun to feel warm,

even dozy. She hoped Corn Hill was a long, long beach, and that Charlie and Syro would be gone a long, long time. She wanted to stay here, hidden. The sun warmed her face, and she felt herself drifting into a kind of twilight nap, awake and asleep at once.

She and Charlie had had a tiff in the car on the way down. Lily had brought up the moment when they were sitting at the kitchen table and Tom had alluded to some pattern, some plan which might emerge from this mire of disaster.

"You don't really believe that now, do you?" she asked. "After everything that's happened, after what's happened to Roy?"

He had looked at her sideways and shaken his head. "You are the weirdest mix of mature, truly spiritual insights and totally babyish superstitions."

"What's that supposed to mean?" she had asked.

"You think that if you're a good girl, then God's supposed to be a good boy? You think when I say *plan* I mean like our plan for driving down here, or your plan for saving the parish, or Dan's plan for Roy's life? What did God say to Job, Lily?"

"Are we playing Jesuit Jeopardy?"

"No. I just want you to tell me what God said to Job."

"A lot of things, as usual," she said.

"Come on," said Charlie.

Lily's voice was hard, almost mocking, as she recited the passage.

" 'Have you entered into the springs of the sea?' " she began. " 'Or walked in the recesses of the deep? Have the gates of death been revealed to you, or have you seen the gates of deep darkness?' " She stopped there, then asked, "And your point is?"

"Don't assume God's plans are always going to meet with your approval. There's a different perspective at work."

"Gee thanks, Charlie. I knew I could depend on you to coddle me."

Hearing her tone of voice again, now, echoing in her mind, she blushed. She would apologize to him when he came back. She needed to talk. She needed to tell him everything.

She woke up with Syro licking her face, his nose gritty with sand and wet with salt water.

"Syro, Syro," called Charlie.

"It's okay," shouted Lily, waving to him, pushing the dog away.

She got up and walked toward Charlie while Syro ran back down the beach. Halfway there, the dog stopped at a mound in the sand and began to uncover what turned out to be a dead skate. Lily and Charlie both headed toward him, waving their arms and screaming, "No, Syro, no." He was notorious for eating garbage and throwing up hours later, in the kitchen, in the refectory, once in the side chapel.

They reached him simultaneously. Lily grabbed the dog by the collar and Charlie grabbed the skate by the tip of its tail. Holding it at arm's length, he ran to the water and threw it as far as he could, which turned out to be not very far at all. It was limp and heavy and broke into pieces midair. Syro immediately pulled out from Lily's grasp and hurtled toward the water. He dove into the freezing bay, paddling with all his strength toward the pieces of dead skate floating on the surface. Charlie sat down on the sand.

"Isn't the beach fun?" he asked sarcastically, gasping for breath.

"Yes and the best is yet to come," said Lily. "We can watch him throw up all the way home."

She sat down next to Charlie and put her arm around his shoulder.

"You're wet," he said, pulling away.

"I'm wet, and I'm sorry. I didn't mean to be so nasty on the way down. I really appreciate your doing this, coming with me, staying with me at the rectory for the past few days. I know you've got a life, and—" She stopped, not sure where to go next.

"Apology accepted," said Charlie, putting his arm around her now. "Let's go eat before the dog starts vomiting."

But Syro had forgotten the skate and was standing in

the shallow water watching them. Charlie called him and he ran up, stood next to them, and shook.

They had eaten the picnic lunch Charlie had brought from the monastery—homemade bread, clementines, cheddar, thin slices of ham, homemade chutney, fresh chocolate chip cookies—and were both leaning against two huge, warm rocks in the niche Lily had discovered earlier. Charlie was crossways, facing the sun, his legs across Lily's knees.

"I think it would be best for you to get it all out," Charlie was saying.

"And it would be best for you to know everything so you wouldn't have to die from curiosity."

"Like the cat," said Charlie.

"Yes. Like the cat," she said. "Actually, a very strange thing has happened—well, not very strange, relative to everything else, but strange. And it works in your favor."

"What's that?"

"I got a letter from Frieda Klass, a longtime vestry member at St. Mary's and, as it happens, a close friend of Fred Barnes and Brother Samuel. I wrote to her a few weeks ago, asking her about Barnes."

"And she answered?" asked Charlie.

"She answered, and she knew a lot. She knew things I didn't think anyone else knew. I couldn't tell you before, because I learned some of it in confession. And other parts just seemed so private. But having it out in the world— getting her letter with the same stuff in it—makes me feel like it's all right to talk about now."

"Did you actually do a confession with Talbot—the whole Reconciliation?"

"Twice—though the first time I could only remember the Penitential Order. But the second time we did the whole thing, there in his hospital room. He asked for me specifically. I couldn't refuse."

Charlie sat up and looked at her. "Listen, Lily," he said. "You know I'm being facetious about this question of information. Of course I want to know, and I really do think it's better for you to be able to share the whole story, not to have secrets about it. But don't say anything you feel uncomfortable telling me."

"Okay," she said and patted his knee. "I think you're right, as usual." She moved closer to Syro, who had slept through lunch on the blanket beside her. The dog felt warm and comforting.

"What you said the other day was right: Dan created a world. He created a past out of whole cloth that had nothing to do with his own past. He married Sally—some money, old name. Then he obliterated the person—how can I say it—the person God would have had him be, the person who had lived *his* life."

"That's quite an accomplishment," said Charlie.

"Yes. But over time he stopped being able to know what the truth was. He believed himself. And the more he believed, the more he invented."

"What about Sally?" asked Charlie. "What did she believe?"

"Hard to tell. I don't think she knew anything was wrong at the beginning, when they met. Then I guess sometime after they were married, she started on alcohol and Xanax—the Talbot drug of choice. The more she drank, the more pills she took, the less the truth mattered."

"That's pretty harsh," he said.

"Sorry. But I—" she stopped.

"You what?"

"She reminds me a little of my mother. I probably do judge her harshly."

"So, Sally . . ." Charlie prompted her.

"Right. Maybe she believed Dan at the beginning, or maybe she liked the sense of—what?—danger, weirdness. But near the end, she began to catch on. She told me a lot about Dan, about the lies. And when she finally understood Roy was in serious danger—if not from his father, then from himself—she pulled it together. She's stopped drinking, for the moment. I don't think it will last, but what do I know?"

Charlie shifted his legs, raised his knees, and sat up. "I keep thinking of that afternoon when Mrs. Hanlon told us her suspicions about Barnes's death. It just seemed so far-fetched."

"It was far-fetched," said Lily.

"It's hard to comprehend, isn't it?" he asked. "It's almost impossible to think about the loss."

The wind had strengthened now. The rocks were not enough shelter. Lily shivered and turned up the collar of her parka.

"I still don't get what drove him to kill someone, whether he meant to or not. He had to know it was a possible outcome," said Charlie.

She turned to face him. "That's where Frieda Klass comes in," she said.

"How?"

"Barnes had been very open with her about a lot of this. Frieda was his spiritual director—or the equivalent. He didn't use names, but he told her the story, especially about his own change of heart."

"And?" Charlie prompted.

"In her letter she wrote that she had been worried from the beginning about his zeal. Before Barnes died, he told her he was going to use the information he had to persuade someone—someone powerful—to reexamine his soul."

"I don't get it."

"Fred Barnes was using what he knew about Dan Talbot to persuade him—force him, really—to change his mind and go along with what he, Barnes, that is, believed was right, right for Roy and right for the church. Fred wanted Dan to help him make everyone else see the light."

"You mean he was, like, blackmailing him?" asked Charlie, his voice tinged with fascination and disgust. "That's impossible."

"I don't think so," said Lily. "I've come to believe it *is* possible."

"What had Talbot done that was so horrible?"

"He had a compulsion, I guess you'd say. He was addicted to prostitutes, one in particular, underage, just a girl. He dropped a lot of money—on the travel, the hotels, and the girl. He'd started to steal from his own company, and from his wife."

"God," said Charlie. "The more I know, the more sense it all makes, the less I understand."

The clouds were moving in and the shoals of the channel were filling with silver water. As she gazed across the sand at the marsh, a great blue heron, then two, rose up out of the tall grasses, flapping their huge wings, then flew across the harbor. She caught her breath and pointed. Charlie followed her gaze.

"I didn't know they stayed here all winter," he said.

"Only a few," she said. "We got lucky."

They were quiet for a while, then Charlie began putting food back in the basket.

"Poor old Samuel," he said, after a while. "He believes that if he had only offered Roy a shelter when Fred first asked him, that none of this would have happened. That the boy would be all right."

"Everyone involved feels the blame. Bishop Spencer feels the same way."

"Why?" asked Charlie, surprised.

"Oh, I've left this part out, but, basically, Spencer knew something strange was going on at St. Mary's. He'd known it for a while. But he saw Talbot and Neville as the enemy, as the prey. He forgot they were his sheep. He set out to trap them, and he used me as bait."

"This is a little too allegorical for me," said Charlie. "What actually happened?"

"Spencer talked me into taking the job so he'd have a spy in the enemy camp. Instead of seeing their trouble as something to which he, or someone, should minister, he saw it as something to be ferreted out. I was his mole."

"Can we stay away from the animal imagery for a minute? Do you mean he knew the parish was in trouble, but didn't do anything about it?"

"He did do something about it," said Lily. "He got me to take Barnes's place so he'd know what was going on, so he could—what—let me think. I can't say 'trap'?"

Charlie shook his head.

"He wanted to get Talbot and Neville in trouble, to catch them in the middle of some discrediting activity," said Lily.

"Is that why you're mad at him?" asked Charlie.

"He used me. He knew what I was like. He knew I'd snoop around and be pushy and impulsive. And he knew I'd come to him when I located the trouble."

"But he also knew you're a priest, a good priest who cares about people, who cares about the world, who can make it through a sung liturgy," said Charlie, throwing the tangerine peels to the gulls.

"Anyway," she said. "He thinks that if he had acted sooner, and with more compassion, none of this would have happened. So he blames himself, too. Which is fine with me. There's plenty of it to go around."

"Do you honestly think you're primarily responsible for this?" asked Charlie.

Lily patted Syro for a minute. "No, not really," she said. "A while ago Tom pointed out to me that feeling completely responsible—for the good or the bad—is just another form of pride. For me, the challenge now is to see just how responsible I really am. I tend toward the all or nothing. The painful part is to see the truth in the middle."

They finished packing up in the thin light. Lily didn't want to leave, but the day was ending. She wondered why the ocean so often made people think of God. Probably because of its size—but size wasn't really the point. *To see Heaven in a grain of sand* . . . Or at least not size alone.

She thought perhaps it was because the ocean's immensity required a shift in perspective. We had to stand back to encompass the sense of vastness. To take it all in— the river, the estuary, the bay, Provincetown, Boston, Greenland, the Arctic and on and on—we had to stand very far away, farther and farther up, on the tallest lighthouse of the world, and farther still, where the parallel lines of two truths, of the world and the spirit, of the church as it was and the church as it should have been, of the bishop as he was and as he should have been, of Dan Talbot's crimes and his grace in the eyes of God, these lines began to curve, to meet.

The ride back was quiet. Syro either felt sick or exhausted or both. The dog stood for as long as he could between the two of them, his front paws balanced weirdly on the parking brake, his head on Charlie's shoulder. The fourth time he closed his eyes and fell onto the gear shift, Charlie sent him into the backseat and told him to lie down. He was asleep in seconds.

"What do you think you'll do now?" Charlie asked. "Are you going to stay at St. Mary's?"

"No. Spencer's already got a replacement lined up, I think. I hope."

"Will you go back to the Women's Center?"

"Yes. Probably. Maybe," she said. "I have no idea."

"You can stay at the monastery for a few days, if you want."

"Thanks. I might. I'll see."

"Did Spencer mention the new Ecumenical Council?" he asked. "They want to focus on anti-Semitism in the church. You know the Holocaust Memorial—"

"Charlie," she said. "Right now I don't know what I should do or where I should go. I think, for once, I'm going to keep it that way for a while. It will be interesting to see what happens if I get out of the way."

She saw him smile. "I'm proud of you," he said.

"Don't be condescending."

"Okay," he answered. "Do me a favor."

"What?"

"You sound so skeptical," he said. "I need you to get something out of the backseat."

"Why?"

"Just do it please," he said. "Pick up the picnic basket. See that brown package?"

"Yeah," she said, leaning over into the back.

"That's for you," said Charlie. "I was going to give it to you at Christmas, but I decided not to wait."

"You always give presents ahead of time," she said.

"I know. But I think I'm justified on this occasion."

She took off the plain brown paper and discovered the triptych from the front window of the antiques store on River Street.

"My God," she said. "How did you—when did you do this?"

"You went on about it that day in the kitchen, so I just stopped on the way home and got it for you. That guy is really nice, too, the owner."

"Oh, Charlie," she said. The images on the right wing of the triptych were faint, some almost invisible. But the two faces in the center panel—the faces of Mary and the angel—remained vivid. The angel, her hands raised palm up in offering, knelt before Mary; her lips were parted, as if she had just spoken. But Mary stared off into some imagined distance, at her youth, at her past, at the life ripped from her by this news. Somehow, the painter had managed to convey longing, resignation, and muted joy.

They were crossing the Sagamore Bridge. Lily raised her eyes and looked out the window at the water in the late afternoon light, the molten blue and orange from the sun, glowing just below the cloud bank, and the small, snug white houses lining the shore. A hawk flew out of the trees on the far side and glided on air currents down the center of the canal. She thought of the herons.

"It's beautiful out here, isn't it?" she asked him.

A single fishing boat sailed directly beneath the bird. For an instant they seemed to be moving in unison.

"Yes," said Charlie. "It is."

She held the triptych in her lap for the rest of the ride home.

When they pulled up at the rectory, a small gray sedan was parked at the curb.

"I know whose car that is," said Charlie.

"Oh yeah?" asked Lily, but she smiled as she said it.

Charlie stopped at the gate, just behind the Honda. Lily gave him a hug and thanked him, then began to gather her scarf and gloves and thermos from the backseat. She put the triptych back in the box and tucked it under her arm.

"I was worried about your being here alone, but I see that's not a problem," he said.

"Would you give it a rest?"

"Are you being coy?" he asked. "Hard to believe."

"I'm not being coy," said Lily. "Not all secrets are bad, you know. Some things are supposed to be private."

"But you two are seeing each other, right?"

"Charlie, I haven't really been in a dating mood."

"Honey, you haven't been in a dating mood since I've known you. I thought that might be changing."

"Actually," she said, as she opened the door, "this is the first time we've seen each other in a while."

"Good," said Charlie. "Enjoy it."

She leaned over and kissed him, then got out onto the sidewalk with her gear. When she reached the gate, she saw Tom sitting on the steps of the rectory. She walked over and sat down next to him.

"Somebody came by a minute ago," he said.

"Who?"

"A girl, a teenager. She didn't look too great. She said you'd given her your name. She found out from Roy where to come, where you were living."

"Did she leave her number?" asked Lily.

"No. She said she'd come back later."

Lily's heart sank. She had thought she was done with this part. She couldn't go through it again. She stared across the courtyard at the church; in the fading light, the building looked abandoned.

"It's not starting all over," said Tom. "You don't have to adopt her. We'll figure something out."

"Right," she said and then realized that she believed him. Her spirits rose. Next to the church spire, just above the roof, the sliver of a new moon emerged in the evening sky. If she comes back, we'll call the hospital, Lily thought. Then she said a short prayer that Lena would be on duty. Somehow, Lily felt sure she would.

Now turn the page for an exciting excerpt from
Michelle Blake's next novel:

*Earth Has No Sorrow*

The six glass columns glowed in the muted light. A cold mist had lifted earlier, leaving a gray cloud cover, appropriate for the ceremony and the day. Lily pulled her red gloves out of the pocket of her coat and put them on, then wrapped a red wool scarf more closely around her neck. Her braid got caught in the scarf; she freed it and took a step forward, toward the Holocaust Memorial, where a man in a black coat stood reading out loud from an inscription on the third column, the one representing Sobibor.

A few hundred yards away, tourists in Faneuil Hall sipped microbrew and wore Mickey Mouse hats with BOSTON printed across the front. From the nearby streets came the noise of traffic and the distant strains of construction work behind high wooden fences. But an air of quiet surrounded the Memorial—the stone walkway and small surrounding park—as if it were set apart and enclosed by the dense reality of its purpose. Lily could hear the man's words perfectly.

". . . a childhood friend of mine once found a raspberry in the camp and carried it in her pocket all day to present to me that night on a leaf," he read. "Imagine a world in which your entire possession is one raspberry and you give it to your friend."

Lily was surprised to find herself near tears. Over the years she had heard so many testimonies, read so many descriptions of the camps, that she had begun to fear she was beyond feeling. She quickly wiped her eyes and stood straighter. These were the moments her height served her best (she was usually the tallest woman in a group and often one of the taller people): Though the crowd was dense, she could see perfectly, and she was spared any threat from the lurking claustrophobia that sometimes jumped her in close spaces.

In front of her, Anna Banieka stood next to Charlie Cooper. The top of Anna's head just reached Charlie's shoulder; Lily noticed the woman's scalp showing through her thin, black hair—dyed and permed, vampish, from another era. Anna's narrow shoulders looked slightly lopsided from the back, but her bearing was erect. Lily couldn't see Anna's face. Suddenly her own tears felt sentimental.

A gust of wind blew grit and sand over the fence of the construction site. Lily turned away, and when she turned back she saw that Anna had taken Charlie's arm. He leaned down and whispered to his companion, then they both moved quietly to the side of the crowd, where Anna sat on a low stone wall near the entrance to the Memorial. Charlie stood next to her, watching the ceremony. Anna's eyes were closed, and her slight smile seemed distant, almost ironic.

Lily turned again to face the Memorial. After the reading, there were a few moments for silent prayer and reflection, then the crowd moved on to the next column, the one representing Majdanek. Lily felt a tap on her shoulder and turned to see Charlie behind her. He was a couple of inches taller than she was, with the same coloring—thick brown hair, brown eyes, pale skin. But Charlie's face was long, shadowed, Goya-like, Lily always thought, while her own face was rounder, almost heart-shaped, not nearly as dramatic.

"Anna wants to start for the Cathedral now," he whispered. "It's going to take her a while to walk there. She's not feeling so great."

"Okay," said Lily, softly, then asked, "Can I come, too?"

"Yes," he said. "That's why I told you. Let's go."

Lily wondered if it was all right for her to leave with Anna and Charlie; the three of them had planned the ceremony and the church service that would follow. But they'd had the foresight to put the Bishop in charge of the day's proceedings, and he was reliable. Besides, Lily was cold and a little restless; reality never quite lived up to her expectations. She followed Charlie without looking back.

Anna walked slowly up the steps to Government Center, her arm linked through Charlie's. She appeared to be leaning on him now, and Lily thought her face looked gray, her lips pale.

"What did you think?" Charlie asked Anna as they crossed the plaza, moonlike with its empty stretches of white concrete platforms and plateaus.

"Of that?" asked Anna. She inclined her head back and to the right, in the direction of the Memorial.

"Yes," said Charlie. "Of that."

She smiled. "It's a good thing to do," she said. "I appreciate the effort. And I appreciate the sentiment behind it."

Sentimental, thought Lily, like my tears.

Anna put her other hand on Lily's arm. "May I?" she asked. "I can't seem to get my breath today."

"Of course," said Lily, then she consciously slowed her pace.

"I've always liked the fact that they put Niemoller— that quotation from him—at the entrance, or is it the exit?" said Anna. "He was an anti-Semite, you know. He preached very ardent sermons on the subject of conversion to Christianity. Then he saw the light, as they say, when Hitler tried to take over his church.'"

"It says on the inscription he was anti-Semitic,'" said Charlie.

"I know," said Anna. "It's the most interesting thing about him."

Charlie laughed. "What's the most interesting thing," he asked, "that he was an anti-Semite?"

"No," said Anna. "That he changed. So few people are really capable of that."

"Do you think?" asked Lily. "I know most people don't change much in their lives. But I believe almost everyone *can* change."

"Yes," said Anna. "Of course, you're right. But it's very hard."

Lily felt pleased, as if she had just gotten an "A" from a favorite teacher. And, in fact, Lily had been a student of Anna Banieka's writing for a long time, long before she had met the woman herself. Years ago, at the end of their first term in seminary, Lily had given Charlie the book *Work Makes Freedom*.

He had considered it the most depressing Christmas gift he'd ever been given. But he'd gone on to read the rest of Banieka's writing: the two studies of anti-Jewish imagery and language in the early Church; the book of interviews with rescuers; the book of interviews with perpetrators; and the three volumes of poems.

Banieka lived and taught in a college town in western Massachusetts. When she came to Boston she stayed with the Brothers at the monastery on Brattle, The Society of St. Peter, where Charlie now lived. Anna and Charlie had gotten to know each other over time. Then Charlie had introduced Lily to Anna, and the circle was completed—or so it had felt to Lily.

After a short walk down Tremont, they reached the Episcopal Cathedral of St. Michael's and All Angels. Anna paused and glanced up toward the building entrance.

"Do you want to go in through the bookstore, around the side?" asked Lily. "There aren't as many stairs that way."

"No, no," said Anna. "I just need to catch my breath."

Her hold on Lily's arm tightened as they started the climb. Lily began to feel concerned now; Anna's skin was still pale, despite the cold wind. But the older woman moved steadily, and they were soon inside, at the north end of the narthex.

Charlie reached out and pulled on one of the smaller doors leading to the north aisle. It didn't open.

"Great," he said. "I knew there'd be some kind of foul-up."

"They probably haven't unlocked everything yet," said Lily. "I'll check the ones at the other end."

But when she tried the doors at the opposite end, she found those locked, too.

"Weird," she said. "Try the main doors."

"Those are never open," said Charlie, but he pulled the large wooden handle and the door swung out silently. "Cool," he said, then bowed to Anna, who stood in the same spot at which they had first entered. Her color looked better, thought Lily, as she walked back to her friends.

She reached the central door just ahead of Anna. Courtesy told her to wait and go second, but something else told her to go first. As she walked into the huge empty space, she heard a crashing sound, something heavy being dropped nearby. Where are the lights, she wondered. And then, as her eyes adjusted, she saw the brilliant red swathe of color draped over the main altar, the black and white swastika centered across the front, and, finally, the body of a child, dressed in the striped uniform of the camps, swinging by a rope from a cross beam above the nave.

# author's note and acknowledgments

St. Mary of the Garden does not exist outside the covers of this book, and it is not modeled on any existing parish. Although there is an Episcopal cathedral on the corner of Tremont and Temple Streets in Boston, it is not named St. Michael and All Angels and it does not, as far as I know, have a basement room with a Ping-Pong table. All the characters are fictional. To quote Dorothy Sayers: "For, however realistic the background, the novelist's only native country is Cloud-Cuckooland, where they do but jest, poison in jest; no offense in the world."

Many people contributed to this book. For their generosity, time, and expertise, I thank Linda Bamber, Linda MacMillan, Linda Mizell, Shelley Evans, Kate White, Anike Dale Thomas, and Lynn Burbridge; Leith Speiden and the Brothers of the Society of St. John the Evangelist; Officer Peter Norton and Marisa Connolly of the Boston Police Department; Mike Durand of COM/Electric; Clarissa Atkinson; Betty Karmitzer; Ellen Keniston; Tellis Lawson; Danny McCormick; Nancy Oriol-Morway; Amanda Powell; Rolfe E. G. Gates; David Siegenthaller; John Traficonte; and Ira Ziering.

Special thanks to my steadfast agent, Gail Hochman, and her assistant, Meg Giles, and to my editor at Penguin Putnam, Martha Bushko. *The Tentmaker* couldn't have been in better hands.

Finally, I thank the members of my family: my father, Thomas Walter Blake, for his support throughout; my sister, Tessa Blake, for her generosity, love, and friendship; my daughter, Katharine Blake McFarland, for serving as my first and best reader; my son, Sam McFarland, for interrupting as little as possible and for being a source of inspiration.

And I thank my husband, Dennis McFarland, who never doubted for a moment, and who shared every pain and pleasure along the way. In you, I am blessed indeed.

# about the author

michelle Blake, *who has also published under the name Michelle Blake Simons, is a poet and a writer whose work has appeared in Ploughshares, Southern Review, and other publications. She received a Master's of Fine Arts from Goddard College and a Master's of Theological Studies from Harvard Divinity School. She teaches at Tufts University and lives near Boston with her husband, Dennis McFarland, and their two children.*

# EARLENE FOWLER

introduces Benni Harper, curator of San Celina's folk art museum and amateur sleuth

## ❑ FOOL'S PUZZLE        0-425-14545-X/$6.50

Ex-cowgirl Benni Harper moved to San Celina, California, to begin a new career as curator of the town's folk art museum. But when one of the museum's first quilt exhibit artists is found dead, Benni must piece together a pattern of family secrets and small-town lies to catch the killer.

## ❑ IRISH CHAIN        0-425-15137-9/$6.50

When Brady O'Hara and his former girlfriend are murdered at the San Celina Senior Citizen's Prom, Benni believes it's more than mere jealousy—and she risks everything to unveil the conspiracy O'Hara had been hiding for fifty years.

## ❑ KANSAS TROUBLES        0-425-15696-6/$6.50

After their wedding, Benni and Gabe visit his hometown near Wichita. There Benni meets Tyler Brown: aspiring country singer, gifted quilter, and former Amish wife. But when Tyler is murdered and the case comes between Gabe and her, Benni learns that her marriage is much like the Kansas weather: bound to be stormy.

## ❑ GOOSE IN THE POND     0-425-16239-7/$6.50
## ❑ DOVE IN THE WINDOW    0-425-16894-8/$6.50